260

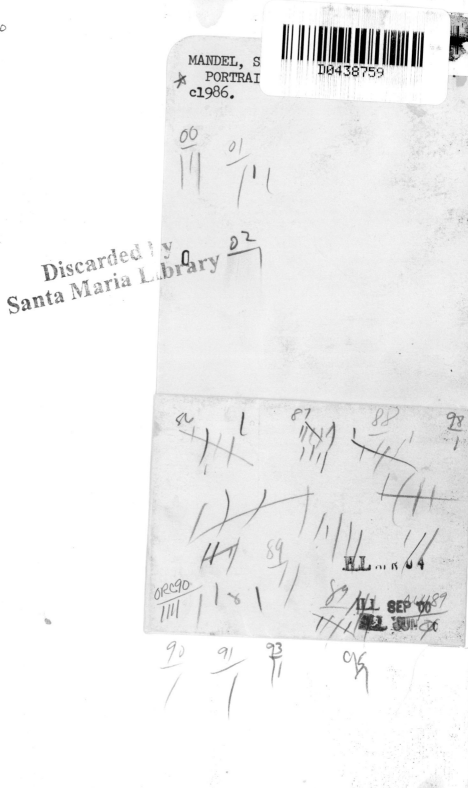

PORTRAIT
OF A
MARRIED WOMAN

PORTRAIT
OF A
MARRIED WOMAN

Sally Mandel

BANTAM BOOKS
TORONTO · NEW YORK · LONDON · SYDNEY · AUCKLAND

PORTRAIT OF A MARRIED WOMAN
A Bantam Book / April 1986

ACKNOWLEDGMENTS
"When I'm Sixty-four" (John Lennon & Paul McCartney)
Copyright © 1967 Northern Songs Limited
All rights for the United States and Mexico controlled
by Maclen Music, Inc., c/o ATV Music Corp.
Used by Permission. All Rights Reserved.

"Do-Re-Mi" Copyright © 1959 by Richard Rodgers and Oscar Hammerstein II.
Williamson Music Co., owner of publication and allied rights
throughout the Western Hemisphere and Japan.
International Copyright Secured.
Used by permission. All Rights Reserved.

3-86 BA 1500

Library of Congress Cataloging-in-Publication Data
Mandel, Sally.
Portrait of a married woman.

I. Title.
PS3563.A446P6 1986 813'.54 85-47799
ISBN 0-553-05079-6

Published simultaneously in the United States and Canada

PRINTED IN THE UNITED STATES OF AMERICA

0 9 8 7 6 5 4 3 2 1

For my mother

PORTRAIT
OF A
MARRIED WOMAN

1

That day Margaret Hollander saw two people dressed as chickens on Manhattan's Ninety-first Street. A young man and a young woman with great yellow-feathered bodies and heavy chicken feet sat on a bench by the Cooper-Hewitt Museum smoking cigarettes. Later, even years later, the strange creatures would come to mind as the harbingers of the unexpected in what was once an orderly life.

Morning started out as always. Matthew, Fred, and Susan sat around the table, each absorbing the shock of a new dawn in his own fashion. The children ate in silence, Fred consuming prodigious amounts of cinnamon toast in an effort to fill his ever-yawning twelve-year-old stomach, and Susan extricating the raisins from her cereal and leaving the bran flakes to grow soggy.

Matthew pored over the first pages of his *New York Times* as if he feared that confronting today with yesterday's *data vitae* would be to venture forth unarmed.

Maggie stood propped in her usual spot at the counter, waiting for the caffeine rush from her first cup of coffee. She was a tall, slim woman, five-feet-ten in her bare feet. Even now, still groggy from the warmth of her bed, she stood very straight. For Maggie, mornings were always wrenching. Nearly two hours would have to elapse before her senses fully awoke. Until then, sounds and images seemed fuzzy to her as if filtered through a gauze screen.

Suddenly the sunny room erupted in a jumble of requisitions. Matthew's deep baritone won out. "My blazer hasn't come back from the cleaners, has it, Mag? I need it for tomorrow night."

"You didn't tell me."

"Yup. And I need longer laces for my black wing tips. Think you could get hold of a pair today?"

"Haul that barge, tote that bail," chimed Susan. Her grin flashed a mouthful of braces.

Matthew reached out with his folded newspaper and tapped her on the head.

"I suppose you don't have a single item to add to my list, Suzie Q," Maggie said.

"As a matter of fact . . ." Susan began.

Maggie interrupted her. "I'm to pick up your costume and drop it at rehearsal at three, and Fred, you forgot to buy Michael a present and his party's this afternoon."

Fred's tongue was rendered helpless by half a banana. "Mrthma bmp?" he asked.

"You want me to get him something."

Fred nodded and took a gigantic swig of juice. "The new *Corpse* tape would be sensational."

"Oh God, all right. It'll be with Sue's stuff this afternoon.

I'm here till seven. Otherwise, feed yourselves. There's lamb in the fridge."

Matthew sent crumbs flying as he opened the Metropolitan section. "I ought to be home by nine. Want to wait and have dinner with me?" he asked with nose buried.

Maggie envied him his powers of concentration. She had once dreamed that she set fire to a corner of the *Times* at the breakfast table. Matthew had simply read faster and faster, racing the flames to the bottom of the page. He held the charred paper between his fingers gingerly until the words fell into ashes. Without comment, and without glancing up, he merely swept the soot away and began the next section.

"Mom's not going to be here to take care of you, Daddy," Susan said. "Hey, maybe you guys'd like my famous hamburgers *au roquefort.*"

Fred clasped his stomach and gagged convincingly.

"Not here?" Matthew asked.

"Jeez, you're out of it sometimes," Susan complained. "It's Tuesday night. Bridge night."

"So it is," Matthew declared. "Whose house?"

"Phyllis's."

Matthew grimaced. He had never liked Phyllis, but Maggie always asked him not to exhibit his antipathy in front of the children.

"She think's she's seventeen, the way she dresses," Susan said.

Maggie shot Matthew a look that said: See what you encourage? But he was reading again.

"She's got great legs," Fred remarked. "I don't see why women have all those rules about what they should wear and what they shouldn't wear. If you've got it, flaunt it, I always say." As he warmed to his subject, Maggie poured herself another cup of coffee and smiled at him. She enjoyed Fred's speeches. Even when he was tiny, he used to deliver solemn lectures to her about why it was advisable to sleep with twenty-two stuffed animals or why the pink gelatinous canned spaghetti was so much better than home-cooked pasta.

"You're all slaves to the fashion industry," he went on. "If some old bag wants to wear something young and sexy, why shouldn't she? You won't catch us men . . ."

Susan cut him short. "Mother, that's your third cup! You drink too much of that stuff!"

"Why don't you lay off, motormouth?" Fred said, stung at the interruption. "God, you're going to be such a nag when and if you ever grow up. I was right in the middle of a sentence."

"You don't even care if Mom gets breast cancer and maybe even dies."

"You think you're the big medical expert just because you got an A in your Personal Health report." Fred's round face was beginning to redden. "Besides, I care about Mom's breasts as much as anybody."

"Hoo *hoo*!" Susan howled.

Fred half-rose from the table to lunge at his sister. She leapt up and flattened herself against the refrigerator, out of reach.

"That'll do," Matthew said. "Your mother's breasts are in no immediate danger as far as we know."

"Well, maybe not from cancer anyway," Susan said with a smirk as she sat down again.

"You're disgusting," Fred said. "She doesn't have one iota of class. You know what she did in lunchline yesterday?"

"Don't you dare," Susan whispered.

"She farted. Everybody heard her, a real ripper. Loverboy Bobby Posner looked right at her and said, 'Can't hold what you don't have in your hand, right, Sue?' It was classic."

"Mom," Susan asked sweetly, "when do little boys stop worrying about castration?"

"Never, babe," Matthew muttered. He stretched, stood up,

and embraced Maggie. "Take care of 'em, will you?" he asked. Maggie wondered if he meant the children or her breasts.

Susan and Fred traipsed out of the kitchen after him with Susan making a running commentary of Matthew's attire.

"Daddy, look how preppy you are with the button-down collar. Très Reaganesque, you know, like you've been embalmed in the fifties or something. Next thing you'll be wearing plaid pants . . ." Her voice disappeared down the hall.

Good, take on your father for a change, Maggie thought. She slumped into Matthew's vacant chair with a sigh. A few moments later, Fred called, "Don't forget Mike's present, Mom!" The front door slammed and they were gone.

Maggie sat with her chin in her hands. She had what her mother always told her were "good bones," which Maggie supposed meant that she was homely. "You'll grow into your face," Mother said, and at age thirty-eight, Maggie was still waiting.

Normally she sat for half an hour after breakfast and skimmed the *Times*. But this morning the silence seemed hollow, as if she were entombed in a cavern so vast that the ceiling could barely be seen for the shadows. She got up and began transporting dishes to the sink. Her body moved automatically, with a kind of swaying grace. She remembered Fred's remark about Phyllis's legs and poked one of her own through her robe. Not bad, she determined. If the face was lacking a certain Hollywood panache, she was still all right from the neck down. She knew the power of an attractive body. At cocktail parties, she was accustomed to men speaking to her chest rather than to her eyes. Sometimes she would amuse herself by recapturing the attention of a distracted male by crossing her legs or moving her shoulder in a certain way. Men were so preoccupied with her breasts or her knees that she wondered if anyone would notice if she were to unscrew her head and place it next to the salted nuts.

A saucer slammed against the rim of the sink and chipped. In the nine years since she had bought the set, this was the first time she had broken anything. The jagged edge of the plate cut her thumb. She found a Band-Aid but as she tried to apply it, she noticed that her hands were shaking. It frightened her to injure her hands. Though it had been years since she had held a paintbrush, there was the wistful notion that someday she would stand in front of an easel again. She flexed her fingers and tried to still the trembling. Maybe Susan was right: too much coffee.

Moving around would help, the faster the better. It was a good day to attack her closet, get out her summer things, clean the shelves, and make a list of the clothing she needed to buy this season. That would take care of the morning. Then there were plenty of errands. Besides the directives she had received with breakfast, there was a note to her ailing father; Mother's Day gifts to decide on; groceries to order; medical-insurance forms to fill out for Fred's persistent ear infections.

She marched toward the bedroom, keeping her eyes averted from the other rooms with their curiously eerie quiet. They had bought the place just before the upswing in cooperative market prices would have barred them from the market forever. It was a pleasant two-bedroom apartment in a brick prewar building on Seventy-ninth between Lexington and Third avenues. It had Maggie's two prerequisites: the ceilings were high and there was a fireplace in the living room. The children had flipped a coin for the extra bedroom. Susan won, relegating Fred to a small maid's room near the kitchen, but it had worked out fine. Fred liked his privacy, and also his proximity to the refrigerator.

Maggie had taken pride in decorating the place on her own in a comfortable not-very-contemporary style. The living room faced south, and was a rain forest of palm fronds and ferns. Maggie often played the stereo for her plants, maintaining they were partial to Debussy. The color green was evident throughout the apartment. Matthew theorized that Maggie was unconsciously trying to reproduce the lush atmosphere of her Stafford, Connecticut, childhood.

Maggie opened her closet door, grabbed an armful of dresses, and hauled them to the bed. She flopped down with them, and found that the dress on top of the pile was her old madras shirtwaist of lilac-and-green plaid. It was hopelessly out of fashion and so faded now that the colors were barely distinguishable. Every year she told herself to quit being foolish and get rid of it, and every year she retrieved it from the giveaway pile and hung it back in the closet.

With the soft fabric between her fingers, she felt her anxiety succumb to a pleasant dreamlike sensation that she had experienced several times in the past week. It was as if periodically she were checking out of the present in order to take a long walk in the past. It had happened in the supermarket waiting in line at the deli counter. That time she was transported back to her wooden desk in the first grade where she could swing her legs without her feet touching the floor. It happened again yesterday in Bloomingdale's giftware department. Suddenly she was in Rockport, walking along the beach with her father as he tried to explain to her about menstruation. A store clerk had startled her by asking if she was ill.

The dress sent her back to that first afternoon with Matthew. It was the beginning of senior year at Radcliffe and the air was so crisp that it almost hurt her eyes. The trees had begun to turn; Harvard Square was littered with awed freshmen and brilliant leaves. Maggie was dashing to the subway for a trip to Filene's, and as she rounded the corner of Boylston Street, she suddenly found herself hooked to the elbow of Matthew Hollander.

"May I have this dance?" he asked. He seemed to have materialized out of the shimmering autumn light. "My name's Matthew Hollander. You're Maggie Herrick."

"I know who you are." Everyone knew Matthew Hollander's earnest handsome face and the lean body that performed athletic feats with simple ease. Like every other woman at Radcliffe, Maggie had enjoyed watching the sheen of sweat on his back and shoulders as he leapt into the air to hurl a basketball through the hoop with a decisive swoosh. But she wondered how he knew her. Surely he hadn't recognized her from the only class they had shared, Renaissance Art, which was a glorified slide show occurring mostly in total darkness.

"Come have a cup of coffee with me," Matthew urged. He still held onto her elbow. Maggie looked down at her watch to hide a burning face. "And a hot fudge sundae. I know you like those." She glanced up at him. "I saw you in the window of Brigham's one afternoon with Phyllis Jacobson," he went on. "You shoved the whipped cream off but ate the cherry."

Maggie laughed and fell into rhythm with his long stride. She hoped she would pass someone she knew. All the way to Brigham's, she kept saying to herself: Here I am with Matthew Hollander. She wanted to remember exactly how it felt.

Pain brought her back to the bedroom. She had been clutching the old dress so tightly that her shoulders ached. With a sigh, she stood and hung it back in her closet. She would keep it awhile longer, even though the wonder and excitement it evoked had faded along with its once-bright colors.

She walked across the carpeted floor toward the window. It was Maggie's habit to poke her head out over Seventy-ninth Street and appraise the air firsthand before dressing for the day, but this morning she felt an odd reluctance. She regarded the window thoughtfully for a moment, then threw it open and looked down.

The air was cool and thick with moisture from an early-morning shower. It washed around her like a gentle whirlpool. The traffic noises rose in bubbles that popped to release their sounds just under her face. The vehicles and pedestrians below were like bizarre sea creatures, their shapes distorted by the glassy surface of the water. Maggie swayed, seaweed drifting. How pleasant to dive into the soft transparent waves. She closed her eyes against a sudden lurch of nausea and stumbled away from the window. Cold sweat clung to the fringes of her hair and plastered it to her forehead as if she had indeed been immersed. Perhaps she was drowning. Perhaps as the water closed over her head, she would continue to relive the years, newsreel style, except that it would take weeks for her to submerge completely.

2

Maggie was on her way out the door for her bridge game when Fred and Susan arrived home.

Susan looked at her closely. "You getting your period?" she wanted to know.

Startled, Maggie shook her head.

"Well, you look weird." Susan moved past her, and Maggie heard the pile of books crash down on the bed.

"Thanks," Maggie murmured.

"I don't think you look weird, exactly," Fred said, leaning against the wall. "But something's wrong."

Maggie felt a lump growing in her throat. "Not a thing," she said. "Gotta go. Don't forget your leafy greens."

Fred gave her a quick kiss. "Knock 'em dead, Mom."

Phyllis's apartment was within easy walking distance, but Maggie dawdled. She remembered last night's television advertisement touting a disaster film about an airplane that plunged into the ocean and sank to the bottom. In the film clip, flames raged, waves crashed, wounded and dying passengers screamed with terror. A stout-voiced fellow, presumably the hero, shouted from the midst of the maelstrom, "Don't panic!" Maggie likened the voice in her brain to that stalwart person; she had been hearing the same command all day. Except that there was no disaster in her life. Everything was perfect, really perfect.

She shook her head and half a dozen tiny seedlets fell to her shoulders. The spring trees were shedding in a strong breeze from the south. A pair of joggers passed, a man and a woman wearing matched shorts. They were laughing. Were we ever like that, Matthew and I? Maggie wondered, and she was off again, back in Cambridge, Massachusetts.

He had called her that same night and asked her out for dinner Saturday night. Maggie refused, because of her long-standing Saturday commitment to Frank Pearson. She felt as if she had just turned down the Nobel Prize, but ten minutes later Matthew called again, this time to ask if she could see him on Sunday. She agreed.

Frank Pearson and Maggie used one another for sex. At first, Maggie had tried to convince herself that she was in love with him, but her roommate, Phyllis, had set her straight.

"He's a good lay, that's all. Don't make it into the romance of the century."

"But he was my first and only," Maggie protested.

"My first was my thirteen-year-old cousin. Think I should marry him?"

Matthew took her to Nick's Place, known at Harvard as the Greasy Greek's. Neither of them spoke much at first. Matthew watched her while under the table Maggie rolled and unrolled her napkin.

"Why are you staring at me?" she asked finally.

"You have an interesting face."

Maggie smiled. "Good bones, my mother says."

"Your mother's right. Do you mind not being pretty?"

"I did when I was fifteen. Not now."

He nodded as if she were confirming something he already knew.

"Do you mind being pretty?" she asked him.

"Yes," he answered instantly. Then they both laughed, and Maggie began to relax.

They had talked about art that night, Maggie remembered, and she was impressed with his sensitivity and profound admiration of creative performance. On the way back to her dormitory, he had tried to kiss her.

She had pulled away. "Why are you doing this?" she asked him.

"Doing what? Kissing you? I like your gap."

"I beg your pardon."

"The gap between your front teeth. It's sexy."

"I mean all of it. Taking me out, giving me the rush."

"You're cute." He tried to draw her close but she resisted.

"I may be many things, but I am not cute. I'm a novelty, that must be it."

"I'd say special."

"You don't even know me."

"I want to. I'll tell you something else. I've been thinking about you all summer."

"Why?"

"I saw your pictures at the student exhibition. I liked them a lot."

"Listen, I'm just an ordinary person with an ordinary talent. I'm no Mary Cassatt."

He held her by the shoulders and shook her slightly. "Why are you giving me such a hard time?"

"Because you could make hash out of me."

He was silent a moment. "I won't do that," he said at last.

"How do you know? It can't be easy to break the beauty-queen habit."

"Exasperating woman," he said, then kissed her and held her very close to him the rest of the way back.

He called her every night, but Maggie, though cordial, told him she was busy.

Phyllis paced their little room. "What does he *say* when you turn him down?"

" 'God damn.' "

"You've got the Adonis of Harvard hot after your ass."

"He doesn't want me really," Maggie explained. "He just thinks he does."

"So what, so what? If you pass up a chance to sleep with that man, I'm transferring you to Mass Mental."

"Phyl," Maggie said, "I like him. He's not just another pretty face."

Phyllis held out her hands in a gesture that said: So, then?

"I'm going to get mangled and shredded by this one."

"Then have a night or two of bliss to remember the remainder of your mangled and shredded life. Am I right or am I right?"

Maggie regarded her silently. Phyllis and Maggie had been paired as roommates freshman year. Maggie remembered being appalled by her language. It was one thing to read the word "cunt" sprinkled among abstruse paragraphs of Chaucer, but quite another to be confronted with the actual spoken word. As the weeks went by, it became clear that Phyllis's formidable mouth was matched by an equally formidable intellect, with which she was just as generous. If Maggie was baffled by a Statistics problem, Phyllis was always there to explain. She shared her Biology lab notes and read all of Maggie's English

term papers, offering patient, tactful criticism. They had continued to room together except for junior year, when Phyllis spent
the year abroad, and Maggie had missed her terribly. When
Phyllis asked Maggie to analyze her reactions to Matthew Hollander, it did not take Maggie long to get up off her bed and
telephone him.

"It's me," she said. "Can I take you out to dinner?"

"Yes," Matthew said, and it began in earnest.

The sight of Phyllis's apartment house roused her from her
reminiscences. The newsreel was happening again, Maggie thought.
Eventually she would work her way up through the years, and
then what? Something cataclysmic, surely.

The linoleum flooring in the lobby was coming up around
the edges. Even the plastic plant by the elevator seemed dustier
and more forlorn than usual. But Phyllis was fastidious about her
apartment. It was decorated in beige and white, sparsely so that
the cramped space seemed larger. There were touches of rattan
here and there, and lots of mirrors. Maggie marveled at the
contrast between the orderly home and the chaotic marriage that
inhabited it.

The others were already sitting at the card table. Three pairs
of eyes stared at Maggie as she let herself in. She found refuge in
Robin's, which were deep brown and, as always, filled with
warmth. Robin was five months pregnant, but even in profile,
her figure barely showed it.

"Did somebody die?" Phyllis asked. The long dark braid of
Radcliffe days had been replaced with an attractive cropped haircut.

Maggie shook her head and sat down. There was a glass of
white wine beside the pile of cards Hilary had dealt her. "Thanks,"
Maggie said, and took a swallow.

"Gee, in all these years, I think you're the only one who's
never been late," Robin said. The soft eyes were plainly worried.

"Sorry. I was attacked by Marcel Proust on the way over."
Maggie hurriedly arranged her cards.

"You going to explain?" Phyllis asked.

Maggie shook her head. "Not to worry." She had a good
hand. The second time around the table she bid two no-trump.

"Oh, Christ, I always forget what I'm supposed to say to
that," Hilary moaned. Even with her face screwed up in dismay,
Hilary Vonderhyde was beautiful. She had thick wavy hair, honey-
colored but streaked pale around her face. Her eyes were light
brown, almost gold, and her skin always seemed tanned. Her
eyebrows and lashes were dark, making the blond hair suspect,
but the fact was, Hilary was one hundred percent natural. She
drew her long fingers through the tangled mane.

"You must be asking for another suit," she murmured.

"No hints," Phyllis warned.

"Oh, three no-trump," Hilary finally decided. The others
passed.

"Damn, I hate playing no-trump," Maggie muttered.

Robin led the six of diamonds and Hilary laid down her
hand. Maggie looked it over in silence. There was a conspicuous
gap in the diamond suit, and, as always, Robin had ferreted it
out. Somehow she always seemed to guess her opponents' weakness. She was the kindest, gentlest person Maggie knew, but she
was deadly at the bridge table.

"I'm sorry, Mag," Robin said mournfully as she ran through
the last of her six-card diamond suit. It was a joke with them
about Robin's card sense. She was good, she was lucky, but she
could not bear the fact that someone had to lose. Sometimes she
seemed almost exultant when she drew a three-point hand and
was unable to bid.

Maggie watched helplessly as the pile of cards accumulated
in front of Robin, and was amazed to feel her eyes sting. She
was losing it all. She glanced up and saw Phyllis studying her.
With shaking fingers, Maggie took the next trick, and then

proceeded to relinquish transportation from her hand to Hilary's strong club suit. She finished the game down four. "Sorry, partner," she sighed.

"I left you in the lurch. Those were sucky diamonds."

"What's the matter, Margaret?" Phyllis asked.

"Nothing," Maggie replied.

"Oh, yes," Phyllis said.

"Getting my period. Whose deal?"

"Mine," Phyllis said, "but I think I'll wait until you tell us what's with you." She tapped the pack of cards on the table while, as always, Maggie doodled on the score pad. This time it was a drawing of a chicken with human features.

"Do you feel as if you've changed?" Maggie asked them. "Over the years, since college, I mean? Oh, I don't know what I mean."

"I've gotten a hell of a lot older," Hilary said.

"That's not . . ." Maggie began, but Phyllis interrupted her gently.

"I remember the energetic, confident young thing who was going to conquer the art world—first Boston, then New York."

"I used to go after the things I wanted, didn't I?"

"You got a case of the regrets?" Phyllis asked.

"I don't know *what* I've got."

"Talent. Which you don't use," Hilary said.

Maggie drew heavy pencil marks through her doodle.

"I don't think she needs criticism tonight," Robin said. "Go ahead and deal, Phyl."

Phyllis began to distribute the cards. "What she *needs* is a lover."

Hilary laughed incredulously.

"All you ever think about is sex," Robin protested.

"All anybody ever thinks about is sex, honey."

"I promise I'll go right home after this and attack Matthew," Maggie said. "You bid a club? I pass."

"I don't think that'll do it," Phyllis said, "but go ahead and give it a try."

"She's got late-thirties ennui. It's practically an epidemic," Hilary said. "It'll pass, Mag, really."

Maggie was beginning to feel dizzy and feverish, as if she had had too much wine.

"Are you okay?" Robin reached her hand out to touch Maggie's arm.

Maggie nodded. "Fine, but I think I'd like to play some bridge."

"Two hearts," Robin said.

"Jump shift, that bastard," Hilary murmured. "I pass in the face of rampant balls."

After that, the hands got interesting and Phyllis concentrated on her cards instead of Maggie. It was past eleven by the time the last rubber was finished and they had chosen Robin's house for the first Tuesday in June.

Matthew was sitting in front of the television set when Maggie got home. There was always restraint between them on bridge night, particularly if Matthew preceded her home, as if somehow Maggie was supposed to be there first, waiting for him. Neither of them spoke of it, but Maggie was always conscious of an impulse to rush if the game lasted past ten-thirty.

"So how's Robin?" Matthew inquired as she dropped her bag and sat down next to him.

"So far so good. This week's five-months."

They were silent for a moment. Maggie thought of her remark at the bridge table about attacking him. It seemed like a pledge. He had changed into his faded brown corduroys, V-neck sweatshirt, and battered Top-Siders. The hair on his chest was soft and pale, several shades lighter than the hair on his head. "How tired are you?" she asked, giving him a half-smile.

Matthew grinned. "What did you ladies talk about over there?"

"Oh, this and that." She leaned against him and turned her face up for a kiss. He reached behind her neck, and at his touch she felt herself grow lethargic. She was sleepy, sensuous, deliciously helpless.

"Come on," he said, taking her hand and pulling her up off the couch. "Let's go to bed."

Maggie stumbled to her feet as if he had roused her from a pleasant dream. "Why?" she asked.

He was halfway down the hall as she trailed along behind him. "More comfortable. And besides, the kids."

They stood naked on opposite sides of the bed. Matthew threw the covers back crisply and climbed in.

"Turn off the light, okay?" Maggie asked. She crept in next to him and he began to stroke her body. Maggie trailed her fingernails lightly up and down his back. She knew that within a minute, he would be kissing her breasts.

Later he asked her what happened.

"Overtired, I guess," Maggie said. Between her legs, she ached from straining to achieve the impossible.

"You seemed interested enough out in the living room." His voice was thick with impending sleep. Matthew could never keep his eyes open after sex. Maggie, on the other hand, found it rejuvenating and would often slip out of bed to balance her checkbook or tackle some long-neglected chore.

"I guess I lost it on the way down the hall," Maggie said.

But he was already breathing deeply. Maggie felt tears leak out from under her closed lashes. She let them come. They trickled into her hair and grew cold. Then she put her hand between her legs as if to soothe a wound and finally fell asleep.

3

The children's key in the lock brought Maggie the usual relief. It was past six-thirty already.

"I've got Zach, that okay, Mom?" Fred asked.

Maggie smiled at the dark slender boy, Phyllis's son. "Sure. I'm kicking you all out in a little while anyhow. Your father and I have ballet with the Brodys tonight. I can't imagine why I forgot to tell you. Here, Zach, let me take your backpack, too." He was a year older than Fred, and four inches taller, but to Maggie, he always seemed rather fragile.

Susan shrugged off her light jacket. "That's two nights in a row, Mother," she protested. "Why can't we ever sit down and have dinner together like a normal family?"

"You always have rehearsals for that dumb play," Fred said. He headed for the kitchen. "What's to eat?"

"*Our Town* is not dumb and you're getting chubbier every minute!" Susan called after him. "Better have a grapefruit!"

"Tell me about it, Jaws!" he shot back.

Susan looked at her mother furiously. "I'm the only person in the whole universe who's got braces at fifteen years old. Why didn't you do it when I was nine and sex appeal didn't count? Fred's don't show at all and I can't even *smile* without blinding somebody. Is there any chocolate cake left?"

"You'd better hurry or there won't be."

Zachary and Maggie trailed after the other two.

"I hope I'm not screwing things up," Zachary said. "Fred says he needs help with his Lit final. . . ."

Maggie laughed. "And on into the next generation. Without your mother, I never would have made it through Radcliffe."

Fred had sliced three squares of cake and set them on the kitchen table. Susan smiled at him. Maggie always marveled at the way her children's animosity converted to goodwill. A display of affection between them, however limited, filled Maggie with a special kind of pleasure, perhaps because she and Joanne were strangers, or worse.

"Is it just because I'm their mother," Maggie asked Zachary, "or are these two extremely engaging?"

"We're extremely engaging," Fred replied.

"It's because you're our mother," Susan said.

"Don't eat any more of that because there's something else I forgot to tell you," Maggie said. "You're invited to eat with Veronica at the Brodys'. You go too, Zach, but call your mother." She dipped her finger in Fred's icing and licked it.

"She's always snorting coke in the john," Susan said.

"I can't believe that. She's just a baby."

Zachary nodded somberly at Maggie.

"I'll go anyway," Fred said. "Mrs. Brody's a great cook."

"How come you're forgetting all this stuff, Mom? It's not you." Susan looked at her mother with concern.

"Momentary lapse, I guess. Do Robin and Jackson know about Veronica?"

"Mother, don't you dare tell them we said anything!" Susan cried.

"Mrs. Brody's not dumb, Sue," Fred said. "I bet she already knows her stepdaughter's a loony-tune. Anyway, stepmothers are required to hate their stepchildren. It's in all the fairy tales. Except stepmothers are supposed to be ugly, and Mrs. Brody's a piece of ass."

"Fred," Maggie complained. She realized with a shock that her discomfort rose not so much from Fred's language as from the knowledge that he was becoming a sexual person. It was happening too fast.

"You're a horny little thing," Susan said, setting her dish in the sink. "First it's Zach's mother's legs and now Mrs. Brody, and she's even pregnant."

"That other friend of Mom's not bad either," Fred said. "Vonderhyde."

"My mom has nice legs?" Zachary asked Fred.

"I can't stand it," Maggie said.

Later on, she sent them off to the Brodys' in a cab. The housekeeper would be there as chaperon, but Maggie still worried.

"We'll be fine, Mom," Fred assured her. "If Veronica wants to rot holes in her nostrils, that's her problem."

"Anyway," Susan added, "as Marie Antoinette said, 'Let them snort coke.' "

Maggie shut the door and heard them chattering on their way to the elevator. Zachary, as always, had been too quiet. The expressions on his face did not provide the open easy reading of her own children. Fred and Susan seemed so confident that nothing terrible could ever happen to them. When Maggie was growing up, she was always convinced that catastrophe was imminent. She read statistics about leukemia, automobile accidents, and spinal meningitis and assumed they applied to her, if not today, then first thing next week. Somehow, her children had eluded the paranoia of her own adolescence. Perhaps it was because they had no older sister like Joanne to create emotional pandemonium. Or parents like Phyllis and Stephen.

An hour later, Maggie arrived at the Café des Artistes. She liked the place, with its lovely murals and dim light that was mysterious rather than oppressive. The European ambience was a respite from the raw pounding energy of the street outside. When Maggie felt like plugging into New York's potent current, she chose one of the bustling Third Avenue restaurants. There, plate-glass windows revealed the mob inside to the mob outside, not like the Café, where even the entrance was covert.

Robin and Jackson were already seated. Jackson, always gallant, rose to greet Maggie and settle her in her chair. Maggie almost expected to have her hand kissed. It would be a natural gesture for Jackson Brody, though she had never met another man who could have gotten away with it.

Jackson was sixteen years older than Robin. He looked like General Robert E. Lee in a Brooks Brothers suit. Tall, elegant, silver-haired, he should have been Savannah-bred, but in fact he was born in Jackson Heights—hence his name—just across the East River. Jackson had spent most of his life scrambling to support his parents, both now dead, and an alcoholic sister. He had met Robin—and Maggie, too—while working as an advertising executive at the mammoth *Woman's Companion* magazine. Then recently separated from his wife, he had lost his secretary besides. When Robin showed up for an interview, tripped over the extension cord, landed in Jackson's lap, and said hello with perfect equanimity, Jackson hired her on the spot. They were married as soon as the divorce went through.

"The kids have an extra baby-sitter tonight," Robin said.

"Aunt Titmouse from Dayton," Jackson explained. Each of Robin's multitudinous relations was named after a bird.

Robin ignored him. "My Auntie Wren is here overnight on

her way to Boston. I'm glad she's around to keep an eye on the nest."

"Do they need it?" Jackson asked.

"Veronica does," Robin replied.

She knows, Maggie decided. And Jackson doesn't, or doesn't want to. The waiter, who had perfect white teeth, asked Maggie if she wanted a drink. She ordered a glass of wine. As another customer squeezed past their table, the waiter pressed against her bare shoulder. After he had gone, the small area on her skin throbbed pleasantly.

"Hello, troops," Matthew said. He kissed the women and shook Jackson's hand. There was always an initial formality between the men, but after an evening together, Matthew invariably declared that Jackson was a terrific guy and he was going to set up a lunch date. Somehow, however, he never got around to it.

"Where'd you get that nice-looking corsage?" he asked Robin as he sat down next to Maggie. Robin wore a small bouquet of exotic blossoms over her left breast.

"Oh, Jackson's always bringing me flowers." In her Midwestern drawl, the word came out "flaahrs."

"I think I last brought a bunch to Maggie when she was in the hospital having Fred. She's not the flowers type."

Maggie stared at him.

"I made Jackson some beaded ones for his office," Robin said. She looked especially pretty tonight, Maggie thought. Part of the glow was due to her pregnancy. After two miscarriages, making it past five months had added extra sparkle to her eyes. Her hair puffed around her face in a bubble that had been the envy of every female two decades ago and was the despair of Robin right now. But Jackson liked it, so that was how it stayed.

The waiter arrived with Maggie's wine. She wished he would press against her again, but dinner was served expertly without so much as a feather touch. The conversations soon split into duets: Jackson and Matthew on real estate; Robin and Maggie on the merits of bearing children.

"Jackson thinks I'm crazy to keep trying and I know he worries," Robin said, "but look, Maggie, you've got your art . . ."

Maggie laughed. She studied the scrap of paper she had been doodling on. She had sketched a cartoon of the waiter with the perfect teeth. "This isn't exactly my idea of art." Maggie crumpled the paper and tossed it in the ashtray.

Robin retrieved it, smoothed it out, and examined it thoughtfully. "I don't have much of a brain," she said.

"You're a killer at the bridge table."

"That wouldn't get me far in the world of high finance. I want babies. Maybe it's because I come from a big family, who knows? I just want at least one."

"You don't have to defend yourself, Rob. I think it's a fine idea."

Robin shook her head. "Do you realize I've been pregnant almost nonstop for two years? And I get nuttier all the time. I lost Jackson's coffee yesterday. I picked up his cup to fill it, went into the bedroom to fetch something, I don't remember what, and when I came back to the kitchen, the cup was gone. We looked everywhere. I was ready to check into Bellevue." She folded Maggie's cartoon and slipped it into her handbag. "I finally found it when I went to change the sheets. It was in the linen closet."

Maggie laughed. "I remember. I always got this thing about open doors. I couldn't bear any door that was even slightly ajar. And I was always drifting off somewhere. I'd wake up and wonder where I'd been. At work, on the bus, it didn't matter." She thought for a moment. "As a matter of fact, it's been happening again lately, a little like that. Only, well, I know I'm not pregnant."

"I was hoping it'd go away once I had the baby."

"A lot of it did for me. Except that once you've got a child, you're not in control anymore, and I don't know if it ever comes back completely. Maybe when they're all over twenty-one. I'm still waiting. Why did you save that cartoon?"

"I always keep your stuff. For when you're famous."

Maggie laughed. The men's voices had risen to an impassioned pitch, so Maggie and Robin turned to listen.

"He bought in sixty-eight—three bedrooms on Park for twenty-five grand!" Matthew exclaimed.

"Jesus!"

"How come you guys get so worked up over a pile of concrete?" Robin wanted to know.

"There's a great deal of magic in the rise and fall of co-op prices," Matthew explained.

"Uh-huh," Maggie said.

They were nearly through with their coffee when a couple drifted past the table. The woman stopped and swooped on Matthew with a little cry.

"Matthew!" Her voice, like her face, was unmistakably that of Helene Sargeant, the actress. Matthew half-rose, but she placed her fingers with their long painted nails on his shoulder. And left them there, Maggie noticed.

"Please don't get up," said Helene. She turned to her companion. "Darling, this is the marvelous attorney who saved me from those dreadful piranhas at Lunar Pictures." "Darling" was obviously doomed to remain nameless, so Matthew made his introductions.

". . . and my wife, Margaret." Maggie watched Helene's face and waited for the inevitable shock. It came, reading: What's brilliant, gorgeous Matthew Hollander doing with a dowdy number like you? Maggie wondered how difficult it would be to peel those white fingers off Matthew's suit.

Helene soon swept off in a cloud of chiffon and subtle perfume.

"Whew." Jackson was awed. "Do they always talk like that?"

"Yes," Matthew said.

"I feel like a lump of pie dough," Robin said, looking down at her pregnant bulge. "She weighs ninety-two pounds with her jewels on."

Maggie watched Matthew curiously. As always, he was unimpressed, by both Helene's celebrity stature and her seductive interest in him. Maggie had attended cocktail parties where glamorous women draped their cleavages all over Matthew. He was polite, sometimes even flirtatious, but only in the friendly manner he applied to his interchanges with the fat Hungarian lady who cleaned his office at night. Maggie would watch with amusement as Matthew's admirers became increasingly frantic in their efforts to engage his libido. Finally, if the attentions grew too heated, his face closed shop and he would move away. He didn't like obvious women, he said, which was his major complaint about Phyllis Wheeler.

"Helene reminds me of Phyllis Wheeler," Matthew said.

"Lucky Phyllis," sighed Robin.

"It's no compliment," Maggie said.

"Helene's much more attractive," Jackson said. "More feminine."

"Phyllis is about as feminine as Attila the Hun," Matthew pronounced.

"Fred thinks she has nice legs," Maggie said. "Anyway, it's getting late. We ought to get the check."

"Better watch out," Matthew went on. "Phyllis'll have our Fred in the sack before he knows what hit him."

"That's a little too young, even for Phyllis," Maggie said carefully. She drained her wineglass and looked around for the waiter. Something moved in her stomach, and she visualized her half-digested pasta coiling and twisting down there in the dark, as ugly as disloyalty. Matthew knew how his contempt for Phyllis pained Maggie. If Maggie were only more like her sister, Jo, she would stand up and deliver a diatribe right here in the subdued murkiness of the restaurant.

"Phyllis came to see me every day when I was in the hospital," Robin said. "She always brought something, a little gift. She acts tough, but she's a softie, really."

"She'd seduce Jackson or me without a qualm," Matthew said.

"That's not true," Maggie protested.

"Well, let's give her half a qualm then," Jackson said.

"You guys don't understand. That's just sex," Robin insisted.

"She's an aggressive bitch, not to mention nymphomaniac," Matthew muttered. "I don't know why Maggie hangs out with her." Matthew now sounded as angry as Maggie felt.

The people at the next table had turned to look at them. Maggie dropped her voice and articulated with clipped deliberation, "She can't help it. It's a sickness with her. She was raped by her cousin when she was eight years old, and she's never gotten it all straightened out. Who could?"

"She probably raped *him*," Matthew said.

Maggie forgot about the curiosity of the neighboring table and blurted out furiously, "You can't stand her because she's not a goddamn clinging vine like the rest of us." As she glared at Matthew, Maggie felt that the only way to stop the trembling of her fingers would be to encircle his neck with them and squeeze hard. The fantasy terrified her. She dropped her eyes and murmured, "I don't know where that came from."

"I suggest you find out," Matthew said in his attorney voice.

Robin was staring at them with the pain of a child watching its parents quarrel. Her lips moved as if she were trying to find the words to make it all better.

Maggie reached over to take a sip from Jackson's wineglass. "It's all right, Robin. I'm all done being a bore."

"My flowers smell like cigarettes," Robin said sadly.

During the ballet, Maggie tried to concentrate on the dancers but was distracted by Matthew's body beside her. He was a shadowy hulk she could barely see out of the corner of her eye, and yet every time he shifted in his seat, she was startled. She felt frantic to do something about that substantial shape but could not think what it was she ought to do. Halfway through the performance, she began to feel trapped. She was four seats from the aisle. What if there was a fire? She'd never make it to the exit. She was perspiring and sick at her stomach. It seemed forever until the ecstatic audience allowed the ballerina to make her final bow.

Robin and Jackson got out of the cab first. In the elevator, Matthew said, "Nice music. Did you enjoy it?"

Maggie nodded.

"Jackson's a good man," he said serenely. "Think I'll call him up and have lunch."

"You do that," Maggie said.

4

Maggie stood on the corner of Fifth Avenue and Fifty-third Street and closed her eyes. When she and Joanne were children, they had often played the blind game, tying scarves around their faces and stumbling about the house to see what it felt like. Maggie had watched her own children do the same thing. But this spot in front of St. Thomas Church at noon on a sunny spring day seemed likely to short-circuit the sensitive auditory system of any blind person. Ornate, exotic languages eddied around her: Chinese, French, Spanish, something Slavic. Beyond the traffic sounds of Fifth Avenue, a vendor hawked T-shirts, announcing designer names like station stops on a commuter train. To her right, a trio—violin, flute, and clarinet, she guessed— performed Vivaldi at the bottom of the church steps, and down the avenue she could hear the plink-plank-plunk of Caribbean kettledrums. She wondered if a blind person could identify his locale simply by listening to the sounds of a given corner. The subdued din of Madison and Eighty-first must differ from a street in SoHo or some busy intersection in the financial district.

As she opened her eyes, the light changed again and she was jostled out into the street. It was pleasant to move along with the crowd, and besides, she wanted to be prompt for her semiannual lunch date with Hilary Vonderhyde. Ordinarily Hilary needed three weeks' advance notice to squeeze a social lunch into her schedule, but this time Hilary had called only yesterday. Maggie was so curious that she canceled the appointment with her gynecologist and agreed to come.

Maggie had not visited CinemInc since Hilary's last promotion. Her new office was vast. It had corner windows and a plush, colorful decor. On the walls were framed graphics of CinemInc's latest films. There were two medium-sized trees on either side of the couch. Hilary stood behind a sleek blond desk. She waved at Maggie and continued her telephone conversation.

"No, get me Phil Kessler. I don't *want* Mason, he's no damn good. I gotta go. Just do it, okay, hon? I know you can. 'Bye." She hung up and came to give Maggie a kiss. Her electric-blue silk blouse and gray slacks showed off her figure. She was as tall and slender as Maggie, though her breasts were fuller. She rarely wore a bra.

"I always like standing next to you," Maggie said. "With Robin, I remember those awful days when I was tallest in the class."

"I know. I wanted to cut off my feet. Or head. Anything. I ordered us some salads. They ought to be here in a minute. Yikes, it's been a zoo around here today. We've got two productions going in Manhattan and there's an awful hassle with the Sanitation Department. Come sit." She led Maggie to the couch and they each took a corner. Maggie leaned back into the cushions and sighed.

"It's a beautiful office. Congratulations."

"Not bad. They were scared shitless I was going to leave, but of course I wouldn't have."

"You're still loving it."

Hilary tapped her knee with her fist. "It's my hedge against chaos, this place. It's only outside I get into trouble."

A young man appeared at the door with two paper bags. He had a beard, a ponytail, and a necktie with bright red tongues on it. His eyes were innocent, ethereally beautiful, but his jeans were very tight. There was a bulge on the left side of his crotch which Maggie tried hard to ignore.

"Be a love, Tom, and don't let them get to me for half an hour."

Tom nodded and left.

"Do you have to be gorgeous to work here?" Maggie asked.

"I think that's one of the reasons I'm comfortable in this place. Everybody's so attractive it's boring already. I don't get looked at here, not like on the street." She pried open a tinfoil container and handed it to Maggie. "The best fruit salad and frozen yogurt in town."

"Is it really so terrible being beautiful?"

Hilary smiled at her. "I'm thinking of getting a nose job. I'm going to find some quack who'll bust it all to hell for me, and while he's at it, he can break a few teeth or rearrange them all snaggled and give me little squinty eyes. Maybe I'll order banana boobs and spindly legs."

"I don't think you'd enjoy it."

"I suppose not, but I'd like to try it for a day or two. You look pretty smashing yourself."

Maggie was wearing the loose black dress that showed off her long legs. Sunglasses with immense round lenses were perched on her head.

"You seemed kind of down at Phyllis's," Hilary went on. "Is everything okay, really?"

"Not to worry."

"She was on your case about your sex life."

"I went right home and raped the elevator man."

Hilary watched her in silence.

"Really, Hil. I'm fine. Lord."

"Okay, but I don't like thinking you're off center. You're the most stable person I know."

"Aren't I entitled to a nervous breakdown like everybody else?"

"How'd you like a job?" Hilary asked abruptly.

Maggie set down her plastic fork.

"Yeah, a job. Full-time. I need somebody to do publicity posters. The guy we're using's a schmuck. Everybody comes out looking like Richard Gere or Elizabeth Montgomery."

"Why me?"

"You can do likenesses. You've had plenty of experience at the magazine."

"Are you doing this because you're worried about me?"

"You just told me not to worry."

"I haven't had a job in ten years. More. I'd have to talk to Matt. The kids."

"What do they have to do with it?"

"Lots. It would mess everything up, me working. I don't even have the room at home, the materials."

"You'll work here, lovey. What do you say?"

"I say . . . God. I don't know what to say."

"The pay's good. Four hundred a week to start."

"I think I made one-fifteen at *Companion*."

"So you'll do it?"

Maggie laughed. "Wait." She sat still while her yogurt melted into sugary soup. "What if you had to fire me?"

"I'd be ruthless."

"What about our friendship?"

"I can handle it if you can. If I dump you, I guess we might have a couple of tense bridge games."

"I'm flattered."

"Don't be flattered, just do it. I need you. Now let's forget it and finish our lunch. Yuck. It's all mush."

"I feel exactly the way I did the night Matthew called and asked me out." She waved her hands in front of her face as if she were erasing a blackboard. "Okay, okay, I'll forget it. You still seeing Bill?"

"I'm doing my best not to. Why am I so magnetized by bastards? It's a classic case of self-contempt. I'm always inflicting these sadists on myself. If they're nice, I just want them to go away."

"What about the detective, isn't he nice?"

"Oh, Lou's all right. I let him touch me above the waist now, but I don't think he'll ever graduate to down below." She stirred her yogurt absently. "Sex has become an awful bore. Here I am in my prime and orgasms are like great big yawns. Maybe I should get into group gropes or necrophilia. Oh, Christ, Mag, I look at you and Matthew and wonder if it'll ever happen to me."

"What makes us so great?"

Hilary leaned forward earnestly. "You're friends. You respect each other. It shows in the way you relate."

Maggie was beginning to feel the familiar panic again. It suddenly reminded her of being stuck between stations in the subway. It was always dark and hot and there was a dangerous smell. Perspiration slid down her sides.

"You're absolutely the best married people I know," Hilary declared.

"What about Robin and Jackson?"

"That's strictly father-daughter. Who needs it? Besides, I'm too tall to be anybody's little girl. Come on." Hilary unfolded her legs. "Let me show you around your new office." Maggie got up and began tidying the coffee table, but Hilary took her arm. "Leave it, you're not at home now."

Maggie followed her down a carpeted corridor to the design department. There was a large well-lighted room with windows reaching practically to the ceiling. Two men and a woman looked up from their drawing boards to nod at Hilary. The men wore beards. One of them was completing a mock-up for the new Sylvia Goodwin picture. His composition was off, Maggie noticed. She longed to fix it.

Hilary half-dragged her out the door and down the hall. "One of the guys is gay, one's happily married, and the girl's an ambitious little thing. Reminds me of me. Ah, he's in." They stood in the doorway of an office only slightly larger than Hilary's. "Jim, this is the lady I told you about. Maggie Hollander, James Perry, our illustrious leader."

Perry came around from behind his desk. He, too, was bearded. Perhaps it was a requirement for men working here, Maggie thought. The women had to be beautiful, the men hairy. Perhaps she ought to try growing a beard.

Perry had a kind young-old face—childlike expression and yet plenty of wrinkles in the forehead and around the eyes. He had probably suffered, but he was not embittered. His handclasp was warm and firm.

"I hear good things about you," he said. "I hope you'll be joining us."

Maggie hoped her smile wasn't idiotic. Hilary walked her to the elevator.

"That's too much," Maggie whispered. "You didn't have to bother him."

"We want you."

"You don't even know what I can do."

"Don't tell *me*. I'm paid to know what people can and can't do. You're the one who doesn't know. Call me tomorrow." It was a command. She gave Maggie a little shove into the elevator.

On the way down, Maggie speculated as to why Hilary wasn't a more assertive bridge player. Perhaps if they tried playing in Hilary's elegant office where she felt most at home, there would be a marked improvement. When Hilary had first showed up as a copy editor at *Woman's Companion*, Maggie had sensed the vine-covered walls and manicured lawns in her background. It turned out that the two women had been educated at neighboring boarding schools and had almost certainly met each other's lacrosse fields. They traded stories about the agony of tea dances, the joy of tiffin, the mysterious forbidden attraction of "townies." One day when Maggie's parents arrived at the office to take her to lunch, Hilary pulled Maggie aside, nearly exploding with suppressed laughter, to inform Maggie that their mothers owned the exact same navy Lily Pulitzer wraparound with the yellow daisy print. Before long, Maggie and Hilary called their parents identical pairs of BYW's—Boring Yankee Wasps.

If these two had been watered in the same garden, how then, Maggie wondered, had their futures diverged so dramatically? Here was Hilary, a glittering success in her career, interviewed in *Time*, photographed for fashion magazines, with nothing but emptiness and discontent lurking one step outside her glamorous office. And as for Maggie, there was the doling out of meals and comfort while her dreams of artistic productivity had shriveled into a tiny painful knot in some obscure corner of her consciousness.

Back in her own kitchen massaging herbs into the leg of lamb, Maggie thought about how it would be if she actually took the job. The idea seemed so radical, and yet women went back to work all the time. But the children still needed her. And Matthew, too. He was hopelessly disorganized outside of his office. Of course, she could hire someone to do the errands. Still, nobody else could do them properly. Who else could have chosen the appropriate present for Fred's friend? Who else could select the exact color of Matthew's shoelaces? What about groceries and menu planning? It was so complicated, with Susan's allergies. By the time she finished explaining everything to a housekeeper, it would be easier to do it herself. And who wanted a stranger around the house? It was such an intrusion. No, she wouldn't take the job. Later, when the children were in college.

Besides, wasn't she supposed to be an artist, the kind who sits in a room by herself and creates things that do more than persuade people to buy things they can't afford? She always meant to make art, not sales. On the other hand, she had never been convinced of the value of her vision. And CinemInc was so attractive. It had been a long time since she'd participated in the companionable activity of a busy office. And she was needed. Hilary made that very clear. Oh, hell, maybe she'd just do it.

She changed her mind a dozen times before dinner. Finally she resolved to let the ultimate decision rest with the reaction of her family. She would assess their response and act accordingly.

It was peculiar for Maggie to be the bearer of news. Normally she listened while the others related the day's triumphs and defeats. Tonight would be different. She would wait and tell them at dinner when they were all sitting down together. She was eager to share it, and yet holding back for a little while was delicious, the way she had hoarded the confirmation of her pregnancy with Fred, lying on her bed and smiling at the ceiling for an hour before calling Matthew.

Finally, when everyone was seated, she handed the platter of roast lamb across the table to Matthew. Fred watched her.

"What's with you, Mom?" he asked.

Maggie reached out and touched her son's arm in appreciation. "I've been offered a job." There was so much music in the statement that it sounded like a chord played by a full orchestra, strings, woodwinds, brass, and all. Everyone heard it differently.

"You don't sound very happy about it," Susan said.

"She does, too," Fred objected.

"What kind of job?" Matthew asked. "Pass the butter, please, Frederick."

"Assistant art director at CinemInc. I'd be doing the promotion posters."

"Jeez, CinemInc," Fred breathed. "Maybe I could meet Harrison Ford."

"Hilary get you into it?" Matthew asked.

Maggie nodded. "She really put on the pressure. Even introduced me to James Perry. He's very nice."

Matthew smiled indulgently. "Jim Perry's a lot of things, but nice isn't one of them."

"How would you feel if I took it?" Maggie asked.

"How you feel is more to the point."

"What if your shirts aren't done on time? What about dinner? What about . . ."

He interrupted her. "Get a gofer. Hire somebody. It's just scut work around here. I assume they'll pay you decently."

Scut work, Maggie said to herself. So that's what I've been doing all these years.

She remembered when Matthew used to introduce her to clients as "My wife, Maggie, the gifted artist." But after a while it just became, "My wife, Maggie," and when he found her sliding paint boxes and empty canvases under the bed for storage, he had said, "Seems a shame," without further comment.

"How *much*, Mom?" Susan persisted.

"Four hundred a week."

"Take it," Matthew said. "It'll be good for you to do something useful."

"Mom's useful," Fred said. He was beginning to look anxious.

"Just like that, just take it," Maggie said.

"Yup," Matthew affirmed.

"You make it sound so easy."

"Shouldn't be hard. It's nice of Hilary."

"I don't know if she's being *nice*. . . ." Maggie began. "She seems to think I can do it."

"Of course you can do it, but you don't have a track record in the field. She could choose anybody at all for an operation like CinemInc."

Maggie sat in silence.

"Will you be home when we get out of school?" Fred wanted to know.

"I don't know. I guess not," Maggie replied.

"I wouldn't like that. I'd live with it for the sake of art, though, I guess."

"Art!" Susan sniffed. "It's a big sellout if you ask me. Mom's work should be hanging in the Metropolitan, not the subway station. Boy, when I'm a writer, you won't catch me writing junk. If it's not good stuff, I won't write at all."

"I thought you were going to be an actress," Fred said. "You're always blabbing away in that goony accent."

"I'm just trying to stay in character," she protested. As the lead in the school production of *Our Town*, Susan had adopted a decidedly New England inflection.

"You'll wind up writing TV scripts for *Dallas*," Fred taunted.

"I'd die first."

"Cool it," Matthew said. "I'll have another slice of that lamb. The decision is up to your mother. Let her struggle with it in peace."

"It isn't only up to her, Daddy. We're her family," Susan complained.

"Why do you talk about me as if I'm not here? I'm not 'her,' I'm 'you.' "

Susan looked confused.

"Never mind," Maggie said.

But Susan turned to address her directly. "Okay, I'm saying that as my mother, you have a responsibility to be a role model and I don't think you're being a very good one."

"Oh, listen to her . . ." Fred began in disgust, but Susan cut him off.

"No, really, she's this homebody type all the time and we all know what that means . . ."

Maggie wondered what it meant.

". . . and now she's going to take this sucky job that just exploits her talent as a true artist, so then she'll be a failure as a woman *and* an artist. What kind of example is that for her children, especially me, since I'm the creative one?"

"That's the most ridiculous junk I ever heard," Fred maintained.

Maggie sat looking at her plate. She was trying to hide the fact that she was crying, but it was difficult because large drops kept splashing onto her vegetables.

The others watched in horror as tiny thuds of tears hit her baked potato. Maggie never cried in front of the children.

"I think you'd better apologize to your mother, Susan," Matthew said.

By this time, Susan was crying too. "I'm sorry, Mommy."

But Maggie shoved her chair back and murmured, "I think I'd better be excused." She fled to the bedroom and shut the door.

Later, as she and Matthew lay side by side in the dark, Maggie said, "I think I might like to try sky-diving someday."

"You're kidding me."

"I don't know if I am."

"Well, take it from me, it's not your style." He rolled over and soon she could hear him breathing with the slow rhythm of sleep.

5

The buzzer sounded next to Matthew Hollander's elbow. He pushed a button. "Send him in, Barbara." Hollis Reardon's papers were ready, and Matthew was pleased. He had pried a reasonable deal out of International Films, a particularly gratifying outcome since Reardon had been screwed at least a dozen times over the years. It was pitiful how helpless creative people could be. In fact, their vulnerability was the reason Matthew had opted for entertainment law in the first place. Writers, performers, painters, it was all the same. Somebody had to protect their interests or they'd never survive.

The one exception was Maggie. She was the only artist Matthew had ever met with common sense. Joanne had the creative temperament in that family. Of course, Joanne was compelled to paint, and with Maggie, art was strictly part-time, though in his opinion, Maggie was more talented.

Hollis Reardon stepped into the office. Matthew rose to shake his hand. "Glad to meet you in person after all those marathon phone calls," Matthew said. Reardon was short, round, and red-faced, not at all what Matthew had expected from the deep booming drawl.

"Some beautiful view," Reardon said.

Matthew glanced out the window. His office was twenty stories up over New York harbor. The building, constructed in 1898, had long ago achieved landmark status. Matthew's mahogany-paneled office had been occupied by lawyers since the turn of the century. "Thanks for reminding me," he said. "I don't think I've looked out that window in three weeks. Have a seat."

"I want to thank you for what you've done," Reardon said. "I really got my ass wiped with the last screenplay."

Matthew smiled. Vulgarity seemed incongruous coming from the rosebud mouth of this small man. Still, Reardon's writing was powerful, often even brutal. Matthew thought of Maggie's paintings. They shimmered with vitality, and yet she was a restrained person, rather formal, not the least bit flamboyant.

"We've built in some percentage points in case the picture does well," Matthew said, "but I think we've got the maximum up front. Once these guys get out of production and into the accountant's office, you end up with zero."

Reardon nodded. "I've been up that rat hole."

They spent an hour poring over the papers for Reardon's contract. Then Matthew leaned back in his chair. A few years ago, he would have made sure his client was out the door the moment they finished, but Matthew had put in plenty of pressure-cooker years. Now he was entitled to savor his triumphs. He snapped the stereo on to WQXR and was rewarded with Rubinstein's Chopin *Preludes*.

"You know what this contract means, besides paying off the

Mercedes?" Reardon asked. "After I finish the film, I'm taking six months off to write poetry."

"My mother was a poet for a while," Matthew said. "She even published a book. A small one."

"That was in the days when people read poems, I guess," Reardon said.

"She was damn good. It was a great disappointment to her that I didn't inherit any of her literary genes. Christ, she used to sit with me hour after hour doing 'descriptions,' she called them. I was supposed to describe things I saw or thought about or dreamed of. But I was one of her least successful projects. I couldn't even write a decent letter home from camp."

Reardon's cherubic face looked so crestfallen that Matthew smiled. "That's probably why I got into this business. I may not possess the sparks myself, but I can be the guardian of the flame." Matthew looked at his watch. The gesture was not lost on Reardon. He rose and held out his hand.

Afterward, Matthew sat and stared out the window. He decided the Statue of Liberty looked like a Staten Island housewife who had fallen into the water with her nightgown on. She rose out of the harbor with her hair in rollers. Helicopters flew past her head like gnats and she had raised a weary hand to swipe at them. Rubinstein switched to Brahms. The sound was complex, passionate and disturbing. Matthew felt eyes on him and turned to see Maggie's face regarding him from her portrait. It was his favorite picture of her, taken when they were first married. Her hair had been longer then, long enough to wear in stubby braids. She was sitting on the gunwale of a sailboat wearing white shorts, one of Matthew's T-shirts, and a wide grin. Come to think of it, he hadn't seen that grin in a long time.

Maybe he ought to take her on a vacation this summer when the kids went to camp. Up until now, there had been so many demands from the firm. Matthew had seen his opportunity to become indispensable. He had achieved that now, as much as anybody could realistically become indispensable. But he deserved a break, and the two of them hadn't been away alone together in several years. Maggie sometimes talked wistfully about London and Paris, but he failed to see the charm in clomping around a city when they lived in one. Maybe an adult tennis camp. Maggie enjoyed being active as much as he did. He'd check it out.

Funny how he couldn't seem to get into his work today. Ordinarily he enjoyed the office. He was eager to plunge in every morning and reluctant to extract himself in the evening. Matthew performed countless juggling acts every day, keeping clients, adversaries, and other attorneys spinning in the air above his desk. For the most part, they returned to earth at Matthew's bidding, to land on the appropriate spot. It had happened that way with Reardon, but there were two other challenging matters that required his immediate attention. However, rather than delve into the files, he swung around in his chair again to avoid Maggie's stare. Home was intruding into his bastion today. Perhaps it was this morning's conference with Susan's teacher, where he was due in less than an hour.

This would be Matthew's first parent-teacher conference since Susan's nursery-school years. During her first weeks, Matthew had walked her to the sunny brick building every morning on his way to work. She was so tiny that he could cup her chin with his hand as they strolled side by side along Seventy-ninth Street. She had clung to him and cried when it was time for him to leave her. Matthew had expected this, but he was unprepared for his own pain.

Then in October, there had been a crisis at the firm. Maggie took over walking Susan, and Matthew had never really participated in her education again. But he still remembered that when he kissed her good-bye outside her nursery schoolroom, she had smelled of bread and butter.

Matthew quickly became comfortable with Maggie's sovereignty in that area of their lives. He trusted her judgment with the children more than his own. What was more, he had come to dislike any trespass from home into the cerebral citadel of his profession. Today, however, Susan's teacher had particularly asked if both parents would be attending the conference. Maggie interpreted this to mean that Matthew's presence was expected. Susan had walked into the kitchen just as the topic arose. She had fixed her eyes on his face, and Matthew found there was no way to refuse.

He peered sideways at Maggie's photograph and could not help smiling. He remembered that they had just made love minutes before he snapped the picture. Christ, they'd been crazy about each other. In those days, Maggie could barely keep her hands off him. Even at the movies, he would feel her fingers between his legs, hidden under an extra sweater or a raincoat draped across his lap. It was the same with him. Her breasts were like small round magnets; even in public places, he was always managing a sly touch.

The first time he had gotten close to her, she was standing at the checkout counter in the Cambridge five-and-dime. Silently he calculated that spot on his rib cage where her breasts would hit him. He liked the way she carried herself, proudly, like a beautiful woman. There was a cloaked quality of specialness about her that he found tantalizing, perhaps all the more because she was, at first glance, rather plain. Matthew was well aware of the bewilderment people like Helene Sargeant tried to mask when meeting Maggie for the first time. Matthew's reaction was inevitably one of smugness. Maggie was secret treasure. No one else knew her sensuality, her talent, her intelligence, her warmth.

He saw her work at the student gallery in May of their junior year. The energy of the compositions intrigued him. At the first opportunity, which turned out to be that sparkling

September day in Harvard Square, he had slipped his arm through hers.

He could still visualize her sitting across from him in the coffee shop. The flat surfaces of her face hid nothing, and yet she took such care in what she revealed with words. She had lightly freckled skin and a wide smile that showed teeth still grooved at the edges like a child's. There was a gap between the front two that created a slight lisp. Matthew found it enchanting. He could see the tip of her tongue as it appeared behind that space when she spoke.

Matthew was accustomed to being gazed at by faces that oozed adulation. Maggie's eyes, however, seemed to be measuring him. Their clear message said: Look, mister, I know you're supposed to be a hotshot, but I'm not impressed yet. From the start, he was eager to earn her regard.

His clock bonged ten times. He would have to get a move on if he was going to make Susan's conference on time. Regretfully, he snapped off the radio.

Matthew was the only man wearing a suit in the subway car. At this hour, it was almost empty. In the corner slouched a heap of filthy rags with a pair of naked blackened feet protruding from the bottom and a rope of greasy hair on top twisted into a grotesque tiara. Two Puerto Rican men rode directly across from Matthew. They talked animatedly in Spanish with much gesticulation. One was angry, the other apologetic but calm. The louder the angry man became, the more silent his companion. Finally, at Fourteenth Street, the quiet man began speaking. He permitted no interruption and restrained the other man's speech by holding his hands down. By Thirty-third Street, he had finished. As the train pulled into the station, they stared at each other. Then the angry man, with tears on his cheeks, reached for his friend and they embraced. Both men's eyes were tight shut. After that, they sat next to each other without speaking until Fifty-ninth, where they got off.

Since subway trips were normally for catching up on reading, Matthew was seldom aware of such interchanges. But something about the relationship between the two men captured his attention. Matthew had no close male friends. There were other lawyers to meet for lunch, men at the Harvard Club with whom he played an occasional game of squash, and there were the husbands of Maggie's friends, yet no one but Maggie was allowed access to his deepest feelings. Perhaps these men were brothers. Matthew was an only child, but he knew from watching Maggie and Joanne what passion siblings could rouse in one another.

Matthew had been born late to busy parents who often left him alone to fend for himself. He became accustomed to long hours on his own when companionship meant books or imaginative games with his stuffed bear. When Matthew was five, his father confiscated the bear and incinerated it, believing his son had become overly dependent upon it. It was the only time Matthew could remember raised voices in his home. Matthew's mother bought him another bear, but Matthew kept it on his shelf and did not play with it again.

He was always well liked and was elected president of his class at Andover every year. There were plenty of other boys around to study with or joke with in the locker room, but nobody ever really knew what Matthew was thinking or feeling. The boys he was drawn to were the loners, the types who baffled the popular group or were despised by them. Matthew admired the solitary boys' independence, their individuality, and he understood their loneliness. One's name was Bobby Hughes, he still remembered, a gawky, sheepish fellow with a genius for botany. Any attempt to become closer to such a boy, however, was ridiculed by the others or met with incredulity by the boy himself. Matthew kept himself busy with schoolwork, extracurricular activities, and finally girls, so that he rarely felt anything was missing. Anyway, Maggie was his best friend now.

The cool air tasted delicious after the sour heat of the subway. Matthew took deep breaths as he hurried along Eighty-sixth Street. Susan and Fred's school was in a handsome stone town house just off Fifth Avenue. Around the Central Park reservoir, joggers made splashes of color like bright tropical birds as they flashed through the trees. What kind of work did those people do that they could take a run in the middle of the day? Matthew wondered.

Maggie was waiting in the reception area. Matthew bent to kiss her, but they parted quickly when a trim young woman approached them with her hand outstretched. The teacher wore her hair pulled back into a ponytail tied with colored yarn. Today the bow was hot pink.

"Miss Lennox. Good morning," Maggie said, and shook her hand.

Miss Lennox drew them into a quiet room away from the reception desk's shrill telephone.

"Is Susan aware that you are here this morning?" Miss Lennox began. The woman never used contractions. Susan did a devastating imitation of her, which Maggie was trying hard to put out of her mind.

"Yes," Matthew replied. "She heard us making plans to come up. She didn't seem disturbed, just curious."

"I think she is depressed," Miss Lennox continued. "There has been a decline in her work this term. She is doing all right, but not as well as she should be. Her demeanor has changed. She sits by herself sometimes in homeroom, and appears to be close to tears. I have checked with her other teachers, and they have all noticed the shift."

"Maybe it's too much pressure from that play," Maggie said.

Miss Lennox nodded. "I did consider that, but then I realized that she really seems like herself only when she is discussing it. Her face lights up, she sits up straighter, and so on.

I wonder if perhaps it could still be her problem from last winter."

"What problem?" Matthew asked.

"You know, Matthew," Maggie said. "When she started her period."

Matthew looked stunned.

"It is harder for some girls," Miss Lennox continued. "It came late for her, which can be upsetting. And of course, Susan is very sensitive. She takes her womanhood seriously."

"What can we do?" Maggie asked.

"I am not sure what is going on, as I said. Perhaps she will snap out of it over the summer. It is such a crazy age. I just hate to see her looking so down, you know? I am very fond of her. It's been a joy having her in my class."

Maggie was thinking that this was the second time this week she had heard the word "down" used as an adjective, and also that Miss Lennox had ultimately surrendered to the contraction.

At the luncheonette on Eighty-sixth Street, Maggie stirred her black coffee with a spoon to cool it off.

"What's the matter with the way that woman talks?" Matthew asked.

"She's very formal."

"I'll say."

"What should we do about our daughter?"

Matthew took a gulp of his coffee. Maggie maintained that the inside of his mouth was lined with asbestos.

"Nothing," he said. "Typical adolescent angst. She'll be fine once she's in camp. When was it again she started menstruating?" he asked casually.

"You've forgotten about it altogether."

"Weren't there a lot of false alarms, ever since she was . . . what, twelve, thirteen?"

"Don't you remember what a state she was in? Ashamed to go to school, everybody would know? How could you forget something like that?"

"February, wasn't it?"

Maggie's face was stony like an ancient sculpture with empty sockets where the eyes were supposed to be.

"I didn't forget," he said.

"Please don't tell me you had a lot on your mind."

"Okay." He put his hand over hers. "Mag, you want to take a vacation with me this summer? There's a really nice tennis camp in Vermont."

"I don't know."

"How come you don't know?"

"I don't know why I don't know. Let me think about it."

"All right." He glanced at his watch and rose. "Gotta run, honey. You sit and enjoy your coffee."

"What about dinner?"

"I'll call you later. I'll probably make it home." He gave her a comradely slap on the back and disappeared out the door.

Maggie took a sip of her coffee and gasped as it seared her tongue. Most likely he would forget to call, or call too late for her to organize dinner. She hated to phone him at the office. His voice always sounded like a tape-recorded message or else she was put on hold. She was left with the usual choices: prepare dinner for the children at six-thirty or ask them to wait until their father came home, just in case he made it. Eat early with them or try to wait until later. Or perhaps he would end up grabbing a sandwich at his desk after all. Phyllis Wheeler served dinner no later than seven P.M. and thereafter declared the kitchen closed. But Maggie found she was incapable of doing that to Matthew when he worked such long hours and came home looking as though he had been sucked dry.

Anyway, today was hardly a time to be looking for extra consideration from Matthew after he had trekked all the way uptown for the conference.

A twelve-year-old girl was looking through the coffee-shop window, and Maggie imagined Susan's face chastising her. Twelve years old was just about the time in her daughter's life when Maggie began to lose control, not in the sense of discipline but in her confidence that she was making valid decisions about Susan. Up until she was twelve, Susan had been deeply involved in art. Suddenly, however, Susan declared that she was finished making messes. She would become an actress or a writer. The art teacher spoke with Maggie about the sudden loss of interest, and Maggie had felt a strange sense of *déjà vu* listening to Susan's protestations that if she could not be great she didn't want to try anymore. She had snatched a watercolor off her bulletin board, ripped it up, and then burst into tears. She slammed her door against Maggie's sympathy, and Maggie had gone into her own room to cry, for the destruction of a quite beautiful painting and for the pain of a young girl who could not tolerate her own talent.

Maggie wondered if psychiatry might help. Matthew would accuse her of overreacting, and yet she was at a loss as to how to help her daughter. Maggie envied Matthew his laissez-faire attitude toward the children, but she wished there was someone she could talk to about Susan. The only person who came to mind as a sensible, sympathetic listener was Fred, and of course, the thought was absurd.

Susan was propped up in bed, coming into the final pages of *Green Dolphin Street.* Maggie slipped in quietly and sat by her feet.

"What do you think of it?" Maggie asked.

"Pretty excellent."

"Honey . . ." Maggie began. Susan's face was buried in the book. Maggie gently removed it, taking care to keep the place with her finger. "You haven't asked about our conference with Miss Lennox."

"Nope."

"Aren't you curious?"

"I guess so."

"She's a little concerned about your state of mind."

"I am okay." Susan began tracing the designs in her quilt.

"Don't mock her."

"I didn't know I was."

"Miss Lennox says you seem depressed."

Susan shrugged.

"Is it your period?"

"That." Her voice was filled with disgust.

"Are you having trouble?"

"I'm getting it, isn't that trouble enough?" The reading light glinted off her braces.

"It shouldn't be trouble. It should be a joy."

Susan burst out, "A joy! That's rich!"

Maggie dipped her head and smiled. "You're right. That sounded like something my ninety-year-old ex-gynecologist would say. Let's call it a mixed blessing."

"Well, I'd just as soon be a guy."

"You seemed so happy when it first came, and then I don't know what happened to you."

"Mom, it's different before," Susan explained patiently. "There's, like, this crazy idea that it's a magic event or something. Everything's going to be perfect when you get your period and it's practically all anybody ever talks about in junior high. You'll be beautiful and, oh, womanly, or something. You wait and wait, and then, God . . ." She shuddered. "Who knew it would just be gory and disgusting."

Maggie fingered the soft tendrils that waved around her daughter's cheeks. "It's not so bad being a woman."

"Mom, I don't want to hurt your feelings . . ."

"But?"

"I don't know how to say this without . . ."

"Never mind. Just out with it."

Susan dropped her eyes. "I'd just rather not end up like you."

Maggie sighed.

"If you're not miserable, you ought to be," Susan declared.

"Why?"

"It's *nothing* here. You wait on everybody, do chores, tuck us all in, and I'm not saying I don't appreciate it. But, Mom, I don't want to grow up and be everybody's nursemaid. I mean, God, Mom, you went to Radcliffe!" Susan's eyes had filled with tears. "I want to be pretty," she went on. "I want to grow up and have babies. I love babies. I mean, when I'm baby-sitting and I hold Meredith, I pretend she's mine. But . . ." Her voice had deteriorated into a strangled choke. Tears spilled onto her nightshirt.

Maggie held out her arms. "I'm not saying it's easy," she said, rocking her daughter. "I guess I'm still looking for answers too."

Susan's voice was muffled against her shoulder. "I don't want to learn with you. I want you to show me. I want you to know."

"But those would be my answers, honey. You have to find your own."

Susan sniffed. Maggie reached for the Kleenex box, handed it to her, and sat back to watch her blow her nose. "God, Mom, sometimes I'm so grim I can't stand myself."

"That's your job. You're a teenager."

"I just want to be happy." She grinned at Maggie. "Tall order, huh?"

Maggie nodded. "It'll require some effort." She picked up Susan's book and skimmed the last page. "You're going to like the ending."

"Don't tell me!"

Maggie gave the damp cheek a kiss. It tasted cool and salty. "I'm nuts about you," she said.

"Well, I'm just plain nuts," Susan replied.

When Maggie crawled into bed later on, she realized that sometime after her conversation with Susan, she had decided to unearth her oils and her easel.

6

Maggie telephoned Hilary in the morning and turned down the job.

"Why?" Hilary asked.

"I'm not ready for that yet. But, Hil, I'm going to get back into it, my work. I don't think I would have if you hadn't prodded me."

"What exactly are you going to do?"

"Enroll in a life class."

"What's that?"

"Where you sketch a live model."

Hilary sighed.

"I know it doesn't sound like much, but it scares me half to death."

"Okay, love, but you tell me the minute you change your mind."

They hung up and Maggie sat in the kitchen and tried to find the courage to take the next step.

It was as if over the past fifteen years she had given herself away piece by piece until there was practically nothing left. A week of all-nighters with a sick child guaranteed the depletion of creative energy. Paintbrushes fell out of her hands from numbed fingers more times than she cared to remember. Or there would be a crucial dinner party for the partners in Matthew's firm. Making art and making hors d'oeuvres did not comfortably coexist. After Susan was born, Maggie had struggled to salvage at least half an hour a day with her paints, but then Fred arrived. He was beautiful and miraculous, just like Susan, and he required everything Maggie had left to give. Every now and then there would be a moment when both children were napping and the house was in reasonable order. Maggie would sit at the kitchen table with her drawing pad and try to make some lines on the blank pages. But her compositions turned out tortured and stilted. After a while, Maggie found that a month would pass without any thought of her work. She told herself that one day it would be there for her again. Now the moment had arrived, and she was terrified that it could all be gone.

She marched to her bedroom, dragged a metal box out from under the bed, and slipped open a manila file marked "Art Classes." Inside were clippings and articles she had squirreled away over the years. Maggie reached for last month's item captioned "Austin Presides at Life Classes on West Side" and went to the telephone. The summer term had already begun, she was told. Maggie had missed only one session, however, and could join the class this evening.

The rest of the day was plagued with panic. It rose in her throat and lodged just behind her larynx. At three o'clock Matthew telephoned with an errand and remarked on the tone of her voice. "You'll do great," he said after she explained. "It'll be like riding a bicycle, you'll see."

Finally she drew a bath and sat in the tub with a glass of wine. Just like riding a bicycle, eh? Well, she would find out soon enough.

The studio was in an old gray building on Central Park West. Maggie arrived early; only the instructor and one other student were there. Eliza Austin was a tall, handsome woman in her late sixties. Maggie remembered her work from an exhibit at the Winer Gallery ten years ago. The teacher held out a long, bony hand.

"They told me we had a new one. I'm glad to see you." She gestured toward the man perched on the window seat. "That's David Golden." The man nodded. "Perhaps David can fill you in on last week's class. This is Mrs. Hollander."

Eliza Austin began busying herself with easels. David Golden sat and stared at Maggie out of an angular face with fierce blue eyes. He could have been anywhere from thirty-five to fifty.

"How old are you?" Maggie asked, then blinked with surprise at herself. "It's none of my business, of course."

"Forty-four," he said.

"I'm thirty-eight," Maggie said vaguely. The man was smiling.

"What are you doing here?" he asked.

"Trying to remember old times. And you?"

"I enjoy Eliza. I'm a sculptor, in fact. But I like to keep my hand in."

Maggie wondered in exactly what way he enjoyed Eliza. It was outrageous to imagine him sleeping with her. Eliza was practically an old woman. Then again, perhaps it wasn't so outrageous. It was hard to guess about a man with such uncivilized eyes.

The class had filled up and the model had taken her place

on a mat in the center of the room. She was an Oriental girl, wrapped in a beach towel. Maggie and David Golden positioned themselves side by side at the two remaining easels. With a little shrug, the model undraped herself. She was slight, but had an exquisite body. Her breasts were perfectly round. Soft, shiny black hair fell to the middle of her spine. Maggie wondered if David Golden found the girl beautiful. Peripherally, she saw that he had already taken up his charcoal and had begun to make long, bold lines. There was intense concentration on his face, but nothing else.

Maggie lifted her hand to draw and saw that her fingers were shaking so badly that even a crude line seemed impossible. Her face was hot, her throat constricted. Tears were building. She glanced to her right and saw David Golden watching her. In a second, he was standing behind her with his right hand around hers, guiding the charcoal along her paper.

"Sometimes it's just a matter of getting started," he said. Then he returned to his easel and continued working. Her paralysis gone, Maggie watched her own hand gliding across the white surface, slowly at first, but with gathering confidence. Something nearly smothered inside her began to breathe. Her hand looked to her like a small animal that had just been released from a trap. It swooped and dove and leapt across the paper. Maggie turned to David Golden, said "Thank you," and began to laugh.

Once or twice during the next hour, she felt the old sensation of power, the heady invincibility, an impression of being suddenly surrounded with clear light. Then she became aware of David Golden standing beside her again. He was so close that she could feel his breath on her ear. He was exactly her height. If she were to turn her head, their mouths would be level. As if she could see out of the side of her head, she was acutely conscious of his jeans, his soft sweatshirt, his battered running shoes. He had the face of a prophet or a maniac, she could not decide which.

David reached toward her picture with a long blunt finger and ran it along the shoulder. Maggie had exaggerated the veil of hair.

"Nice. You're very good."

His arm brushed Maggie's. She began to tremble. The finger moved along her drawing, down across the perfect breasts, down the soft line of the belly. Maggie was beginning to feel physically sick.

"Not so dark here," David Golden said. His fingers gently brushed the shadow between the legs. Finally the finger dropped, creating a small breeze.

Maggie took a deep breath and tried to smile. "Thanks. I see what you mean."

"Now tell me what you think," David said. He took her elbow and drew her over to his easel. He held her arm for a moment, then released it to point to the model's head on his drawing. "I didn't see the hair your way. It's almost hidden."

The picture did nothing to minimize the discomfort in Maggie's knees. It was powerful, sensuous, earthy. "You must be a good sculptor," Maggie murmured.

Eliza Austin joined them now. She said nothing about David's work, just touched the drawing near the feet. David nodded. The instructor's comments to Maggie were kind and respectful.

Matthew had not come home when Maggie arrived. Fred was asleep and Susan was reading in bed with her eyes at half-mast. When the phone rang, Maggie assumed it was Matthew.

"Hi," she said into the phone.

"Hello. This is David Golden."

Stupefied, Maggie answered, "Oh, hello!" in an overly hearty voice as if he were some dear friend who had materialized after a long absence.

"I neglected my responsibilities tonight. I was to fill you in on the first class. Can I see you?"

She struggled for words. At last she answered, "I don't seem to know what to say to you."

"Well, as I see it, you've got two choices. 'Yes' or 'no.'"

"I appreciate the offer. It's very kind of you. But I think 'no.'" She hated the sound of her voice. She heard her mother telling the gardener he needn't come on Saturday.

"Okay. See you next week, then." He did not say good-bye.

She sat by the phone and went over the conversation again and again. The way he had said "Can I see you?" The request had seemed to hold some urgency. She was probably imagining it. He had a very soft voice with little modulation. She listened to it again: "Can I see you?" An odd thing to say to her when he was supposedly calling to do her a favor. She jumped when the phone rang again, stared at it until the third ring, then picked it up.

"Hello?"

"Hi, Mags." It was Matthew. Her heart stopped crashing around in her midriff. "Be home in an hour."

She was surprised at her disappointment, but then, she comforted herself, Matthew had not even remembered to ask her about class. He was well aware of her ferocious anxiety. When Matthew was worried about a problem at the office, Maggie always thought to ask how it all turned out, not necessarily from interest but at least to let him know she was concerned with his emotional comfort. Obviously, her preoccupations did not carry the same weight with Matthew.

He was very late getting home, by which time Maggie had fallen asleep.

She woke the next morning feeling angry. She glared at Matthew all during breakfast, waiting for him to ask about her class. He was almost out the kitchen door when Susan stomped in wearing her exercise sandals and inquired through a yawn, "How'd it go last night, Mom?"

"Oh yes, how was it?" Matthew asked from the doorway. He looked a little guilty.

"It was fine," Maggie answered, keeping her eyes on Susan.

"I expect to hear all about it tonight," Matthew called on his way out.

"You expect," Maggie echoed. Then she busied herself with the children's breakfasts and tried to stop hearing the words: *Can I see you?*

7

Robin's apartment always made Maggie feel claustrophobic. The place was festooned in crafts: needlepoint on the throw pillows, macrame hanging from the walls, hooked rugs on the floor, crocheted blankets on the sofa. Even the doorknobs had little knit covers on them. Being in Robin's living room was like being hugged to death by a wildly affectionate giant panda.

"I used to think you were supposed to douche standing up," Robin was saying. "I did it in the shower."

"Oy yoy yoy," Phyllis commented.

"Well, how was I supposed to know? Gynecologists never tell you that kind of thing."

"Mine tells me I should have no trouble maintaining a perfectly normal sex life," Hilary said, arranging her cards.

"Hoping desperately for a few details," Phyllis added.

"Exactly."

"Are we ever going to play?" Maggie asked.

"Ah, the first words from Margaret Hollander this evening," Phyllis said. "You look kind of odd tonight. Are you pregnant?"

Maggie laughed. "Two hearts."

"Two! She said two!" Robin cried with dismay.

"Yes, darling, I heard," Phyllis said.

"Well, I pass, darn it," Robin said.

"You'd better have points up the kazoo," Hilary said.

"My kazoo is loaded," Maggie answered. Phyllis gave her a sharp look. Maggie smiled benevolently while Hilary answered her bid with three spades.

"You sure you're not pregnant?" Phyllis asked again.

"Yes, but I'm going to small slam. Six hearts, ladies."

While Hilary set down her hand, Phyllis murmured, "Matthew's having a sexual renaissance, that's it."

"I'm ignoring you," Maggie said. "Whew, I can only lose one trick."

"Why are you on her case anyway?" Hilary asked Phyllis.

"Look at her," Phyllis urged. "She's glowing like a ripe mango, and her blouse is unbuttoned two slots lower than usual."

"Phyl, how am I supposed to concentrate?" Maggie asked.

"Let me tactfully observe," Hilary said to Phyllis, "that you, on the other hand, are a mess. What did you do to yourself?"

Unconsciously, Phyllis had been caressing her neck where there were two dark blotches parallel with the line of her jaw.

"My macho husband," she explained. "We got a little carried away over the weekend."

"Don't tell me," Hilary said with horror, but her eyes kept straying to the bruises.

"Actually, Stephen's coming to pick me up tonight," Phyllis said. "Maybe he has a girlfriend in the neighborhood."

"You know something, Phyl," Hilary said. "I can't figure out why you two stay married."

"We challenge each other," Phyllis said.

"How does beating up on each other present a challenge?"

Robin sighed. "I don't think we should even bother playing bridge anymore."

"Well, I don't mind," Maggie said, sweeping up the last trick. "We'll end on a high note."

"Sex is aggression," Phyllis said. "You can repress it all you like, but in my opinion, there's something to be said for letting it all hang out."

"And getting a broken jaw in the process," Hilary remarked.

"It's just as likely to be his broken jaw as mine," Phyllis said.

"Isn't sex supposed to be an expression of tenderness?" Maggie asked.

"Well, maybe in the beginning," Phyllis said. "I can't remember back that far. But I do recall that it got pretty dull after a while, and a little harmless whack now and then livens things up a lot. It's the element of danger, I guess. It's very stimulating. I recommend it."

"What does your psychiatrist say?" Robin asked.

"I've never discussed it with him."

"Phyllis Wheeler!" Maggie exclaimed.

"Well, shit, he'll just tell me it's based on neurotic patterns and ruin all my fun."

Hilary leaned back, stretched, and yawned. "I'd like to find myself a sweet and gentle man."

"You've found half a dozen," Phyllis said. "They bore you stiff and you know it."

"A sweet, gentle, interesting man, who'll challenge me intellectually instead of physically."

"Jackson is very gentle," Robin said.

Hilary looked at Maggie, waiting.

"If you want gentle," Phyllis advised, "you'd better find yourself a gay guy. Or another woman."

"I don't think I'm into that," Hilary said. She touched her own cheek in the place where Phyllis's was bruised. "Of course I remember back in boarding school, I had my doubts."

"Me, too," Maggie said. "All us girls were madly in love with one another."

Hilary laughed. "For me, it was my geometry teacher. At least I chose the most masculine-looking person on campus. I remember she gave me a book once, *Puzzles for the Math Genius.* It was like a holy relic."

"Did anything ever happen?" Phyllis asked.

"That would have wrecked it," Maggie said. "You were supposed to worship from afar. It was all very tragic. I was infatuated with a senior. We'd stare at each other beneath the trees and sigh a lot."

"Exactly," Hilary said. "And if anybody actually went over the edge into physical stuff, there was an awful scandal."

"Boy, it's all a far cry from my high school in Ohio," Robin said. "Did you keep in touch with these people?"

"No, once they let us start spending some time with boys, it was all over for poor Miss Dunne. I noticed that she always had perspiration stains under her arms. God, I wonder whatever happened to her."

"Maybe now's the time to look her up," Phyllis suggested, and Hilary gave her a shove.

"Boarding school ruined my life, I'm sure," Hilary said. "I blame all my man problems on those godawful tea dances with Choate and Hotchkiss. By the time I got to college, men were an alien species. I didn't have the vaguest idea how to talk to them. How come you didn't get warped, Maggie?"

"I'm not warped?"

"You found Matthew."

"Just luck. Besides, if it weren't for my Rooms here, I wouldn't have gone out with him."

"Such a schmuck she was, I can't begin to tell you," Phyllis said. "Will somebody deal? I'm humiliated by our defeat, Robin."

"I figure humiliation ought to be a terrific turn-on for you," Hilary commented.

"Oh, shut up," Phyllis said.

The buzzer sounded. Robin rose to answer it.

"That's Stephen already," Phyllis said. "He'll be in heaven. Four women all to himself."

Robin let him in. He was a medium-sized man of sturdy build, with a shadow of whiskers that no razor could ever erase. He stood in his trench coat with shoulders hunched forward, legs apart, lending him a faintly belligerent demeanor.

"Hello, girls," he said. "What a pretty picture."

"I told you," Phyllis said.

"Who's ahead?" Stephen asked.

"Maggie just whipped our little behinds," Phyllis said. "Small slam."

"I don't think I've played bridge since Oxford days," Stephen said.

"Notice how he gets that in," Phyllis remarked. "We never stray far from the halcyon days of our Rhodes Scholarship, even twenty years later."

"Why don't you sit in?" Maggie asked. "I'd just as soon quit while I'm ahead."

"Okay, sure," Stephen agreed. He shrugged out of his raincoat and took Maggie's seat across from Hilary. His rolled-up sleeves revealed forearms covered with curly black ringlets. "Whose deal?"

Robin began doling out the cards. As always, Stephen's presence made her uncomfortable. Maggie noticed that she kept glancing at him with alarm.

"How're you feeling, Robin?" Stephen asked.

Robin jumped a little. "Uh, fine," she replied.

He reached out to pat her belly. "You're getting there."

"Stephen should have been an obstetrician," Phyllis said. "Or certainly a gynecologist."

"You're full of astute observations tonight, my darling," Stephen remarked.

"Aren't I always?"

Maggie watched the hand with interest. Stephen was a skillful player.

"How's Matt?" Stephen asked.

"Fine. Working hard."

"I sent him a client, one of our people who's getting into motion pictures. He must have mentioned it."

"No, actually," Maggie said.

"It may come as a surprise to you, Stephen," Phyllis said, "but contact with you is not a major event in Matthew's life." She explained to the others. "When Stephen grows up, he wants to be Matthew Hollander."

Robin was squirming in her seat, but when Maggie glanced at Stephen to gauge his response to Phyllis's gibes, she was startled to catch him regarding his wife with appreciative amusement.

Hilary swept up the last two tricks and smiled at Stephen. "Thanks, partner. Set 'em, down three."

"Another?" Stephen asked.

"Sure, why not?" Phyllis said.

Maggie saw Robin look longingly at the front door while Hilary dealt.

"One club," Hilary began, then contradicted herself. "I mean one no-trump. Oh, sorry, I'm such a tit. I mean, nitwit. I forgot to ask you if you're the short-club type, Stephen."

"Nothing short about him," Phyllis said.

But when Phyllis bid four hearts, Stephen and Hilary bowed out. "The hell with it," he said. "Pass."

"Don't chicken out now," Phyllis admonished him. "Faint heart never won fair lady. Or whatever."

"It's okay," Stephen said. "Hilary and I will fix your tushies."

Stephen led the jack of diamonds. Phyllis covered with Robin's king from the board. Hilary played her ace and took the trick, led another diamond, which Stephen trumped with a low heart.

"Wow," Hilary breathed appreciatively.

"I'd say we've got a damn good communication going here, partner," Stephen said.

Hilary smiled at him. "Maybe I'm not such a tit, I mean, *nit.* God, what's this preoccupation with tits?"

"It's because you've got such nice ones," Phyllis said. "You'd just like Stephen to know."

"Oh, for Christ's sake," Hilary said.

Robin got up with a red face. "Excuse me. Ladies' room."

"Look, you got Robin all flustered," Stephen said. But Maggie could see he was delighted.

"You still going out with that detective?" Stephen asked Hilary with his eyes on Robin's exposed cards. He threw the ten of hearts on the table. "When in doubt, trump."

"Now and then," Hilary said. "He's too nice."

"We've been analyzing Hilary's affinity for nasty men," Phyllis explained.

"We have?" Hilary asked.

"But we decided that men are hopeless and she should try a woman for a change."

"I've always held to that philosophy myself," Stephen said.

"A devotee," Phyllis said.

The game ended with Phyllis down one. Stephen grinned at Hilary. "That was fun."

He made no move to rise, but Robin stood in the middle of the living room and announced in an impossibly cheery voice, "Well, let's call it a night for this time."

Phyllis laughed. "We're being thrown out."

"I'll get raincoats," Maggie said.

Stephen took Hilary's arm. "I'd like to play again sometime."

"Any time, dear," Phyllis said. "You liven up our little group."

"How are you going to get home from here?" Stephen asked Hilary. "Don't you live down in SoHo?"

"Cab," Hilary said. "It's not bad at this hour, right down the East River Drive."

As Hilary arched her back to put her arms into her raincoat sleeves, Stephen's eyes fixed on her breasts.

"Coming, Mags?" Phyllis asked.

"Yes," Maggie answered. But in the elevator, she wished she had stayed behind with Robin for a little while. The sexual tension in the plummeting rectangle was so suffocating that despite the late hour, she walked home, alone, and let the cool summer rain cleanse her.

8

Maggie sat on her bed and savored the thought of art class, where she was due in less than an hour. Her anticipation was so tangible it felt like a delicious taste in her mouth, a long-awaited treat that was sweet and satisfying after weeks of self-denial. Class could hardly live up to this, she thought; she might as well enjoy her pleasure as long as possible. Maybe tonight she would find that she could not draw a convincing line after all. Maybe David Golden would not be there. She took a long, leisurely bath, then pulled on a pair of old corduroy jeans and a cotton sweater. No dressing up for David; he would see the real Maggie. She was late now. She grabbed her handbag, dashed to the front door, and caught a glimpse of herself in the front-hall mirror. She laughed at the flushed, youthful woman she saw there. It had been a long time since Maggie had dashed anywhere. Hurried, hustled, rushed, yes. But never dashed.

Class was already in full swing. Maggie caught her breath with gratitude when she saw the empty easel beside David. She took her place and waited for him to say hello, but he only studied her quietly. His features were softer than she had remembered.

"I'm sorry I was such a fool on the telephone," Maggie said. Then she laughed. "Oh God, I'm doing it again." He just continued watching her with a half-smile on his face. "Help me out, will you?"

"How?"

"Say something."

"All right." He paused thoughtfully. "I like the way you look."

"That wasn't exactly the kind of thing I meant."

Maggie glanced at the model sitting at the far end of the studio. She was a middle-aged, plump, coarse-looking woman. Her breasts were pendulous with large dark nipples, and her legs were tracked with varicose veins. But she had extraordinary hands. She held them in her lap tenderly as if they were a pair of precious white birds. Maggie immediately thought of the Stieglitz photographs of Georgia O'Keeffe's hands. She picked up her charcoal and began to sketch, losing herself in this intriguing display of homeliness and beauty. After twenty minutes, she stretched and stood back to look at what she had done. David was standing beside her.

"Georgia O'Keeffe," he said. She stared at him. David went back to work, but Maggie found it difficult to concentrate after that. She imagined an invisible current transmitting her thoughts to the silent figure standing a few feet away.

At the end of class, Eliza Austin inspected Maggie's work, made a comment about tension, and suggested some exercises in quick line drawing to loosen her up. Maggie could see David preparing to leave as Eliza continued. He was going to get away before she could speak with him. She could barely breathe from panic, and here was Eliza Austin telling her to close her eyes and let her hand "sweep the page, sweep effortlessly, no, quickly, don't stop. . . ." Eliza was patient—endlessly, agonizingly patient. When Maggie opened her eyes again, the model had dressed and David was gone. Panic turned to grief.

"You're very gifted," Eliza said.

"Thank you," Maggie replied, thinking wryly what those words could have meant ordinarily. He must be out of the building by now. Finally Eliza said good night. Maggie tried not to hurry as she left the room, but when she saw the crowd at the elevator and noted that David was not among them, she bolted for the exit sign at the end of the hall. She took the stairs two at a time, dashing again.

She saw him on Central Park West more than a block away. He had a loose stride, legs slightly bowed, arms cocked and swinging. Maggie started running. A tiny voice in her head sang: *What are you doing? What are you doing?* But it was easy to ignore under the rasping noise of her respiration.

"David!" She caught him at Eighty-first Street, just north of the Museum of Natural History. He spun around and reached out to steady her with both hands on her arms. "Let me buy you coffee!" she shouted.

"All right," he said.

"I'm a very reserved person," she explained, panting.

They both laughed and began walking toward Columbus Avenue. After a moment he said, "Your art's not reserved."

"That's different."

"Shouldn't be."

"You're right," she said. "It shouldn't."

It was dark now, but the soft summer dark that is still a little gray around the edges. In unison, they both said, "You are what you paint." They stopped in their tracks and gaped at one another.

Maggie whispered, almost dismayed, "Does this often happen to you?"

"No."

"With anybody?"

"No."

"What's going on?"

He shook his head and drew her arm through his.

In the coffee shop, Maggie ordered a glass of juice. Her central nervous system was far too agitated to cope with caffeine.

"How long has it been since you worked?" David asked.

"Years. Close to ten, I guess."

"I find that difficult to understand."

"What's that accent?" Maggie asked.

"Leftover New Orleans."

"New Orleans," Maggie said. "What a wonderful place to be from."

"Not if you're a sculptor."

"Do you have a family there?"

"Parents. A brother."

"Tell me about them."

"My father has a dry-goods store. He feels the same way about yard goods as I do about stone."

"What does he think about what you do?"

"I suspect he's decided I'm homosexual."

"Is that supposed to follow?"

"Artists, you know. But he's not unpleasant about it, just regards me with a kind of bewildered disappointment."

"And your brother?"

"Very upstanding. Plays golf on Sundays, drives a station wagon. He works with my dad, but they don't get on. Robert wants to bring in computers for inventory, and my father would rather check things off on his yellow legal pad."

"Does your mother work too?"

David held up his hand with a smile.

"I'm grilling you. Sorry," Maggie said.

"I'll tell you my entire life story if you can stand it. Sometime."

Sometime, Maggie thought. That meant there would be another time. She felt the sudden sweet taste in her mouth again. "Were you always a sculptor?" Maggie blurted, then laughed at herself. But he was patient.

"I tried to be a painter at first. But I guess I always liked messing around with the materials more than making images. Now tell me about you. When did you begin?"

She sighed. "Oh, God, I was making pictures before I had words. I think it was my way of being safe in a scary world." She shifted her legs under the table and accidentally nudged his foot with hers. She wondered what his bare toes looked like. "I used to have this dream," she continued. "There was a hideous monster, a massive shadowy thing with huge sharp teeth and claws. He would trap me in a room. I was terrified and desperate, but then I would put my finger on the wall and draw, no crayon or anything, just my finger. I would make this even scarier monster, even bigger, and it would come to life and destroy the one that was trying to kill me." He was watching her over the rim of his cup. She shook her head and smiled. "I haven't thought of that in a long, long time. And it wasn't only fear. All kinds of feelings. Like anxiety. When my father had to go to the hospital for an operation, I built him a bed tray. I guess if I could build something, make something with my hands, I felt as though everything would be all right. I had some kind of control."

"Then what's kept you safe these past ten years?"

Maggie had no answer. She looked away. There was a fly walking up the fake wood paneling beside David's left ear. How simple to be a fly, she thought. Buzz, eat, an anonymous coupling now and again. A fly does not concern itself with the flyswatter, poised and vibrating, ready to slice through the air and obliterate.

"Carving is my adventure," David was saying. "A wild

exploration. Pushing something past its limits, almost further than I think it can go. There can be no preconceived notions about how it's going to come out, that's a kind of death. Allowing the inconceivable to happen is what's crucial. Sometimes it means being very brave. Do you know what I mean?"

She nodded.

"Tell me about your husband."

The fly did a little hopping dance on the sugar bowl, then veered off for the kitchen. "He's a fine man. A lawyer. Good at what he does, very ethical. We have two wonderful children." The sound of the word *we* reverberated in Maggie's head. *We, we, we . . . wee, wee, all the way home.* David was listening to it too. She saw the sudden pain in his face. "Do you know how long it's been since I wore these jeans?" Maggie asked suddenly.

"What do you usually wear?"

"Dresses, skirts, things to . . ." She trailed off.

"To what?"

"To get him to tell me I'm pretty," she whispered. "I'm such a fool."

David took her hand, flattened her fingers against the table, and traced them on the cool marble surface. "I want you to model for me," he said.

"I've got to go home."

"Please don't," he said. "Don't be afraid of me."

"I'm not."

"Let me see you tomorrow."

"No. I don't know." She wanted to kiss his mouth.

"Go ahead," he said.

She looked at him astonished. "I don't know how you do that. It's an invasion of privacy."

"See me."

"David, I'm so fucking respectable. I don't *ever* say 'fucking.'"

"Let me call you."

Maggie examined the check dropped on their table by a weary waiter long ago. She put some money beside her saucer and stood up. After a moment, David followed her out.

"Look, I'm getting into a cab," she said outside in a trembling voice. "Just walk away from me now. Please."

He nodded, put his hand against her cheek for a moment, and walked off. He turned to watch as a cab pulled up.

The waiter inside the coffee shop observed from the front window. He shook his head morosely. No money to be made off people like that. Lovers never eat much.

9

"Mom, can I come in?" Fred looked pale and solemn outside the bedroom door.

"What's the matter, honey?" Maggie asked.

"I've got stage fright."

Maggie smiled. "Me too." She smoothed the collar of his blazer. "You look marvelous. Where's Zach?"

"Watching TV." Fred sat down on the edge of the bed. "What if she blows it?"

"She won't. She was great last time and she'll be great tonight."

Our Town had made such a hit in March that a special end-of-school performance had been scheduled.

"I think I'm gonna puke."

"Maybe we ought to take airsick bags."

Matthew emerged from the bathroom wearing a towel around his waist. "You've got two different-color socks on, Frederick."

"Leave it to you to notice, Dad," Fred said. The door clicked shut behind him.

"Just exercising my acute powers of observation. Maybe we should all go out somewhere afterward to celebrate." Matthew shed the towel and slipped into his underwear. His body appeared exactly as it had eighteen years ago, except perhaps his chest was slightly hairier.

"You're feeling festive."

He grabbed Maggie by the shoulders and wrestled her to the bed. "My daughter's a star. Shouldn't I feel festive?"

"Hey, cut it out, Matt, you're hurting me."

He rolled her over on her stomach and pinned her arms behind her back. "Gotcha," he exulted.

For a man so trim, it was surprising how heavy his body felt. Maggie knew that no amount of struggling would free her from the grip of those sinewy arms. She lay very still.

"No fight in the old girl tonight?"

"I've told you I don't like being manhandled," Maggie murmured with her face pressed into the mattress.

Matthew whacked her rear end playfully and stood up. He sighed. "I don't know. You used to be a good sport. How come Zach's coming along? Shouldn't this be a family affair?"

Maggie rose slowly. The folds of her bathrobe fell open, revealing her bare breasts. She snatched it closed around her and belted it. "Phyllis and Stephen have a bar mitzvah in Pennsylvania," she said. "I didn't think you'd mind."

"Kid's here more than he's at home."

While Matthew's back was turned, she plucked her clothes from the closet and slipped into the bathroom. It was still warm and steamy from Matthew's shower. Her slip stuck to her thighs, but at least she was alone.

There was a time when Maggie was able to laugh at Matthew's roughhousing. Even enjoy it. She tumbled and wrestled with him, never mind the bruises. But lately she had begun to feel like prey, never knowing when Matthew might spring from behind a closet door to grab her bottom. She thought of David Golden's hand, gentle against her cheek, and suddenly began to cry in deep twisting gasps. She turned the cold water on full blast, grabbed her towel off the rack, and buried her head in it. But after a few moments, the sound of all that water being wasted induced such guilt that she quickly turned off the faucet and pulled herself together.

When they reached the auditorium, Fred, Matthew, and Zachary found seats while Maggie went to deliver Susan's necklace, left behind in the last-minute rush. Years ago, Maggie had bought her a chain with a tiny gold shamrock. Susan swore it was insurance against forgetting her lines.

Backstage, costumed performers rushed about, their faces under heavy makeup hinting at features familiar to Maggie since Susan's kindergarten days. Maggie had fed them snacks, patched wounds with hand-decorated Band-Aids, comforted them on their first sleepovers, and had transported the pudgy actress playing Mrs. Gibbs all the way across town at two A.M. when severe homesickness struck.

Maggie edged her way through the circus to a long mirror where Susan sat applying final touches to her mouth. Her costume rendered her nearly unrecognizable, but Susan's transformation penetrated beneath the makeup and mascara. She gave Maggie a remote smile.

"Thanks, Mom. Can you put it on for me? My hands are all grease." The New England accent had become expert.

Maggie closed the clasp around Susan's slim neck. "You okay?"

"Yeah, I guess. But I can't talk now, you know?"

Maggie nodded, bent down for a quick kiss, and left. On her way out, she heard the director admonishing some other interloper: "No, you mustn't disturb Susan now, not before a performance."

Maggie took a seat between Fred and Matthew and wondered where her child had disappeared to inside that quiet, contained figure at the mirror. "I thought it would be easier this time," she whispered to Matthew.

"She'll be fine," he said.

"Fred, you all right?"

"Sure, I popped ten 'ludes in the boys' room."

The houselights dimmed. Maggie's heart began to thunder. She grasped Fred's hand, which was as cold and damp as her own.

"Don't be nervous, Mrs. Hollander," Zachary said, leaning around Fred. "Sue can handle it."

Susan appeared alone onstage, wearing a felt hat, pipe in hand. She walked slowly, comfortably, like a man taking a stroll on a Sunday evening.

"This play is called *Our Town*," she began. "It was written by Thornton Wilder. . . ."

Maggie let out a long breath and settled down. The first time she had watched Susan perform as the Stage Manager, Maggie could barely concentrate on the play. Every stammer, every pause, sent trickles of sweat running down her sides. Tonight she was determined to absorb the performance. It was apparent that Susan was in full control. No matter that Mrs. Gibbs shouted every line, that Emily Webb was saccharine, that poor George kept anticipating his cues. Susan maintained her composure. At one point, George Gibbs stood in panicked silence with eyes rolling wildly as if he might encounter his lines etched in the air somewhere above his head. Susan quietly folded her arms and fed him the words, *sotto voce*, but loud enough for

Maggie to note that even when prompting a fellow actor, the New Hampshire accent remained intact. "Mr. Morgan, I'll have to go home. . . ." Susan prodded George, the "Morgan" coming out "Mawg'n." Maggie glanced at Matthew, but he was scribbling on a small pad: *Ferris v. Smith, 1978,* followed by three question marks.

The first time Susan had performed in a play was in the third grade. She won the lead in an original musical written by the school drama teacher. For three weeks the Hollanders endured her songs at breakfast and dinner. One of them Maggie still remembered was sung to the tune of "Don't Fence Me In": "Gimme smog, gimme dirt, gimme egg creams for dessert—New York's my town!"

On the day of her performance, Susan's confidence had dissolved into tears and sweaty hands. On the way to school, she had stopped dead in front of the dry cleaner's on Madison and Eighty-fourth Street.

"I think it's my appendix," she said.

"Real nervous, huh?" Maggie asked.

"I've got a stomachache. Well, it doesn't really ache, it's jumping all over."

"That's called butterflies in the stomach."

Susan smiled. "That's good. Just what it feels like." Then the smile turned to a grimace. "Let's go home."

"What is absolutely the worst thing you can imagine happening on that stage today?" Maggie asked.

"I'll fall down and forget my lines and mess up the songs and then I'll just die."

"Will you really?"

"I'll wish I could."

"And then what?"

"We'll go back to music class." She thought a moment, then said, "You know what, Mom? I think a few butterflies just flew out of my mouth."

Maggie had given her a squeeze, and they went on to school and triumph. Watching Susan now, Maggie imagined her surrounded by a cloud of butterflies, a delicate snowstorm on the stage. The image was so intense that Maggie felt her fingers twitch with the need to get it down on paper.

The Stage Manager was making a speech about marriage, about the natural urge to live life "two by two." But was it so natural? Maggie wondered. Here she sat next to a man who seemed at this moment no more related to her than the paunchy stranger across the aisle. Wasn't marriage an artificial alliance, and weddings an empty rite that bound two incompatible species together in something aptly termed wedlock?

Their wedding had been outdoors. A blue-and-white striped tent was erected on the Herricks's back lawn for refreshments in the event of rain. But the early-August day was bright. Maggie had lingered in bed that morning thinking about how little she knew herself and how she knew Matthew Hollander even less. And yet pairing off this way had been going on for so long there must be some merit in it. Even apes chose special mates, she had reassured herself, gazing at the white ruffled curtains that softened the morning light at her window. Then she had reached out to her bedside table for the worn Raggedy Ann she inherited from Joanne and clung to it. No more little girl, no more daughter. She would be Matthew Hollander's wife. Who the hell was he? She sniffed, still clutching the doll, sat up on the edge of the bed, and stared at his photograph. He was so handsome. Square face wearing the expression of a Viking warlord standing at the prow of his ship. But there wasn't a shred of vanity in him. He was direct to the point of brutality, so that when he said he loved her and thought her beautiful, she knew he meant it. He was the first person outside of an art class who truly appreciated her work, and the fact that the mere proximity of her body kept him in a continual state of arousal had its charm as well. But mainly she was marrying him because nothing bad could happen to somebody with that face. And as his wife, nothing bad could ever happen to her either. This man was as close to perfect as anyone she was ever likely to meet.

There was a tap at the door. Joanne poked her dark head inside. "Nice day for a hanging," she said with a grin. "Are you ever getting up? Your presence is required downstairs in Panicsville."

"I'm up." Maggie yawned.

"Think he's actually going to go through with it?"

"Who, Matthew? Maybe." But Maggie knew he would.

Joanne came in and tugged at the doll under Maggie's arm. "You still have this old thing?"

"I wish I could take her with me," Maggie said.

"Old Matt wouldn't mind." She put her hand briefly on Maggie's head. "You're a good kid. All the best." Then she fled.

After the triumphant curtain calls, they went to the Summerhouse restaurant on Madison Avenue. Susan asked to be seated by the front window beside the old painted wooden rocking horse. She was flushed and agitated. Her eyes were huge under dark splotches of makeup.

"Oh, God, did you hear old George Gibbs, I mean, Adam Newman? Oh, God, he was grotesque! Scared to death, just frozen solid, poor thing. I had to rescue him a million times. And I screwed up something rotten in Act Two with the wedding. . . ."

"What would you like to eat, Stage Manager?" Matthew interrupted her.

"Oh, God, I couldn't eat a thing! Oh, well, maybe I'll try the *crème brûlée*, it's so *elegante*. Oh, God, did you see how everybody cried when Emily passed into the great beyond? The place was absolutely awash!"

"Yeah, that must have been when Dad was making notes for tomorrow's meeting," Fred said.

Susan's monologue stopped short as if someone had flipped the Off switch operating her tongue. Maggie stared at Fred. Susan stared at her father. Zachary looked down at his plate.

"You didn't watch," she said.

"I did," Matthew replied. "M-most of it."

Maggie had never heard him stammer.

"Oh," Susan said. "Well, I guess since you'd already seen it before . . ."

Maggie looked away from the shamefaced Fred and gazed at Matthew. He was struggling with something. After a moment he said haltingly, "You forgot your line for a second and I couldn't stand it. I was too nervous." He put his hand over Susan's. "I'm sorry. I'm very proud of you."

Maggie chided herself for ever harboring uncharitable feelings toward Matthew. She knew how difficult it was for him to break through his natural emotional constraint. He loved his daughter. Maggie would never go to that art class again. David Golden was not reality. Matthew was reality. And her beautiful children, one radiating triumph and the other struggling with envy, they were reality. It was enough. It ought to be enough.

10

Matthew had just disappeared out the front door when the telephone rang. It was Robin.

"I'm bleeding," she said in a very calm voice.

"I'll be right there," Maggie said.

"I can't get it to stop."

"Hang up, call the doctor, and lie down. I'm coming."

Downstairs, Maggie pleaded with a harried businessman to let her take the taxi that had stopped out front.

"Lady, there aren't any other cabs," he protested.

She slid into the back seat while he held the door open in confusion. "It's an emergency. Sorry." She slammed the door. Fortunately, traffic was light and they made it to Robin's apartment house in six minutes.

Robin met her at the door with a bath towel packed between her knees.

"I can't get it to stop," she said again.

"Come on," Maggie said, holding out her arms. "The cab's waiting."

"I can't go like this. Let me get something clean."

"Screw that." Maggie took off her cardigan and tied it around Robin to cover the blood-soaked cloth.

During the ride to the hospital, Robin leaned her head on Maggie's shoulder. Her eyes were closed. A film of sweat covered her face, making the freckles glisten. Her arms, crossed under her belly, tensed with each jolt of the cab.

"Is Jackson still in Chicago?" Maggie asked.

Robin nodded. "I keep telling it to move, and it won't move," she whispered.

The emergency staff helped Robin onto a mobile stretcher. "I'll take care of admitting," Maggie said. She smoothed a lank piece of hair off Robin's forehead.

"It's still not moving," Robin said.

"You'll be okay, honey," Maggie said.

As the attendant started to wheel Robin toward the elevator, her eyes filled with tears. "Don't leave me," she pleaded.

"I'll be right there," Maggie said.

They deposited Robin in a labor room. Maggie could hear the cries and groans from a cubicle next door as a woman worked hard to bear her baby. They don't call it labor for nothing, Maggie thought. But for Robin it's always been for nothing.

A resident approached Maggie with clipboard in hand. "Where's her husband?" he asked.

"Out of town."

"Can he be reached?"

"I can try. Is she miscarrying?"

"Looks that way."

"May I stay with her?"

"Far as I'm concerned. But give me a few minutes to examine her."

He disappeared into Robin's room. The entire floor seemed hushed suddenly. The eerie silence lasted a few moments, then the resident came out. "I don't think there's a whole hell of a lot we can do this time around. You can go in."

Maggie sat down next to the bed. Robin opened her eyes.

"Hi," Maggie said.

"I love you," Robin said. Maggie grasped Robin's hand and held tight.

"I always thought you looked like Katharine Hepburn," Robin said after a while. "That first day I met you at *Woman's Companion* and you were so nice and took me to Schrafft's in your navy-blue dress."

"Katharine Hepburn. Thank you," Maggie said.

"People always thought I looked like Doris Day. I never could warm up to Doris Day."

"Why not?"

"She always played dippy ladies who can't stand on their own two feet. I don't want to be like that." She sucked in her breath and wrung Maggie's hand as another contraction struck.

"Can I get you something?" Maggie asked. "I'm sure they'll let you have something."

Robin shook her head. "Nothing really helps unless they put you out. Maggie?"

"Yes?"

"Don't let them throw it away until I've seen it."

"Maybe it won't come to that," Maggie whispered.

"It will."

Robin began to cry softly. "It's not the pain," she explained.

"I know," Maggie said. She laid her head next to Robin's on the pillow until the obstetrician came and asked her to leave.

---

*

After Fred and Susan went off to do their homework, Maggie told Matthew that Robin had lost the baby.

"I'm sorry. Is she all right?"

"Physically."

"Damn shame. That's the second time, isn't it?" He snapped on the news: Roger Mudd reporting from Washington.

"Third," Maggie said. She got up and went into the bedroom. Lying there mourning for Robin's baby, she remembered the births of her own children. Susan's arrival was obscured by the paralyzing numbness of Pentothal. There was still pain. Maggie was aware of the hurt, but the person who hurt was somehow not exactly Maggie. The birth itself seemed depersonalized as well. About three days afterward, while her hormones were doing their wild dance, she became convinced for a few hours that Susan was not really her baby.

When she found she was pregnant again, she decided that this time she would not be robbed of the experience.

She had been told that her second labor would no doubt be half the duration of the first. But Fred was a big baby. Maggie even wondered if a part of her was trying to hold him back inside, this final child. Matthew sat beside her labor bed and coached her through the various types of breathing. But her contractions were erratic. Just when she thought the peak had come and gone, another wave of twisting, wrenching agony would tear into her. It went on that way for twenty hours. Matthew, pale and frightened, pleaded with her to take a spinal block. But Maggie had not endured all of this only to relinquish her ultimate participation. Finally the obstetrician announced that she could push. By this time, her abdomen was transformed into a solid block, no longer yielding and round, but squared like an immense fist. Everything in her lower body worked to urge the baby out. After several pushes, she could feel the fetus loosening, swimming down into the birth canal. The sensation elated her and gave her the energy to keep on. She was bringing this baby into the world. What joy to be giving life with her own courage, her own body.

In the delivery room, it took only three more pushes for the head to crown. There was such pressure that Maggie felt she would surely split up the middle, but the terrible pain had disappeared. The doctor performed an episiotomy, which was also painless. Another push, out came the head, then one more giant shove and he was born. The thrill was almost sexual, like some spectacular orgasm.

Soon Fred began to howl, and turned from pale sickly blue to bright red. Maggie comforted him until he stopped yelping. He lay across her belly with solemn eyes wide open and his tiny fist crooked around Matthew's finger. After the umbilical cord was cut, they took him from Maggie.

"Where is he going?" she protested.

"Just to get weighed and have his feet printed. You don't want to take home the wrong baby, do you?"

"I couldn't. I know him now."

When they gave him back, he was bundled in a soft white blanket. He felt solid and warm. Both of them were transferred to a clean bed and pushed down the hall to the recovery room. Matthew brought champagne. Then Maggie and Fred drifted off to sleep with Fred nursing expertly at Maggie's breast.

Looking back on that golden day, Maggie wondered if sharing Fred's violently intimate beginning had influenced her feelings about him forever after. There was something direct and warm in her relationship with him that she missed with Susan. And yet the intensity between Maggie and Susan stimulated and challenged her. Oh, how she loved them, and how she grieved for Robin lying alone in her hospital bed with an empty womb.

11

After ten minutes in Zabar's, Maggie always found herself sailing off into a kind of trance. So much food, so many people. It was very pleasant. She had been lingering and swaying over the stuffed veal when she felt a hand on her bare arm. She turned and blinked into David Golden's face. He was grinning, the stark lines lifted in delight.

"What are you doing over here?"

"My kids are going to camp tomorrow. I'm loading up on favorite things."

"I'd like to see your kids."

On the one hand, Maggie felt like whisking him home to meet Fred and Susan this instant. On the other, she wanted to bar him completely from her life on Seventy-ninth Street. But to protect whom? she wondered.

"I'll help you. Then come see my place. You're only a couple of blocks away."

"I can't."

"Can't why?"

"I made this promise. It's too complicated to explain."

"Try me." They were jostled by a shopping cart. David held her around the waist as if they were dancing.

"You know those rash things you say in moments of severe stress . . . to whatever might be up there in the heavens?"

He smiled.

"A pregnant friend of mine was about to lose her baby. First I promised God that if He let her keep it, I would never see you again. Except in class, of course."

"And what happened?"

Maggie shook her head.

"I'm sorry."

"Then I had this feeling," she continued, "that she was being punished for *my* sins and I shouldn't see you anyway."

"But you don't think that now."

"No." Too fast, Maggie thought. Altogether much too fast.

"I want you to look at my work."

Maggie caught sight of her reflection in the meat-counter glass. A sensible face, rather haunted, not happy, getting older.

"All right."

On their way down Broadway, David held one shopping bag and she the other. Their unhampered arms were linked. Maggie thought briefly about being recognized and dismissed it. She was too giddy to care.

"I hope you appreciate my self-control," David was saying. "I haven't called you."

"I noticed."

"I hoped you'd be pleased."

"Disappointed. Grateful." Maggie could not identify what it was in David that made her feel so outrageously free.

He lived in a once-elegant building on West End Avenue near Seventy-eighth Street. He followed her up the five flights of marble stairs. Her light summer dress swept against her legs with each step. She felt his eyes on them, and her breasts grew tight as if they were swollen. By the time they reached the top, she was gasping and glad for the long ascent to excuse her discomfiture. They stood in front of his door while Maggie's pulse thumped. She told herself she could still turn and walk back down. But instead she watched David's hands unlocking the door—long brown muscular fingers.

At last the key turned, the door opened, and he ushered her inside. The sun was high in the west over the Hudson. Light blasted in through tall windows that ran the length of one huge room. The floor was polished and gleaming. There was an unobstructed view of the narrow strip of green that was Riverside Park, the Seventy-ninth Street boat basin, and the river. New Jersey was a black shadow on the other side of the sunlight.

Part of the room was a living area. There were a chair and a reading light in one corner. Against the near wall was a small built-in kitchen, a table and chairs. Beyond the table, a mattress lay on the floor. Maggie averted her eyes, but not before she had seen that the bed was unmade. A pile of books stood on the floor next to the bed and there were bookshelves running all along the bottom quarter of the wall like wainscoting.

But the living quarters seemed incidental in the apartment, as if all the necessities of daily life had been only grudgingly allotted territory. Easily two-thirds of the room was given over to David's completed work. Stone shapes, marble, sandstone, alabaster. There were busts of faces here and there and one immense torso, but mainly the carvings were free-form. They were forceful, multi-textured, and pleaded to be touched. Maggie felt a lump in her throat. She turned to David, who was watching her anxiously.

"Thanks," he said.

"May I take a closer look?"

They moved among the pieces while he introduced each one as if it were a friend.

"This," he said, caressing the surface of a white lustrous piece, "is very recent."

Maggie understood that the work had something to do with her. She examined it curiously. It was smaller than many of his other sculptures, only about a foot high. It was pear-shaped with a voluptuous rounded bottom. Out of the top, the suggestion of a curved shaft appeared, then tapered and disappeared into space. Maggie suddenly wished she could sit down before her knees gave way.

"What's it made of?" she asked.

"Carrara marble. I did it after we had coffee. It was something about the way you got into that cab, those jeans . . ."

She knew he was going to kiss her. She stiffened, but his mouth was so tender, so undemanding and gently inquisitive, that she found herself responding. He held her for a long time, in the bright light with the dust motes dancing around them. Finally she leaned back in his arms. "I guess I don't have to tell you that I don't usually perform this way."

"Why do you do that?"

"Do what?"

"Apologize."

"I wasn't."

"You really think this is a performance?"

"Oh," Maggie said. "No. This is just not possible," she murmured.

"You can't be the artist you are and talk to me about impossibilities," David said.

"Ah, David, you've got your work cut out for you," she said. "I've been living in negatives for a long time." She disengaged herself. "May I have a cup of tea or something?"

"Yes." He tucked a piece of hair behind her ear. "May I do your ears sometime?"

"I'm beginning to think you can do anything you please."
She laughed. "Like I mean . . ." She laughed again. "Oh, Lord, I
sound just like my fifteen-year-old daughter." She stopped, testing, but even the thought of Susan did not sober her. She sat at
the table and watched him move around the tiny kitchen. He
spooned loose tea into a tea ball and hung it inside a squat
earthenware pot.

"Does a dormouse live in there?" she asked.

"Yes."

"Margaret Herrick Hollander."

He looked at her quizzically.

"That's me." She shook her head. "What *am* I doing here?"

"You don't sound unhappy about it." He handed her a mug
that had phases of the moon painted all around it.

"I'm thrilled with myself." They both laughed.

"Are you looking for an explanation?" he asked, sitting
down opposite her with his tea.

"Yes. All the time. Today it seems metaphysical. My friend
Robin lost her baby and now I'm being born."

"It's probably futile to analyze," David said. "It's just here,
and we'd better figure out what to do with it."

Maggie's stomach lurched. She put down her cup and tried
to forget the unmade bed on the floor behind her back. "I don't
know you. Maybe you killed your mother and chopped her up
into little pieces."

"I'll admit to the fantasy."

"You just have the one brother, no sisters?"

"Yes. What have you got?"

"A sister. An artist. She's the talented one."

"Excuse me?"

"Oh, I have a gift, but Joanne would be a great artist if
she'd discipline herself."

"That the party line?"

Maggie looked startled. Then she began thoughtfully, "I

wonder if maybe a good girl can never be a great artist. Do you think? Maybe one has to be a maverick. Joanne's like that. Doesn't give a damn about convention. God, she's pretty miserable."

"Does that go with it too, the misery?"

"I don't know. I suppose there have to be some happy artists."

"I know I've said this before, but it's hard for me to imagine you not working," David said.

"It got edged out, I guess. There didn't seem to be time for it. I told myself it wasn't important, not as much as it would be for somebody like Joanne. Didn't you ever stop?"

He nodded. "In the army."

"You in the army? Heavens."

"Yes, but they let me design things—garages, a recreation room. And it was good for me, being in the service. It made me feel lucky to be what I am. I always knew I'd get out and have control over my own life. There were so many others. . . ."

"Did they cut off your hair?"

"Yes."

She tried to imagine him in a crewcut. It seemed impossible. Suddenly she needed to know what he looked like in every phase of his life. "Do you have a photograph album?"

"No." He was smiling.

"Someday when you're out I'd like to come up here and go through this place. I want to know what brand of socks you wear, what your checkbook looks like, whether you've got a collapsible umbrella or a long skinny black one . . . although come to think of it, I bet you don't own one at all."

He laughed. "I don't." He poured some more tea from the brown pot. "What kind of art does your sister make?"

"Representational. Portraits, mainly. She earns a lot of money when she works at it."

"You like her paintings?"

Maggie thought for a moment. "Not really. Everyone always has the same kind of sour expression. She's great with color. Acrylics."

"You don't approve?"

"For me, I can't stand them. They don't feel right or smell right. Oils are so delicious. I'd just as soon eat them as paint with them."

"Let me get you some more tea."

"I've got to go." They watched each other. Maggie had the sensation that she was staring into a mirror. "Do we look alike?" she asked. "That might explain it."

"A little narcissism?"

"Yes."

He shook his head and rose with her. "I want to wait on you. Do for you. Will you let me?"

"I'm not used to it."

"Get used to it." He held her by the shoulders. "You'll be back here again." She was silent. "You're a very strong woman. You can handle it."

"I don't feel strong."

"Be strong enough. Don't shut the door on this." He kissed her. She could feel the tension and power in his back, and yet he was tender. He smelled of marble dust. "Maggie, Maggie," he whispered against her mouth.

She wrenched herself from him and imagined a beautiful rich tapestry tearing in two. At the top of the stairs, she turned to see him framed in the doorway, a clean form like the pieces of stone behind him, shimmering in the light like fanciful shapes at the bottom of a transparent sea.

Maggie stumbled out onto West End Avenue and stood blinking on the sidewalk, letting the heat wash over her. Then the roar of the Seventy-ninth Street bus reminded her that a cool green apartment awaited her on the other side of the park. She walked the short block to the bus stop, stepped up onto the bus, and took a seat in the back. She could not stop grinning. A trim woman who embarked at Broadway gave Maggie the brief suspicious glance New Yorkers reserve for lunatics. But Maggie's smile broadened. She had experienced David Golden and life would never be the same. His connection to her was a fact of natural law, as absolute and basic as the principles that governed the solar system. This afternoon, she had had a revelation worthy of Charles Darwin or Sir Isaac Newton.

It was not until she got off the bus that she wondered what she would say to Matthew and the children. She was nearly forty-five minutes late already. She could say that she had run into someone from her art class, started talking, and time had just flown away. It was not a lie; and it was a monumental lie. Maggie had always regarded herself as a truthful person, and yet David had made her realize that she had spent decades lying to herself. Wasn't denying herself the worst kind of falsehood, the most pernicious betrayal?

In the elevator she imagined herself explaining, "Well, children and Matthew, today I discovered that I have a Siamese twin. Remarkable, isn't it, that I never knew I had one? My parents kept it from us, and we just happened to bump into one another, this fellow and I. Separated at the heart when we were born, actually . . ."

She put the key in the door and took a deep breath. It was Fred who scared her the most.

"I'm home!" she called.

" 'Bout time," Susan yelled from her bedroom.

Maggie walked into the kitchen and began unpacking the shopping bags. Matthew appeared, looking rumpled, as if he had been asleep. She felt a sudden rush of affection for him. She wanted to tell him. He was practically her oldest friend, after all. She turned the full radiance of her face on him and waited to see what would happen. Her heart was pounding crazily at the insides of her ears.

"Must still be hot out there," he observed. "You're all sweaty."

"Yes," she said. So easy.

During dinner, Fred asked her why she was so quiet.

"I'm thinking about you kids being away for eight weeks," she lied.

"Well, you don't look very depressed about it," he complained. "I haven't seen you this happy since Nixon was impeached."

At six-thirty A.M. on the corner of Forty-fifth Street and Vanderbilt Avenue, Matthew stood beside the Camp Poqomashee bus with his palms sweating. Maggie and the children were twenty feet away talking with the Wheelers, but there was such a crush that even if Matthew had felt sociable, he would have been hard put to join them. Instead, he distracted himself by counting fishing rods. So far, there were sixteen, each gripped in the small fist of a boy. This was a co-ed camp, and yet not a single girl carried a fishing pole. Biology will out, he supposed. Phyllis Wheeler's psychiatrist would say the rods were phallic symbols.

The camp director held up his arms as if he were about to make an important announcement. Nausea gathered in Matthew's stomach. Everyone else seemed so festive. Not one crying child. But of course these were all older. Matthew had been six when he spent his first summer at camp.

He remembered the bus trip. It had seemed a great adventure to climb up the steep steps, wave good-bye to his parents, and set off for the Adirondack Mountains. The very name was exotic and thrilling. Upon arrival, he had gone swimming in the clear cold water that tasted sweet without a trace of either chlorine or ocean salt. He had even caught a bullfrog down by the waterfront. But after the campfire, after lights-out, he had lain very still on the top bunk in the pitch-black cabin and thought that it had been a very fine day, and tomorrow his mother could come and take him home. But she didn't come, not tomorrow or the next day or the next. In fact, his parents never made it to visiting day that first summer. Something came up, he couldn't remember what. Matthew had admired his counselor, who always called him "Sport." Matthew felt obliged to live up to the nickname. A person named "Sport" would certainly not call out for his mother in the dark.

There had come a time, finally, when Matthew began to look forward to spending his summers up in the mountains. He liked the rough cabins that were set back from the lake in a grove of pines. The fragrant pine needles cushioned his footsteps as he explored the woods, imagining himself an Indian brave. He spent many hours sitting on his special rock beside the lake watching the surface of the water, how its depths reflected an endless variety of colors: turquoise, silver-white, blue, purple, and black.

Because of his physical coordination and maturity, he was soon allowed to participate in overnight hikes with the older campers. The final trip of the summer had been a three-day excursion up Mount Marcy. Near the summit on the second night, a violent electrical storm had struck. The campers clung together in the lean-to all night long, listening to the downpour and watching the lightning illuminate the forest like millions of exploding flashbulbs. That summer had been Matthew's introduction to the majesty of natural forces. His urban life seemed a long way from those early primitive communions with the woods, but even now on the rare occasion when he was wakeful at night, he would find himself remembering the lake and its moods. The memory comforted him still, so that finally with the sound of water lapping against the shore, he would drift into sleep.

He coughed as the bus started its engine and sent clouds of foul exhaust into the air.

"Daddy, we have to get on the bus now," Susan was saying.

"Oh," he answered. He wanted to tell her: No, not this summer. Stay home.

"Don't look so sad," she said. "In ten minutes you'll be ecstatic we're gone. Think about it, just you and Mommy."

"I guess so." He hugged her. She was the oddest combination of sturdy and frail. His arm went all the way around her rib cage so easily. And yet the flesh that covered the birdlike bones was so firm. She wriggled free.

"Fred!" she called. "Come say good-bye to Daddy. He's having a breakdown."

Fred and Maggie pushed through the crowd together. Fred extended his hand.

"Fat chance," Matthew said, and pulled his son close for a bear hug. Here was a substantial person, not as pudgy as he looked. That bulk was mostly muscle.

Then Maggie held them both for a moment and they were away, up the steps and behind the tinted glass that turned all the campers into identical silhouettes with raised fluttering hands. Matthew put his arm around Maggie.

"Shit," he muttered.

Maggie looked up at him. "You're crying," she said, astonished.

"I'm going to miss them."

"Yes," she answered.

But that night when ordinarily she would have felt depressed and lonely in the aftermath of their departure, she lay in bed with a trembling sense of excitement. Susan and Fred were gone, they were safe, and she was free. David existed a mere half-mile on the other side of the park.

———

She searched for her guilt. It had to be there somewhere, lurking in the memories of her resplendent day like slugs clinging to the roots of a fabulous tropical flower. None. Matthew lay breathing softly, unaware that the wife beside him was no longer the wife of yesterday. Maggie's regret was that she could not rouse him gently, hold his hand in the dark, and tell him about her happiness.

She dreamed that she was a mermaid with long streaming hair. She dove through the turquoise water, flipping her graceful tail, and when she sang in her soft sweet voice, tiny fish in many bright colors sprang from her mouth.

12

While Maggie lay dreaming, David Golden was letting himself into his studio on Broadway and Ninety-fifth Street. At this hour, the ground-floor stores were closed and heavily gated. There was a bakery, a small grocery store, a dry cleaner, and a shoe repair. In the elevator to the fourth floor, however, David could hear the throb and thump of the latest rock band to rent space here. Among the other inhabitants were a psychotherapy center which specialized in primal screams, an evangelical organization, and a dating service which matched singles of indeterminate sex. David rejoiced in his neighbors because they left him to himself. In fact, if there was one item in his life about which he felt savagely possessive, it was this room. When David had first arrived in New York, he had shared studio space with a group of artists. David was faster and stronger than the others and did things they told him were impossible. "It won't balance," they would warn him. Or "Alabaster can't take that kind of abuse." David ignored them, but he longed for privacy. Finally, when he began to sell his pieces, he scraped together enough money to rent his own place.

The first studio was spacious, but it was a three-floor walk-up. After a year of hauling two-hundred-pound blocks of rock up and down the stairs, David began looking again. An apologetic real-estate broker had finally brought him here. Despite its shabby ambience, the place had everything: a large freight elevator; a window for ventilation; floors sturdy enough to support several tons of rock; twenty-four-hour access. Even now, five years later, David felt gratitude when he slipped his key into the door.

He stood blinking in the bright fluorescent light, breathing the rich musty smell of stone dust. In defiance of David's efforts to protect the shelves with plastic and canvas drapes, the fine gray film seeped into everything. Even the inner crevices of his supply manuals were grainy with it. Pompeii probably looked like this, David thought, as he gazed at his shrouded statuary.

David walked to the window and snapped on the powerful fan. It would suck out clouds of powdered stone, which thereafter sifted down onto the two stunted bushes in a courtyard below. Every few weeks, his conscience needled him into trekking down with a watering can to clean off their encrusted leaves.

A massive piece of raw white stone loomed on his worktable. David walked around it, feeling his excitement grow. Normally, he ordered his material directly from a quarry in Italy. But last week, he had spotted this five-hundred-pound slab of Bianco marble at his favorite supply store on Nineteenth Street. It was expensive, almost six hundred dollars. David had gone to battle with himself. His pneumatic air drill was broken and required a costly new part. His toaster had expired, and he was getting tired of toasting bread in the oven. Besides, this difficult stone demanded a brand-new set of carbide tools. It took about half a minute to decide. Maggie Hollander was in that rough marble somewhere and David was going to find her.

He had never carved a woman's torso before. A man's once, as an exercise. Women had somehow always become abstracted into free forms that later seemed cerebral and cold to him. David caressed the rough surface of the rock and wrestled it over onto its side. He picked out a toothed chisel and the hammer that was so perfectly weighted it seemed more an extension of his arm than a tool. He slipped a safety mask over his face and started taking down the stone, beginning with the shoulders and working back. Five or six shots, then rest. Five or six, then rest. The first few bites into rock always hurt him, as though he were piercing flesh, but soon he began to feel that he was working with the stone, that they were creating something together. The marble was even more lovely than he had anticipated. It was webbed with pale gray lines like the translucent veins in a woman's skin. He thought about the underside of Maggie Hollander's arm as she had reached behind her head to smooth her hair.

He remembered her standing in the doorway of Eliza's studio illuminated by tangerine light. There was an extraordinary tension emanating from her slender body. She was clearly afraid, yet seemed determined to master her fear. The light flickered off the hollows and curves of her face as she spoke with Eliza. David had wished she would stand still so that he could sketch her.

Maggie had walked toward him like a dancer, head high, back straight, yet somehow liquid. As she shifted her shoulder to shrug off the strap from her handbag, he could see the shape of her breasts under the cotton sweater. Her stomach would be a long curve slipping into the shadow between her legs.

Close up, her face was almost severe. But when she spoke, her mouth was soft and curled up at the corners in a child's smile. She was hesitant, self-conscious, and brave. She was unaware of her own courage, but David found it immensely moving.

When class began, David had watched Maggie freeze. Suddenly she was a George Segal sculpture, lifelike in all respects except for the dead eyes staring at the easel. At once, he understood. Every artist experiences that particular numbing horror. That it is gone. Whatever the mysterious impulse that makes it possible to create something out of nothing, whatever the elusive power that connects an artist to his environment through his mind, his eyes, his hands, that it has vanished forever. David went to Maggie at once, took her hand, and warmed the terror out of her fingers.

Once loosened, how they flew, darting, diving, trailing bold streaks of charcoal. There was nothing tentative about this woman's art, no restraint, no apology. She had already forgotten him, absorbed in a kind of ecstasy. David had felt he should shield such naked joy from the others.

In one evening, Maggie had engaged every crucial part of him: his creativity, his intellect, his sexuality. But she escaped from him that night. He looked for her in the groups of people on the street outside, by the bus stop, in front of the museum that stood ghostly and secretive in the dark. Finally he had walked home and telephoned every Hollander in the book until he heard her voice.

The rough approximation of shoulders began to emerge from the stone. David was sweating heavily now, and he could feel the dust collecting in the back of his throat. It was curious that he had never asked Sharon to model for him. Eight years of living together, and the notion never occurred to him. Perhaps it was because in some essential way, Sharon had remained outside his art. He remembered how she would wander among his sculptures in the apartment, touching them cautiously, her small face bewildered. Her questions irritated him. "What

does this bulge here mean? Does it represent something real?"
She never asked him why he needed to carve, but the issue
hovered in her eyes. David was continually on the defensive.
Either he found himself defending Sharon to his carvings, making excuses for her obtuseness, or else apologizing to her for
their ubiquity and even occasionally talking of getting rid of
them. Such discussions always left him feeling sick with himself.

When Sharon had moved out, the silence she left behind
seemed sunny and clean. He felt unaccountably elated. For the
first time in eight years he was alone with his most intimate
friends—his carvings. But after a few weeks, desolation settled
in. David began to miss her so profoundly that the inside surfaces of his arms tingled with the need to hold her. He could not
sleep. He wadded his quilt up into a ball and hugged it in a futile
attempt to fool himself into unconsciousness. He fought with
himself about asking her to move back in. He knew she would
come. He also knew that ultimately he would want to cast her
adrift again. Sharon had been beautiful, bright, articulate, but so
haunted by her nightmare childhood that she required perpetual
comforting. David had ministered to her the way he attended the
choking plants in the courtyard beneath his studio window.
While he struggled over telephoning her, he began to realize that
he had used her. He needed someone to care for, a family,
children, and Sharon had been a sponge to soak up the overflow
of nurturing impulses he sometimes felt would drown him. Once
he understood the basis of his need for her, the longing began to
dissipate and he was saved from the cruelty of reaching out for
her again.

The truth was, David had always been rather indifferent to
women. They interested him sexually, but by the time he met
Sharon, he was over thirty and had never been deeply attached
to anyone else. At one time, he had considered the notion of
homosexuality, and when his good friend Evan, a fellow sculptor, made subtle overtures toward David, he decided to give it a

try. But after the first embrace, David had begun to laugh, not out of discomfort, but because the entire procedure seemed so awkward and comical. He was profoundly apologetic to Evan, and the two men had remained friends.

In the first decade after David's arrival in New York, the only apartment he could afford had been a roach-infested hole in the East Village. Congregations of junkies murmured and nodded in front of abandoned tenements while David hurried past trying to avert his eyes from the incessant assault of ugliness. He missed the intimate, drowsy atmosphere of New Orleans, the scents of tropical flowers, sweat, decaying garbage, strong coffee. But once he entered the artist's world, he believed he would never settle anywhere else but New York.

It began with the chaotic shop on Nineteenth Street where David bought his supplies. The owner, Ben Ginsburg, was a hulking lumberjack of a man. He took David on a tour and watched carefully as the young sculptor watered down particular stones and ran his fingers over their surfaces. Afterward, Ben invited David into his office, which was a wild collage of invoices, checkbook stubs, tax forms, calendars, and bills here and there disciplined into piles by paperweights that were carvings made by Ben's many friends. Ben pressed a buzzer on a half-buried telephone, asked to be left alone for an hour, and he and David talked, about art and whose work David should see, about New York, and loneliness, the philosophy of work versus leisure, and Chinese restaurants.

Finally Ben had stood up, held out a huge paw for David to take, and said, "Hey. A bunch of folks show up here on Saturday nights. Carvers mostly, but a few painters, too. We put away a six-pack or three and sort out the world. Come along if you feel like it."

David had left feeling that he had passed some important test. Over the years, he watched Ben measure other newcomers, and the fact was, each person Ben introduced to the inner circle had some contribution to make to the group. Someone with an abrasive personality would turn out to produce work of such monumental genius that the brash package no longer mattered. And Ben was always there to extend advice and credit. "Pay when you sell something," he'd say, which could be never. He had even found David his teaching job at the West Village School for the Arts. In those early years, David rarely missed a Saturday night at Ben's. David had gravitated hungrily toward the gifted. Artists with special vision electrified him, and he felt their influence upon his own work in a new intensity and willingness to experiment.

Maggie Hollander's breasts appeared under the steady blows of David's chisel. The need to possess her was so powerful that it frightened him. If there had been no white stone waiting for him here in the studio, he wondered if he could have controlled himself with her this afternoon in the apartment. He thought of that soft skirt brushing Maggie's legs as she climbed his stairs. An erection pulsed against the stiff fabric of his work pants. The hammer struck, beating rhythmically, tiny bits of rock flew about him, and he was past happiness into a kind of rapture.

It was dawn when David finished blocking out the torso. He was aching and covered with dust. The insides of his mouth and nose were thick with it and his eyes burned. But he liked what had emerged under his hands. The torso rested on its hip and curved upward with breasts pressed forward, shoulders back. There was energy and powerful sensuality in the rough stone. David was too exhausted to clean up. He snapped off the fan and the lights, stretched out on the gritty floor where he could see the outline of Maggie's body, ghostly through the soft dust clouds, and slept.

13

Matthew loaded the car early Friday morning in anticipation of holiday traffic. The Fourth of July was traditionally spent with Maggie's parents, in part because Maggie's birthday fell on the third. Until two summers ago, it had been a hectic trip, transporting the two children. Maggie had spent the hours refereeing disputes that began somewhere west of Bridgeport and continued all the way to Stafford. She had not yet accustomed herself to the simplicity of traveling as a couple.

Nevertheless, she enjoyed long trips in the car, particularly when she was not required to drive. She liked to look out the window and let the colors blur together. She would play tricks on her vision, first narrowing her eyes, then widening them quickly. Telephone poles, woods, houses alongside the road, leapt and squatted and contorted themselves into fantastic shapes.

Today the interior of the car was hushed. But the inside of Maggie's head was whispering, shouting, chortling, arguing, and carrying on lengthy discussions with itself. What if she were actually to embark on an affair with David? The word "affair" seemed so crude, so ordinary. Entering a relationship with him would be to plunge into a mysterious wonderful world. A few short hours with him and already she had begun to discover hidden pieces of herself, as if she were a diver upending encrusted old rocks to reveal the sunken treasure beneath. She imagined them submerged together, twisting, arching, curling in the shining light, coming together to embrace with long slick limbs, kissing and slowly rising to the surface.

Matthew slammed on the brakes as a battered station wagon veered suddenly into their lane. Maggie stared at him. His reflexes, as always, were quick and sure, a quality she admired in Matthew. In fact, he had many commendable traits. Shouldn't admiration be sufficient? Why did her heart keep stretching to accommodate David Golden?

Matthew glanced at her. "What's up?"

"Nothing, why?"

"Do I need a haircut or something?"

"No, you look just fine."

"Phooey, I bet you say that to all the guys."

My Matthew, she thought. Her mouth moved; she almost said it: *Matt, there's a man named David Golden. He thinks I'm beautiful. Isn't that something?* Instead, she said, "La *la*."

Matthew grimaced. "What was that?"

"I'm singing," Maggie said. "La la *la*."

"You can't sing. You're tone deaf."

"Doe, a deer, a female dear . . ."

"Spare me," Matthew said. But he smiled at her.

I won't do it, Maggie thought.

*

Her lightheartedness began to falter as they got off the highway and drove through the Stafford town square. It was a neat village, like an eighteenth-century New England town fabricated by Walt Disney Productions. The fringe of grass along the sidewalks was perfectly trimmed. The little gazebo that sat on the green was freshly painted. No litter, no sprawling drunks. Even the old shade trees appeared to have been pruned. There was not a dead limb or drooping branch to be seen.

They passed the high school, a pristine Georgian structure with white columns. The scent of cut grass struck the car like a soft green wave.

"Far cry from P.S. 102?" Maggie said, thinking of the graffiti and broken windows that blemished the junior high on Seventy-fifth Street.

Matthew turned off onto Barnstable Road.

"Oh, dear," Maggie sighed.

The Herrick home was set far back off the road. The groomed lawn was untroubled by weeds or patches of garden. Two maple trees of nearly equal height loomed one to each side of the brick walk. The house itself was a handsome white colonial. It stood unperturbed and cool in the sun, as permanent and unyielding as some great gleaming boulder deposited by the glaciers twelve thousand years ago.

Norma Herrick came down the front steps to greet them. She was nearly six feet tall with no excess flesh to pillow the no-nonsense architecture of her frame. Her kiss felt bony. Standing near her mother always made Maggie feel insignificant. It was an illusion that Maggie had to stand on tiptoe to kiss her, but it seemed true enough.

"Hello, children," Norma said. Maggie shrank another inch. "Good trip?"

"Yup," Matthew said. He and Norma did not kiss. Matthew had gone straight to the trunk to unload.

"Your father's at the airport picking up Joanne. They should be here any minute. We're barbecuing, so as soon as you're settled in, come down to the yard."

"Ah, the scene of the crime," Matthew said. Maggie knew he meant their wedding. She grabbed her overnight bag and went into the house.

She paused in the living-room doorway. Sure enough, her mother had redecorated again. Every two or three years, Norma reupholstered the sofa, the side chairs, and bought new curtains. This time, the colors were predominantly peach and green.

"What do you think?" asked Norma next to Maggie's elbow.

"Very pretty. The nicest, I think."

"Oh, I don't know. I'm not sure it does what I hoped it would do."

"Well, Mother, you never give up anyway." Maggie understood that Norma was trying to achieve some measure of warmth. But the immaculate room with its perfectly restored antiques and polished floors spoke with a cool voice. Maggie thought of Robin Brody's apartment and smiled. Robin's place was so warm it made Maggie sweat; her mother's house gave her the chills. Next to Robin, Maggie was a hypothyroid freak; next to her mother, she was a dwarf. Suddenly it struck her that other people might not measure themselves this way, by using the rest of the world as a yardstick. It seemed a revelation. She wished David were here. It was the kind of observation that would interest him.

"How was it for you, being tall, when you were growing up?" she asked her mother.

"In what way, dear?" Norma asked.

"Being the tallest girl. You must have been, straight along."

"Oh, yes." Maggie watched her mother's face as it went on a long-unaccustomed journey into the past. After a moment Norma said, "I made it a point never to slouch."

*

There was a tray of liquor and mixers on the table in the backyard. Matthew was showering, Norma was in the kitchen, so Maggie poured herself a gin and tonic and lay down in the lawn chair. Unlike the front of the house, the backyard was wild with the sight and scent of flowers, as if it was important to keep this excessive display of color and aroma hidden behind an austere facade. The rhododendron bushes made Maggie think of Phyllis, who had once announced that she thought of her friends in botanical terms: Robin a buttercup; Hilary a calla lily; Maggie a rhododendron. Maggie had inquired how she classified herself, and Phyllis replied without hesitation, "Venus's-flytrap." Phyllis understood them all so thoroughly. How outrageous to have David Golden billowing like sea grass just beneath the surface of her life and Phyllis knowing nothing of him.

Maggie and Joanne's Snow Tree still stood beneath Maggie's bedroom window. One Sunday morning in early May there had been a freak blizzard. Maggie had awakened to see two inches of snow like vanilla frosting on the lilac bushes, the daffodils, the tulips. Below her, the little cherry tree glistened. Among its dazzling branches sat a pair of cardinals, some sparrows, a blue jay, and a finch. Maggie ran to fetch Joanne and together they gazed at the magical tree with its bright chattering decorations.

Maggie let her eyelids droop. Soon her father would arrive with Joanne and there would be no peace. Her thoughts drifted like the dandelion fluffs floating above the lawn. Her very first memory of life emerged on a day like this. Maggie remembered being on her back and looking out through golden pillars at something soft and green. She had felt comfortable and happy, and yet tantalized by the greenness beyond her grasp. She theorized now that she must have been in her playpen gazing out at the wooded area past the toolshed.

She took another sip of her drink and heard the dreamy buzz of ladies' voices, the clink of ice in glasses, laughter. Norma used to hold her bridge-club parties out here in the early summer. Maggie had liked to help set up the chairs and place the decks of cards on each table with their score pads and stubby pencils. There was always the picnic table with goodies on it, too: cool drinks, limes, lemons, and little cakes. Maggie enjoyed the sight of the bright-colored summer frocks, even sometimes broad sunhats with ribbons.

One July day just after her ninth birthday Maggie was reading in her room upstairs when she heard great hilarity explode on the lawn below her window. She leaned her arms on the windowsill and looked down to investigate. Her mother seemed to be the focus. She had paper in her hands, lots of white squares which she was passing around. Suddenly Maggie felt her face burning. Norma had found her drawings, her secret collection of cartoons that were hidden on the top shelf of her closet behind the shoeboxes. There were drawings of her parents, of Joanne, of her teachers, even of some of the women present. Most of them were unflattering, but they were her diary, her method of releasing outrage, irony, even adoration. There was a cartoon of her favorite teacher, her beloved Miss McAdams. It hurt Maggie the most to imagine those women laughing and pawing at her movie-star rendition of that kind young lady.

She felt like screaming at them: *How could you?* But instead she pulled down the shade and threw herself on the bed and sobbed. The collection reappeared in its nest that evening. Maggie took each drawing out and ripped it into tiny pieces. Then she flushed them down the toilet. Norma never mentioned the empty hole on the shelf.

Maggie sat up and took a deep swallow of her drink as her mother came through the back door with a trayful of crackers and cheese.

"Having a nice sunbath, dear?" she asked.

Maggie switched herself into the present tense. "Lovely. I didn't check the barbecue. Should I have?"

"No, let's wait to see the whites of their eyes."

Norma stood looking down at her. Maggie tried to shade her eyes against the bright sunlight, but her mother's features were blackened and dazzled with multicolored dots.

"Have you been going to exercise class?" Norma asked.

"No. Good Lord, no," Maggie answered. "Why?"

"You look . . . I don't know, Margaret. Different. Rather glowy."

"Well, you know how fast I tan," Maggie said, but she was pleased. Norma was rarely complimentary. She was always rearranging Maggie's collar, tucking in a blouse, checking her stockings for runs.

Matthew, Colin Herrick, and Joanne trooped out the back door one at a time with enough space between exits for the stiff spring to slam the screen each time with a loud snap. Here they come, Maggie thought. Husband: SNAP! Father: SNAP! Sister: SNAP! There was a ritual quality about their arrival that seemed appropriate. Maggie stood up and swayed from the sudden elevation.

"Hello, Dad, you're dapper as always." She kissed him on the cheek, but was suddenly nearly toppled over by a hug from Joanne, who had grabbed her around the middle. "Whoa!" Maggie yelped. The sisters did a little dance until Maggie regained her balance. Then she held Joanne away from her and took a good look. Joanne was medium height, but her roundness made her seem shorter. She had full breasts, but never wore a bra, so that she sagged and bobbled with every movement. Her hair was wild, wiry and black with reddish-brown frizzled ends so that she looked as if her head might recently have been set afire. She had a pouty child's face and bit her nails.

"You look smashing," Joanne said.

"Thanks. So do you," Maggie replied.

Joanne shook her head impatiently. "I don't, but that's all right. You look *really* smashing. Are you pregnant?"

Matthew hooted. "She'd better not be."

Joanne disengaged herself and made a futile effort to smooth her hair. "Well, y'all're doing something right." Maggie noticed the Southern accent. Wherever she alighted, Joanne quickly adopted the local intonations.

"Where did you fly in from this time, Jo?"

"New Orleans."

Maggie's heart lurched. "Where's Hob?" At the time of her child's birth, Joanne had been deeply immersed in J.R.R. Tolkien's *The Lord of the Rings*, hence the name "Hobbit" for her baby.

"With his father for two weeks. He'll come back all freaked out," she said with a shrug, "but it's nice to be free."

Maggie had never noticed that Hob in any way cramped his mother's style. He went along in a backpack when he was small enough to carry—to peace marches, all-night parties, gallery openings. Later on, he got left at home along with the telephone number of some reliable neighbor to keep him company. Maggie kept waiting for the dire effects of Hob's haphazard upbringing to surface, but the last she had seen of him, he appeared well-adjusted enough, if prone to a somewhat unorthodox diet. Maggie had once watched him eat Mallomars and canned tuna for breakfast.

"Drinks, anyone?" Colin asked. His face was round and pink, but the softness was deceptive. He had been sufficiently shrewd and tough to make a success of his investment firm amid the established Connecticut financiers.

"I'll have a vodka, straight up, Daddy," Joanne said. "A little more . . . fine, that'll do just fine." Maggie noticed that the drawl was becoming more pronounced. Joanne plunked herself down at the foot of Maggie's lawn chair. "Now let's hear what y'all've been up to," she said.

Matthew shot Maggie a look of amusement at the same time that Norma and Colin exchanged glances of faint disgust. Then all four looked at Maggie. For a wild moment she wondered what would happen to those four pairs of expectant eyes if she were to say: Hey, listen, I've met a wonderful man and I want to sleep with him, but it goes against everything I've ever thought I believed in. What do you think I should do? Instead, she said the next-best thing.

"I'm getting involved in art again." Maggie waited for some shock waves, or at least a few ripples.

"Lucky you," Joanne said. "I think I've just burnt myself right out. Nothing's happening anymore."

"I thought you just finished an exhibit in Santa Fe," Norma said.

"Yeah, yeah, but nothing sold. Nobody wants representational stuff anymore, especially portraits. Unless they're somebody's kid or favorite aunt."

All right, Maggie thought. She would try again. "I'm taking a life class with Eliza Austin," she said, rather loudly.

"Didn't I see her work in an exhibit on Newbury Street in Boston once?" Colin asked.

"Yes, you probably did, back in the sixties."

"I'm not wild about her stuff," Joanne said.

Norma turned to Maggie. "Maybe you know some people in New York who might be interested in Joanne's work. If you're involved in the art world these days."

"I'll look into it," Maggie said quietly. She looked down at her hands. Perhaps she could have brought up David Golden after all. No doubt Joanne would respond that she had once had such a lover, or that she had not had one and wished she had. The conversation continued about the sad state of Joanne's finances while Maggie imagined herself standing up and calmly stripping off her clothes. No one would notice unless somebody needed something. Then all eyes would turn to Maggie. Even then, they would see what they expected to see. Maggie visualized herself as a vending machine. Each little window displayed a particular body part: an ear for listening to tales of woe; a selection of mouths—one for kissing bruises, one for deep sexual kisses, one for advice; a hand for performing the necessary tasks like drying the dishes or writing checks; a foot for walking to the dry cleaner's and the grocery store; two breasts, one lactating, one not. She began to get very excited. Her fingers were tingling in the old way. She stood up abruptly, spilling her drink on the arm Joanne had draped across her knee.

"Excuse me," she said. "Bathroom."

There was a moment's pause in the conversation, but by the time Maggie had taken a few steps toward the house she heard her mother talking to Joanne again. It was the tone Norma reserved for addressing people who were very young, very old, or handicapped. For the first time, Maggie began to wonder which of Norma's children was better off. Perhaps in this household it was preferable to be ignored.

Maggie went up to her old room and rummaged through the desk for paper and a pencil. Quickly she began sketching her vending machine. A profusion of shapes was emerging, an intriguing balance of curves and sharp edges. If she pushed the idea just a little further, perhaps it could really mean something. She was working very fast now, trying out various combinations. She sketched the ear toward the center, but somehow that destroyed her focus. She realized with surprise that there was no eye here, but then she understood the significance of the omission. This was a blind machine.

Finally she achieved a drawing that pleased her. And yet something was missing. She stared at the strong black marks on the white paper and was struck with a tremendous sense of excitement. Scissors! That was it! She wrenched open the drawer and hunted down a pair of child's blunt scissors. Then she began cutting out the drawing, but not exactly conforming to its edges, here and there slicing across the sketch itself. She was so elated that she did not hear Matthew come in.

"What the hell are you doing? I thought you were sick or something," he said.

"I . . . wanted to do this. It was the scissors I needed. . . ." Maggie stammered. She felt jarred, as if she had been awakened from a delicious dream by being shoved out of bed onto the floor.

Matthew leaned over her shoulder and peered at the cutouts. He made no comment about them, just told her that dinner was ready and left the room.

"I hope this is still your favorite birthday dinner, Margaret," Norma said. Maggie watched her mother's reflection in the dining-room mirror as she dipped into the mixed salad and portioned it out onto five salad plates.

"Wonderful," Maggie said. "But I've still got a few more hours of being thirty-eight."

"Five to be exact," Matthew said. "Then you'll be starting your fortieth year."

"Lordy, my sister almost forty years old," Joanne said. "That must mean I'm a grown-up too. How revolting."

Colin arrived from the backyard with a huge steak still smoking and sizzling from the grill. "I'm sorry we couldn't celebrate on the actual day," he said. "It's this affair at the club. With my being president and all, I couldn't really."

"You don't worry about being grown up, do you, Joanne?" Norma asked with a smile, or the facsimile of one. Maggie supposed the intention was to dilute the effect of any words that might offend. Norma almost always smiled when she spoke. In fact, Maggie had noticed the same tendency in many women. They could say the most appalling things with a bright smile stretched across their faces. Maggie had listened to the mother of one of Fred's classmates describe her husband's affair with the baby-sitter. The woman grinned throughout the entire narration. Maggie had found it difficult not to respond with a ghoulish smile of her own. She had begun to catch herself at it now and then. Good sport at all costs, she thought. Watch us smile as our souls splinter.

Colin was holding his wineglass up in a toast. "To my daughter Margaret on her thirty-ninth birthday. May she taste the sweetest fruits life has to offer." He drained his glass and sat down. Maggie searched his face and thought she discerned sadness there.

Joanne spoke first, into the hush. "Hear, hear," she said. "But, Daddy, what are the sweetest fruits?"

Maggie noticed that her mother was looking down at her plate.

"That depends on Maggie," Colin answered. He speared a slice of steak. "Medium or medium-rare, Maggie?"

Maggie thought of David's voice, David's face. Forbidden fruit, and surely sweet. "Rare," she answered.

Norma had embarked on a monologue about vandalism at the golf course. "Perhaps there's malice in it, but I rather think it's more casual than malicious," she was saying. "They drive their cars straight across the greens and dig these great yawning chasms with their treads. Children are no longer being endowed with consciences. It's the parents' fault."

Maggie noticed that her father maintained a glazed countenance when Norma was talking. He held his head tilted toward her in apparent attentiveness but the eyes were operating in a different sphere altogether. Maggie resolved to appraise her mother's face when Colin began to speak.

"There were some pretty conscienceless people in your generation too, Mother, after all," Joanne said. "Look at Nixon and that tribe. No wonder kids behave like delinquents."

"Oh, Nixon again," Norma sighed.

"I have a young man in my office," Colin began. "A Negro fellow, or black, I should say. He came to us through one of those programs that encourage businesses to hire ex-convicts . . ."

Maggie quickly glanced at her mother. Norma was rapt. Maggie imagined her mother's ears vibrating with the effort to capture every syllable Colin Herrick uttered. Maggie pictured Matthew reciting passages from a bicycle-repair manual and she, Maggie, kneeling at his feet, gazing up at him with total concentration. We are children, Maggie thought. My mother is still a little girl and so am I. It suddenly became clear to Maggie why she felt so utterly confused about David: she could not ask Matthew to make this decision for her.

A large box was placed under Maggie's nose. She had entirely missed Colin's story about the ex-convict.

"Happy birthday, Margaret, from your father and me," Norma said. Her gift packages were legendary. Norma claimed that her gift-wrapping talent was her sole contribution to the artistic ability of her children. This present was decorated with sprigs of flowers from the yard, and it smelled as good as it looked.

Inside the box was a dark gray cashmere sweater, V-neck cardigan with pockets on the sides. "It's very . . . practical," Maggie said. She failed to track down an appropriate facial expression, so she smiled.

"I thought it was handsome," Norma said. "I should think you'd get a lot of wear out of it."

Maggie glanced at her father. This was not a sweater in which to taste the sweet fruits of life. Maggie remembered her pink ruffled dress, the most treasured item in her fourth-grade wardrobe. It had been a gift from Maggie's grandmother.

"I can't imagine Mother sending you a ridiculous piece of fluff like that," Norma had said.

But Maggie had loved it. When her ninth birthday arrived a few days later, she put it on.

"You're not going to wear that to your party," Norma said.

"But I like it," Maggie protested.

"Take it off," Norma said, and began undoing the buttons at the back.

Maggie wrenched herself away. "No! It's pretty! I never get to wear anything pretty!"

"Margaret!" Norma had shouted. "What in the world has gotten into you? You get ahold of yourself this instant if you want your party, and take off that ridiculous dress. Look at your legs sticking out under those flounces. You look like an ostrich." Norma withdrew with a white face, leaving Maggie to stare at herself in the mirror. Her legs *were* long and skinny. So were her arms. What was more, her face was funny-looking. Silently she unbuttoned the pink dress and put on the paisley jumper and white blouse with the Peter Pan collar.

"I've got something for you, Mags," Matthew said. "I was going to wait until tomorrow, but . . ." He handed her an envelope embossed with the name of his law firm: Berwick, Saunders & Ross. It was certainly not the new Georgia O'Keeffe book Maggie had hinted about and then finally asked for outright. Somehow she had not wanted to buy it for herself; she wanted it to be given to her. She opened the envelope. It was a check for five hundred dollars. She noticed that the five had been changed from a three.

"Thank you, Matt. You're very extravagant."

"I didn't think a book was quite enough," Matthew said.

"There was not one second to shop in New Orleans," Joanne was saying. "I'll find you something fabulous and mail it up."

There was silence. The words "It's okay" were hurling themselves against Maggie's clenched teeth, fighting to get free. But Maggie knew that Joanne would forget, or would send some totally inappropriate item, like the plastic lizard pin that arrived two weeks after Christmas, complete with a jewel in its mouth and instructions as to how it was to be worn on one's shoulder. And now there was this awful sweater, and Matthew's hastily produced check. They were all staring at her.

"You know what?" she said to Joanne. "Don't bother."

"Excuse me?" Joanne said. Her speech was clipped, with no reference to the Deep South.

"Don't send a gift. It wouldn't have anything to do with me."

"Margaret," Norma said.

"No, Mother, don't get nervous. I'm just speaking my mind." She turned to her sister. "You didn't remember, Jo. Well, that's not so terrible, though it would have been nice, since I always remember yours and Hob's."

"But I almost always do eventually," Joanne protested. "I just sent Matthew's birthday present."

"Yes, two months late. And six silk ascots?"

"Maggie, I don't mind," Matthew said.

"You should," Maggie retorted. "Matt, you wouldn't wear an ascot if God himself ordered you to."

Maggie had a sudden sensation of cool air surrounding her, as if the air conditioning had been switched on. She began again, softly, to Joanne. "I'm asking you to think a little. That's what being thoughtful means, being full of thought for another person. I'm always doing it for everybody else. Couldn't you do it for me now and then?"

"All right, Mags." Joanne's eyes were damp.

Maggie reached across the table and squeezed her sister's hand. Then she got up. "If we're all done, I'm going to go call the children."

In bed, Matthew asked, "What was all that about with Joanne?"

"It seemed immoral somehow to let it go on and on."

"They were horrified."

"So were you."

"I'm not used to your doing that sort of thing."

"Well, I don't suppose it'll happen very often."

"A blessing."

"Why is it a blessing to let Joanne get away with behaving like a self-centered child forever?"

"I just think you're better off saving the moral indignation for the really important stuff."

"Oh," Maggie said. He had the most uncanny knack for making her feel trivial. It was so much simpler just to release the easy words: *It's okay. Don't worry about it. No problem. I don't mind.*

She woke up sometime in the middle of the night. The illuminated bedside clock said one twenty-five A.M. The room felt alive with another presence, someone vital and greedy and hot. Well, David Golden, she thought, I'm thirty-nine. One more year and I'm forty.

14

The telephone rang at eight-thirty Wednesday morning. Matthew grabbed the receiver on his way out of the kitchen, said hello, and then stood poised in the doorway for a moment. Maggie could tell from the way he was listening that the caller's voice was unfamiliar. He held the phone out to her.

"For you. Who's David Golden?" But he did not wait for her to tell him, just set the telephone on the counter and started off down the hall. Maggie sat still and stared at the white object that held David's voice. Then she picked it up gingerly and rested it against her shoulder awhile before answering. Finally she said hello.

"It's David. I want to see you."

"Class," Maggie said. "Tonight. Isn't it?" She was trying to squeeze the syllables out through paralyzed lips.

"I mean before. Come to dinner. I'll fix you something here."

"God."

"What is it?"

"Just fear."

"You're not afraid of me, are you?"

"No, it's not you."

"Will you come?"

"All right."

"Five-thirty. See you then." He did not even say good-bye.

Matthew was calling from the hallway. "See you!"

"Okay," she answered; then, "Wait!" She wondered what would come out of her mouth when she reached Matthew looking all slick and pressed and self-contained by the front door.

"I won't be here for dinner before my class. Are you coming home early?"

"No. About ten."

"Fine."

"Got a hot date?" He grinned.

"A few of us are getting together."

"Well, have fun." He kissed her and was gone.

Maggie leaned against the wall and slid slowly to the floor. She wanted to laugh and yet was not sure it was laughter that was caught in her throat. She sat on the hard parquet in her bathrobe and took stock.

David, this man she had kissed, had spoken on the telephone to Matthew, her husband of eighteen years. Absolutely nothing had happened. Not only had the telephone not exploded, but Matthew appeared devoid of suspicion, or even curiosity. Next, Maggie had told Matthew she would be out without even checking first to see if he needed her at home to cook dinner. And finally, she had lied. "A few of us . . ." she had said, and it had slipped out so easily. Lies were ugly, odious. So why then did she not feel corrupt? Why instead did she feel almost proud?

What kept billowing up through the questions and confusion was one fact: she would see David. Alone. Soon.

She was supposed to meet Phyllis for lunch, but the idea seemed impossible now. First of all, Phyllis would surely notice Maggie's excitement. Second, Maggie felt a profound need to be alone with her happiness. She wanted to be the miser who locks his doors, pulls his shades, and gloats over his golden treasure in peace.

"Up, Margaret," she said to herself aloud, and then giggled. "Losing it, I must be losing it." Other than the occasional blasphemy after stubbing her toe, Maggie could not remember ever talking to herself. "Probably because I simply had nothing to say," she murmured on her way to the kitchen. "Oh, shut up," she told herself, and stood by the telephone trying to figure out what to tell Phyllis.

"Matt needs me at his office," Maggie said. "I'm sorry. Can we make it next week?"

"You sure everything's all right? You sound odd," Phyllis told her.

"Yup. Fine."

"Yup?"

Maggie coughed. "Got a frog in my throat this morning."

"What's he want you for?"

"Oh, uh, something with a client. I'm not really sure, but it's rather urgent."

"You going down there to get laid?"

Maggie coughed again. "Nope," she said in a strangled voice.

Phyllis was silent. Maggie could almost hear gears clicking and meshing through the receiver. "Okay, hon. Let's talk Monday and we'll set something up."

"Thanks. Talk to you soon. Sorry. 'Bye." Maggie hung up and told herself she would have to do better than this. Phyllis had antennae that could pick up the sexual impulses of a gnat.

133

At the last bridge game, Phyllis had asked twice if Maggie was pregnant. The notion had seemed absurd at the time, but this morning Maggie felt just that way: full up, swelling with something beautiful, wonderful, mysterious. Special, as if she were the only woman in the world to be so blessed.

At five o'clock she changed into her white sundress with the spaghetti straps and dropped a bottle of wine into her straw bag. Out front, a doorman was hosing down the sidewalk in the sunshine. Maggie said good evening, and as she stepped across the puddles, wondered why the water did not instantly turn to steam around her feet. She was high-voltage, crackling, sparking. In the cab across town, she told herself she was not ready for an affair. Danger, she said. Danger! Yet there was nothing menacing in the memory of David's face. It promised excitement, yes, but shelter and comfort as well. The future lay trembling and full of color, just out of reach.

Each time David looked at her, he grinned as if the sight of her was a thoroughly unexpected surprise. He had led her to a chair at the round table and seated her almost formally.

"Here, sit while I unpack this stuff." There were two grocery bags on the counter. "I was out all day." He turned to smile at her again. "I was afraid you might call and back out, so I stayed in the studio and worked."

"I didn't call."

"How about a glass of wine?"

"How about the entire bottle?" But the truth was, she felt relaxed. The sun streaked in the window at the company of statues, which made fantastic shadows across the floor. Maggie could see every hair on David's hand as he uncorked the wine and poured them each a glass.

"Sit with me a minute," she said. "We've got plenty of time to eat before class."

He sat opposite her. His feet were bare, and he captured her ankles between them under the table.

"Tell me about your trip," he said. "I thought about you."

"Oh, my parents . . ." Maggie sighed. "My first great unrequited love."

"That bad."

"Have you ever been to the Museum of Holography down in SoHo?" He nodded. "It was a little like that. I felt as if I could walk around them all right, view them from all sides. They have three dimensions. And yet, well, they're not solid somehow. There's no reality to them. I could stick my hand out and it would pass right through them without encountering anything."

"And Matthew?"

She dropped her eyes.

"You don't like me to mention him."

"You talked to him this morning."

"Yes."

"Did it feel odd?"

"Not the way you think," he answered. "I didn't feel guilty."

"I guess that's what I meant."

"No," he said. "Angry. Jealous."

Maggie looked at him incredulously.

"He's got you and I haven't," David explained.

"I don't know if that's exactly true."

They stared at each other for a moment. Then Maggie said, "I never plan on talking to you this way. How come we always seem to get right into it?"

"What should we talk about?" he asked.

"Oh . . . art, I guess."

David stood abruptly. "I've got something for you." He opened his bureau drawer and removed a package.

"I don't remember telling you I had a birthday," Maggie said.

"No. This is just something I think you should have, if you don't already."

Maggie opened the gift and caught her breath. It was the Georgia O'Keeffe studio book. She covered her face with her hands and began to sob. David knelt beside her and stroked her hair.

"What is it?"

"I'm happy. I can't even tell you," she choked. "Oh, David, I feel so lucky." She kissed him on the mouth, a long full kiss.

"How hungry are you?" he whispered.

"Very," she said hoarsely.

They kissed again. His hands followed the line of her body from her neck down her bare shoulders and arms. He slipped the straps off her shoulders and unzipped the front of her dress. He pushed the fabric aside gently, releasing her breasts. Maggie felt his name catch in her throat as he kissed her nipples. So gentle, his mouth and hands were like butterflies against her skin. She felt the heat rising from a part of her that had long been cold and dark. He was a magician, drawing fire with the lightest touch.

They undressed each other, frenzied now, with frantic kisses and hands searching. Finally David was inside her. Maggie cried out, a moan, a sob, a kind of deep laughter against his mouth. And soon they lay together, two long naked bodies clasped like a companion piece for the other stone figures, serene and complete in the sun.

"David, I'm so happy I don't care if I die this second." They were on his bed on the floor now, exhausted and glistening with sweat.

"Please don't."

She was silent a moment. "What if we hadn't signed up for that class, David?" she went on. "What if only one of us had? God . . ."

"I would have found you anyway, by the smoked salmon at Zabar's."

"You don't really believe in fate."

"I never did, but I have to tell you I've been giving it some thought lately."

"You make me want to work," Maggie said, watching their fingers twine together on his chest. "What do other people do when they feel something so strongly, *so* strongly that it won't stay inside their bodies? When there's not enough room to contain it?"

"I don't know how many people feel things that way," David replied.

"It can't only be creative people. Children do, I think."

There were patterns on the ceiling now, the windows' outlines stretched into long rectangles. "You see that?" David asked, taking her fingers and pointing at the shapes. "That's the very first thing I remember in this life. Patterns on the ceiling above my bed, or crib, I guess. There were leaves and slats from the blinds, all moving. Beautiful."

"Any color?"

"Grays, I suppose."

"Funny . . ." Maggie began, then stopped.

"What's funny?"

"No, it's just that something's happening. I'm not sure what. With making art, I mean. The shapes. I've never been involved much with that . . . more with color. Form, too, but . . . I can't explain. It's almost as if suddenly I'm more interested in the margins around the pictures than the pictures themselves. I did something at my parents' house, unlike anything I've done before. With scissors and glue." She laughed. "Like a child with cutouts. Only it was so exciting. I can't stop thinking about it."

"You'd better explore it."

"I guess I'd better."

They lay quietly for a while. Finally Maggie said, "David, I'm in love with you."

"I know."

"Are you going to make me dinner?"

"All right."

She stood up and held out a hand to help him. "But let's not get dressed. We should always be naked."

"Wait till January and my landlord turns off the heat."

They stared at each other, both wondering where they would be in January.

"When I was talking about holograms," Maggie said, "my parents?"

David nodded.

"That used to be me, too. But not anymore."

He reached for her and held her for a long time.

15

Fred's small room was the perfect size for a studio. Maggie liked being confined while she worked; that way her ideas hung close around her in the air and could not escape beyond her reach. Her old accomplices had recently disappeared. The tortured tubes of oils were heaped in a cardboard box in the closet. No brushes poked from cans on the windowsill. The stinging scent of turpentine had been replaced by the sweeter aroma of glue. Her easel stood neglected against the wall like a reproachful spectator. Maggie sat at Fred's desk surrounded by a wild array of colored paper: tissue, cardboard, newspaper, ribbon, tags from new clothes, dry-cleaner receipts, the chopsticks wrapper from a Chinese restaurant. It was midmorning, but she was still in her nightgown. The breakfast dishes were unwashed, the newspaper unread, even the mug of coffee beside her had turned cold as she snipped, pasted, arranged, and rearranged.

Last week from David's apartment, Maggie watched a flock of birds over the Hudson River. Those near the surface circled relentlessly, as if caught in the funnel of a water spout. But soaring in the sky with the sun setting behind them were three who had broken free. They sailed and dipped and dove in a sea of salmon-pink light, as if they had exploded upward, out of the merciless pattern of the others. The beauty of their swirling freedom had moved Maggie. And now she sat staring down at a square of deep rose-pink Christmas wrap. The paper was a glossy foil whose reflective qualities suggested to her the brilliancy of a sunset over the river. She had cut white triangles out of various types of paper and had arranged them so that the heavier weight shapes were near the bottom of the shiny square. Those near the top were sheer tissue, which she wrinkled slightly as she pasted them down. She imagined becoming so light, so diaphanous, that the wind could lift her effortlessly and send her spinning into the air in a wild, free dance.

The telephone rang. At first she ignored it, remaining suspended like the birds. But soon the sound began to tug at her. She was to see David this afternoon. What if this was he, calling to cancel their appointment? She let it ring again. What if it was the camp in Vermont reporting an accident? She leapt up and dashed to reach the telephone before it stopped.

"I knew you were there," Phyllis said.

Maggie was too breathless to respond.

"I want to know why you won't see me," Phyllis said. "It's okay, you can catch your breath. But I'm not hanging up until I have an explanation."

"I've been, ah, busy, you know I'm working again," Maggie began. "I mean, not a job, of course, but making art . . ."

Phyllis interrupted. "The kids are in camp, Matthew's at the office, you can't possibly create masterpieces every minute of every day. What the hell is going on? I haven't seen you since bridge at Robin's and neither has anybody else."

Maggie felt as if the telephone receiver had melted and stuck to her ear, that no matter how hard she tried to pry it loose, it would hang there forever on the side of her head like a grotesque appendage.

"Listen, roommate, if you don't have lunch with me today, you can kiss me right off. Are you my friend or not?"

Maggie was to see David at two o'clock. But Phyllis's voice, despite the upbeat banter, could not disguise its urgency. "Okay, Phyl. An early one, twelve at Mortimer's?"

"Fine. See you then."

When Maggie arrived, flushed and panting, Phyllis was waiting at the bar on a tall stool.

"You're late," Phyllis commented.

"Sorry." Maggie glanced at her watch. "Only seven minutes."

The maître d' was able to seat them immediately, allowing Maggie the chance to compose herself by consulting the menu she already knew by heart. Once they had ordered, however, there was nowhere to hide. In the bright light of the table overlooking Lexington Avenue, Maggie felt as if she were on display to Phyllis and the rest of Manhattan.

"So how are you, Phyl?" Maggie asked, leaning forward on her elbows. A good defense is a strong offense, Matthew always said.

"Oh, no, you don't," Phyllis replied. "You can't get away with it, Hollander."

Maggie tried to look bewildered.

"Don't insult my penetrating intelligence. The subject of today's luncheon meeting is Margaret, not Phyllis."

Maggie sat back and drained her glass of white wine. She

knew it was no use. "All right," she admitted. "I know I've been sort of unavailable lately."

Phyllis hooted and signaled to the waiter for two more glasses of wine. Then she looked at Maggie for a long time with a smile on her face. "Listen, Mag," she said when Maggie had begun to squirm. "I know you're seeing someone."

Maggie's mouth opened and closed but no sound came out.

"No, it's all right, you don't have to talk about it if you don't want to."

"What on earth makes you think such a thing?" Maggie asked.

"Don't get clutched. I'm sure nobody else has any idea. It's only because I've known you such a long time. And besides, I can usually tell. There are signs." She looked around at the noisy fashionable crowd. There was a sprinkling of famous faces at the choice tables. "Some people can spot a nose job or a face lift," she went on. "I'm an expert at love affairs."

Maggie swallowed a third of the wine in her glass.

"Oh, every once in a while I get muddled between pregnancy and adultery. Pregnancy lends a similar voluptuous look to people sometimes, in the beginning, a smugness. I know you're not pregnant, and you're positively oozing sexuality. I bet you've got men following you on the street like dogs these days."

Maggie was concentrating very hard on maintaining eye contact. If she looked away, it was capitulation. But Phyllis was right. In the space of five blocks between her apartment and Mortimer's, she had been whistled at twice and saluted with an awful sucking noise by a van driver on Seventy-sixth Street.

"I don't suppose there's any point in denying it," Maggie said finally. "You really want to believe this."

Phyllis smiled and shook her head. Then she reached out and covered Maggie's hand. "Honey," she said softly, "I don't mean to torture you. I only wanted you to know I knew so you wouldn't hide from me anymore. I've missed you. Besides, it can be pretty rough sometimes. If you ever need to talk or if there's anything I can do . . ."

Infuriatingly, Maggie's eyes brimmed. At the sight of Maggie's tears, Phyllis's eyes grew moist as well, and the two women began to laugh.

"So let's change the subject," Phyllis said, wiping her eyes carefully so as not to disturb her mascara. "What's going on between Robin and Jackson?"

"I don't know what you mean."

"They're having problems."

"Well, there was the baby . . ."

"No, I don't think it's that. I called Robin to ask about the Vermont trip. She was strange."

"You know something? I bet it'd be too painful for them this year, spending parents'-day weekend up there surrounded by our kids."

"I didn't think of that," Phyllis said. "I guess it just seems like a tradition after all these years."

"What did she say, exactly?" Maggie asked.

"I can't put my finger on anything in particular. Her voice was peculiar and she said 'I' a few times instead of 'we.' Robin's always been very big on 'we' and 'us.' I bet she wants to adopt and Jackson's refused."

Maggie sat twisting her napkin guiltily. It was no use telling herself that Phyllis was imagining things. Maggie had all too profound a respect for her friend's intuitive powers. And the truth was, Maggie had not phoned Robin in two weeks.

"Don't look so miserable, Mag," Phyllis said. "You know that whatever Jackson decides, Robin will eventually convince herself he's right and she'll live with it."

Maggie picked at her salad. Phyllis watched her for a moment, then said, "How about another neutral subject?"

"Yes, please."

"So what do you hear from the kids lately?" Phyllis asked.

Maggie laughed. "Not a whole lot, of course. Fred scrawls a line now and then with requests for things, mainly food. But Susan's suddenly turned into a correspondent. I got two pages this morning."

They spent the remainder of the meal discussing their children. Then Maggie glanced at her watch. "One-thirty already. I think I'll skip dessert and coffee today."

Phyllis gave her a suspicious look, then sighed. "Me, too. I love their homemade ice cream but it just melts right onto my thighs and sits there. Let's get the check. I can see you're about to have an anxiety attack."

Outside on the street, it had begun to rain. "Oh, look at this," Maggie cried in dismay. "Wouldn't you know it would rain? I didn't bring my umbrella, and God, the traffic." A siren wailed. Looking up Lexington Avenue, which was jammed with cars, Maggie could see the flashing lights of an ambulance. Unexpectedly, it pushed south past the entrance to Lenox Hill Hospital. As the emergency vehicle reached Seventy-fifth Street where Phyllis and Maggie stood, the light changed. Traffic began to move across town, ignoring the scream of the ambulance.

"Jesus, Phyl," Maggie said. "They don't even let it through."

"New York," Phyllis said.

"Idiots!" Maggie stepped off the curb into the intersection and held up her hand. "Stop, you creep!" she cried at a taxi driver. The startled cabbie slammed on his brakes and hung out the window to shout at her. But in the meantime, the ambulance managed to squeeze behind Maggie and move on down the avenue.

Back on the sidewalk, Phyllis gaped at her and shook her head. "Well, I'll be goddamned," she said softly.

Maggie was to meet David at the West Village School for the Arts, where he taught sculpture three afternoons a week. In the cab, she was struck by a powerful ambivalence. She was eager to be included in this other mysterious sector of his life, in anything that would enrich the texture of him so that she would know him inside and out, inch by inch. But on the other hand, what if David were a dreadful teacher, inarticulate or nervous or foolish? What if they were both embarrassed?

The school was in a small brownstone on West Thirteenth Street. She followed the sound of chisels tapping against stone, and slipped into a large fluorescent-lit studio containing David and six women. David was leaning over the shoulder of a middle-aged lady with blue-white hair. The discussion was intense, Maggie could see, with the woman shaking her head in bewilderment and David being insistent. Finally he stood up. He looked in Maggie's direction but did not appear to have seen her.

"Hold it a minute!" he shouted over the din. As he spoke, he paced back and forth, back and forth. "Mrs. Ridgeway here has a problem. It's a familiar dilemma for sculptors and I'd like to throw it out to you." He paused. Everyone gazed at him respectfully and Maggie relaxed. He was obviously in full control. "Sometimes you'll get a stubborn stone. Maybe there's an imperfection in the marble or maybe it's some elusiveness in your own vision. You have to come to an agreement with your material, and you're the one who has to make the adjustment. It takes patience sometimes. I've had stones stare at me for months before I figured out what I'm supposed to be doing. You must be flexible, but don't compromise. Adjust. Can you understand the difference?"

There were a few slow nods, but not from Mrs. Ridgeway. She seemed close to tears.

"A word about polishing," David said, "since some of you are at that point now."

"Thank God," said a stringy young woman near the window.

David smiled. "Yes, it means, really, that your struggles are over, it's all been resolved. I regard polishing as my way of apologizing to the stone for all the abuse I've given it. It should be a bit like making love. Your carving will reward you with a wonderful soft glow." He shot Maggie a tiny smile. So he had seen her after all.

"That's it for today. Make sure everything is put away in the proper slot. No points with chisels, please. See you Friday. Please stay for a moment, Mrs. Ridgeway."

After the others had left, Maggie stood uncertainly in the doorway. But David had drawn the woman over to the window and was already deep into conversation with her. She was crying openly now, and David held her hand, all the time speaking urgently in a low voice. After a while, Mrs. Ridgeway got up heavily, blew her nose, and left, passing Maggie wordlessly. David waved at her to join him.

"My goodness," Maggie said.

"I told her it was no use," David explained.

"Oh," Maggie said.

"The woman has absolutely no ability. Look at that." He swept his hand toward the sandstone lump that represented several weeks of Mrs. Ridgeway's attention. "She was all set to sign up for another semester."

"Maybe she just enjoys it."

"Oh, she does. I don't know why. She was with me last term and she did another couple of awful things. But it's criminal."

"What's criminal? Her spending money on the class?"

David seemed surprised at the question. "No, her producing these ugly hunks."

"What's the harm, David, if she gets pleasure out of it? Nobody has to look at it except her."

"But, Maggie, it's what she's doing to those beautiful pieces of rock. It's like child abuse. I've even had nightmares about it."

"You're an uncompromising man."

"About some things, yes."

Her eyes accused him silently.

"Maggie, do you think she was devastated?"

"Yes. But it was nice of you to hold her hand."

146

"I wasn't aware that I did."

"I hope you don't ever feel that way about me," Maggie said fervently.

"How could I? You're a wonderful artist."

"No, I mean that you wouldn't know if you were touching me."

"Not likely."

He took her hand and kissed the palm.

"I liked that part about making love to the stone."

"I was thinking about you at the time. And trying to figure out the fastest way to get uptown."

"I'll treat you to a cab."

"A deal."

They lay on David's mattress in the gray light listening to the rain sweep across the windows like waves breaking. Today they had not delayed making love by lingering over mugs of tea; they were far too greedy. David's body was ready for her before they reached the top of his stairs.

"What is it that's so wonderful about summer rain?" Maggie murmured sleepily.

"Makes things grow."

"Like this." Maggie held his penis, miraculously soft and yielding, stone transformed to flower. "How frightening to carry all these important things on the outside. I'm glad mine is hidden away in the dark."

"Not all of it," David said. A gentle throbbing had begun in response to Maggie's curious fingers.

"It curves," Maggie said, watching him grow erect in her hand.

David laughed and pulled her over on top of him. The wind sent another spray of raindrops against the windows. "Like making love beside the sea."

"And I'm riding a dolphin," Maggie said, bending down to kiss him.

They stood naked, looking out over the Hudson River. Sometimes the clouds were gray and impenetrable, sometimes they were wispy enough to permit a glimpse of a ghostly high-rise on the New Jersey side. David had opened the window so that the mist could cool their bodies. "Just the two of us, alone in Atlantis," he said.

Maggie leaned her head against him. "You're the only person I know who could turn Fort Lee, New Jersey, into an underwater utopia." She was silent a moment. I've been wondering about Sharon. Do you mind talking about her?"

"No."

"I'd like to know more."

"She was . . . small. A small person who made little rustling noises, like a mouse in the breadbox."

"You don't make her sound terribly significant."

"She wasn't."

"But all those years."

"Maggie, I didn't know you. It was another life. When I met you in class that night, it was like entering a new dimension, as it was when I discovered art. All the definitions changed. Nothing will ever be the same."

Maggie thought about Matthew. He had been the earth and she a satellite spinning around him, governed totally by his field of gravity. And now he was a shadow who moved in and out of her world. She fed him, spoke to him, but he no longer had substance or vitality. "I'm getting cold," she said.

He draped a sheet around her, then stood back to take a look.

"A David Golden original," Maggie said. "Elegant in its simplicity." She watched his eyes move over her body with the cool obsessive scrutiny of the artist. "All right, I'll do it," she sighed, understanding that he would want her to pose for him this way. "Sometime. But I get to do you nude."

He grinned at her. He hated sitting still for her sketches. "Bargain. Come on, I'll make you some tea."

Maggie sat wrapped in her sheet while he filled the kettle. He wore an old-fashioned tank-style undershirt. There was barely enough flesh on him to cover muscle and bone. While his back and shoulders rippled as he busied himself in the kitchen, Maggie gazed into the essence of him. She could see ligaments twisting as he reached over his head for the sugar bowl. His lungs swelled and shrank rhythmically, his blood marched through his veins in short pulsing steps, the bones in his long fingers flexed and straightened as he poured boiling water into the teapot.

He looked up at her suddenly. "What are you thinking?"

"Why?"

"I feel like I'm being X-rayed."

Maggie laughed. David's uncanny perceptions no longer stunned her, but there was always delight when he availed himself of his direct route into her thoughts.

He poured the tea out into mugs, taking care to give Maggie her favorite with the moon design. They sat quietly for a while, enjoying the warmth of hot tea and intimacy.

"Know where these flowers come from?" David asked her finally, indicating the red carnations Maggie had brought him a few days ago.

"Holland," Maggie guessed.

He shook his head. "The Andes. They grow very high up. It's desolate, nothing green at all, just scrubby brown villages here and there in the mountains, and then suddenly these brilliant patches of color, field after field of carnations in rose, pink, white. They're shipped off to the States by the ton."

Maggie imagined the barren peaks adorned with blossoms, like bony old ladies whose necks were draped with jewels. "That's what I want to do with my work," she said.

"You mean the surprise?"

"Yes, that, and also the beauty. I don't want to make ugly art. I don't see the point. Life is grim enough as it is."

"You want to celebrate the good stuff."

"Yes." She glanced at David's sculptures. "You, too."

"We're propagandists, I suppose," David said.

"Yes, but aren't all artists trying to make people see things the way they do?"

"That's part of it, sure," David replied. "But for me most of the impulse comes from trying to work something out for myself. It's more self-discovery than getting a message across."

Maggie thought about her new fascination with constructions. It was an adventure in building rather than copying out what she saw. If nobody ever saw her work, she would still be driven to do it, and yet there was an effort to communicate as well. The long-dormant part of her was demanding attention now. She wished she understood it better.

"David, what were you doing in the Andes?"

"Peace Corps."

She shook her head. Facts about David kept rising to the surface and popping in her face like bubbles. "The Peace Corps *and* the army?"

"I'm a patriot." He drew his chair next to hers so that they were sitting thigh to thigh. "Besides, I could never figure out what to do about a job."

"You put your face very close to people when you talk to them," Maggie said. "Is that Southern?"

"I only do it with you." His mouth was two inches from hers.

"No, you do it to everybody. There was that poor lady in Zabar's when you were telling her where to get bagels. She looked alarmed, because you kept closing in on her until she was stuck right up against the Russian coffee cake."

"I'll have to watch it."

"It's very sexy." She kissed him.

He drew his hand through her hair. "Maggie."

"What?"

"Move in with me."

She stared at him.

"I didn't mean to say that. I'm sorry. I'll take it back if I can." He held her hands between his. "Do you have any idea what it's like for me when you've gone?"

"Yes."

"I drift around like an empty husk, and every minute I'm thinking about the next time."

"It's the same for me, David."

"Then please."

"Oh, God."

David stood up. His chair scraped harshly across the wood floor. "I wasn't ever going to do this. I have no right. I'm not the one with a family. This is my family." He gestured angrily toward the carvings. "I don't even know what it means to be a part of something like that. I'm jealous of it, Maggie." His face was anguished. "I want too much. I want everything, and I'm pressuring you. I'm sorry."

"Don't you know I think about it all the time too?" Maggie said. "It's so easy now, with the kids away. I imagine just packing my bags."

"Do it."

"And send the children a postcard with a pretty picture of the West Side explaining that Mommy has left them?"

David turned away from her to stare out the window. "What about you, Maggie? When are you ever going to start thinking about you?"

"But I am thinking about me. Thinking about them *is* thinking about me." He was silent. She put her arms around his waist from behind and leaned her head against his back. "Sometimes I believe I'm losing track of reality."

He spun around. "Reality is you and me." He took her

hand and touched it to his mouth, his heart, his crotch. "And this, and this, and this." She began to look frightened. "Ah, Maggie," he went on softly. "I never cared for a woman before, and now I want you with me every second." He held her quietly for a moment. "But if we had to go on like this for the rest of our lives, it would be enough. I could handle it."

"Things don't stand still like that."

"They will if we make them, if we want it badly enough."

She shook her head. "David, I'm such a conventional person, really."

"You're not as conventional as you think."

Maggie eased back in his arms. Sometimes it seemed to her that his face was just two immense burning eyes. "What do I give you, David?"

He looked surprised. "You know me. No one else on this earth knows me except you. You live inside my head, my guts, sometimes I don't know where you leave off and I begin or who thought what. We recognized one another that first night, remember? It didn't take more than a couple of minutes and I knew who you were, what you could mean." He shook her gently. "Shit, Maggie, maybe there's some other language that has words for it."

She knew that it was nearly time for her to go. "I want us to work together," she said, grasping for something they could both look forward to. "If you're just polishing now, couldn't I be there at your desk?"

"I'd like that. But when is it going to be?"

Now came the excruciating part. Matthew's mother was due this evening. It would be difficult to get away. "I don't think I can come again until a week from tomorrow."

"Oh."

"It's my mother-in-law. Sometimes she hovers and sometimes she ignores me totally. I can never predict which it's going to be."

"Will you call me if you can come before?"

"Yes. David, I hate this more than anything."

"I know."

On the way across town, Maggie put her hands to her face and took a deep breath. After she had been with David, her fingers always had the clean dry scent of stone dust.

"Hello, my darling!" Rhoda Hollander threw her arms around Matthew's neck. Maggie watched him flinch. The older woman pulled back and examined her son's face. "But a trifle peaked, *n'est-ce pas?*"

Matthew reached behind to unhook the veined fingers that were crusted with rings. "I'm fine, Mother. How was the trip?"

"I've just been telling Margarita. Ghastly. Stuck on that hideous bus in the Lincoln Tunnel with all those noxious fumes. The state of New Jersey has finally invented the supreme method of torturing its mature citizens. Denying us the right to drive." She flung herself dramatically onto the sofa with a sigh.

Matthew took his drink from Maggie with a grateful smile. "Only those mature citizens who drive over eighty miles an hour on the Garden State Parkway," he reminded his mother.

Rhoda leveled a painted fingernail at him and shook it. "Don't nitpick with me, Matthew. If I'd been eighteen years old, they would have marked a few points on my license and sent me on my way. Don't you agree, Margarita?"

Rhoda Hollander had always called Maggie everything but "Maggie," which she claimed was a name that smacked of Tennessee Williams and corruption. Sometimes it was "Meghan," sometimes "Marguerite," even "Peggy." A clue to Rhoda's current affinity for "Margarita" could be found in today's Mexican attire—multicolored cotton skirt and heavily embroidered blouse. But even at seventy-three, Rhoda was authoritative enough to carry off such costumes. She traveled incessantly—

restlessly, Maggie thought—and inevitably arrived home sporting the native dress of whichever country she had just visited. Maggie secretly explained Rhoda's aversion to Japan by the fact that nowhere in Tokyo was there a single pair of *kutsu* size ten triple-A.

Maggie was always struck by the similarity between Matthew's physiognomy and his mother's. There was the same square shape, same bold nose and widely set eyes. On Matthew, the features were handsome, on his mother, formidable. When Rhoda made her infrequent appearances, Maggie always found herself searching Matthew's face for intimations of his father, who was known to her only through photographs from which he peered with vague kindliness. Edward Hollander had been an administrator in a prestigious small hospital in Princeton. Rhoda always referred to him as "poor Edward," presumably in reference to his early death from emphysema.

At the dinner table, Maggie watched the two identical mouths chew broiled chicken with jaws moving in unison and decided that Rhoda's genes had been far too intimidating to permit the contribution of hereditary characteristics from "poor Edward" or anyone else. In the engendering of Matthew, his father had been as close to unnecessary as was scientifically feasible.

Rhoda regaled them with the travelogue of her trip to Mexico, although as always, the narrative tended to feature greater detail about her travel companions than the exotic landscape.

"What I appreciate about Marion," she said, "is her decadence. One sits on a tour bus beside this tidy little old lady with her hair in a bun, just like Helen Hayes, you know, and suddenly she's talking about fellatio. It's quite refreshing."

Maggie had often expressed admiration to Matthew regarding his mother's extravagance, conversational and otherwise. Her own parents seemed so ordinary. But Rhoda was an original. "I wonder what I would have been like if your mother had been my mother," she had said to him.

"God forbid," he replied.

"Well, I think she's wonderful. Irritating, maybe, but she's never dull."

"Jesus, Mag, it was like having Auntie Mame for a mother. Freshman Week at college she showed up with a handbag full of joints and sat around the dorm smoking grass with my classmates."

Maggie laughed.

"That was her anti-alcohol phase. She figured we were bound to get high once in a while, and marijuana was preferable to booze."

"It was a protective impulse anyway," Maggie said. Ever since that conversation, Maggie had wondered if Matthew had married her because she was his mother's opposite: repressed, conventional, withdrawn, and colorless.

"I disapprove of summer camp," Rhoda was saying. "Get me some Sweet'n Low, won't you, dear?" she asked Matthew.

"Mother, you just swallowed seven hundred and fifty calories' worth of pecan pie."

"All the more reason for the Sweet'n Low."

He got up and Rhoda turned her attention to Maggie. "Unless it's a music camp or one of these ethics places where they teach potting and acid-rain testing, that sort of thing. Those dreadful sports factories ruin American children, just turn them into mindless robots who wind up watching Monday-night football every week and never read a book."

Matthew returned with the Sweet'n Low. "Thank you, dear," she said, and emptied three packets of the fine powder in her coffee. A pale cloud rose around her fingers. With a sense of shock, Maggie noticed that Rhoda's hand trembled as she reached for her spoon. The woman had always seemed magnificently impervious to the cruelties of time. This first evidence of vulnerability filled Maggie with sadness.

"Though I suppose camp is somewhere to acquire friends," Rhoda went on. "You don't realize until you're an old wreck how valuable companionship is, except that everyone's continually dying on you." She turned to Matthew. "Myrna Billings keeled over last week in Shop-Rite beside the produce counter. Humiliating to go out that way, clutching a head of lettuce."

"I'm sure she doesn't care."

"You think not? I wonder." For a moment Rhoda was silent. The next words out of her mouth were unexpectedly tentative. "I've been thinking. About death, I mean." She paused again. "One does, at my age. Obviously." She waved her hand as if with impatience at her own weakness. "I was remembering poor Edward only last night. I don't know how long it's been since I thought about him." Her eyes met Matthew's briefly, but he quickly looked away. "Sometimes I wake up in the night and turn toward that side of the bed. . . ." She waved her hand again. "Silly after all this time. I hope I'm not getting Alzheimer's. Promise me you'll put me in a home if I ever lose it." The staunch shoulders hunched forward, leaving a hollow between breastbone and gay frilled blouse. "I understand you're back at work again," she said in a voice so abruptly brisk that Maggie nearly jumped.

"Yes. I've been trying . . ."

Rhoda scraped her chair back and stood. "Well, come on. Let's see what you've been up to." She followed Maggie into Fred's room. "Criminal to allow such talent to flounder. Matthew never permitted his gifts to emerge. I can't think why."

"I don't have any gifts," Matthew said in a tired voice.

"Let's not get into that again," Rhoda said, picking up the sunset collage.

"I think I'll catch the news," Matthew said.

Rhoda inspected the work from all angles. "Interesting, Margarita. But don't you think a touch primitive?"

"It's 'Maggie.' "

"I beg your pardon?" Rhoda said.

"My name. It's 'Maggie.' I'd appreciate it."

For the remainder of her visit, Rhoda never addressed Maggie by name. She just pursed her lips resentfully, leaving spaces where Maggie's name should go, and looked deprived. She left two days early, and as soon as the door shut behind her, Maggie was on the telephone to David.

"How was your mother-in-law?" he asked, holding her at the top of his stairs.

"She makes me think of the Colosseum."

"Why's that?"

"Because she's a beautiful old ruin but it's important to keep in mind that terrible things happened to the lions and the Christians in there."

"Poor Matthew."

"Yes. Come to bed."

16

At a certain moment while she was packing for the trip to Vermont, Maggie plucked the old madras dress out of her closet and stuffed it in the wastebasket. The rush of elation that followed made her so giddy that when Matthew came into the room she was tossing his rolled-up socks into the suitcase from across the bed.

"How many points for a foul shot?" she asked.

Matthew appeared not to have heard her. He strode directly into the bathroom. She could hear him removing his shaving things from the medicine cabinet. There had been a few seconds when she had feared that he might notice the discarded dress. But then, he had always teased her about her reluctance to throw it away, and besides, he was obviously preoccupied. He

---

could be stone deaf when he was involved in an interesting case.

When they had crossed the Connecticut border, Maggie thought about the dress again. There was such satisfaction in having tossed the old relic away, freedom and a titillating sensation of nakedness.

"How do you suppose snakes feel when they shed their skins?" she asked Matthew.

"I don't think they feel anything much, do they?"

"They look so shiny when they crawl out of those dry old husks. I would think they'd have to feel something. Fresh, unburdened, clean—something."

But he was away again, concentrating on the traffic, which had thickened as they approached the turnoff heading north. Though Maggie drove well, Matthew always preferred to take the wheel. She could not remember his ever having relinquished the driver's seat, even on their three-week honeymoon across the country.

It was uncanny what had happened to her, she thought. She had become two entirely separate women. There was the David-Maggie—sensuous, confident, spontaneous. Today she was Matthew-Maggie, the cautious, withdrawn, efficient mother-of-two. She imagined Matthew-Maggie as the freeze-dried version of herself. When she crossed the park to the West Side, a magic transformation took place: just add David and stir. Presto! The essential Maggie Hollander, full-bodied and steaming.

There was a place where both Maggies coexisted. In Fred's room, her little studio, all the ingredients blended into a rich stew. Everything poured out into her constructions: the longing for David, the deep attachment to her children, the turbulent feelings for Matthew, the need for creative isolation and the contrasting magnetism of family and friends. Ambivalence and conflict thrived in that room. Sometimes the atmosphere became so thick that she was forced to the window for air. But she was never frightened there. Her scissors and glue and odd fragments of paper made her omnipotent. It was venturing outside that filled her with dread. She understood that the two Maggies must not mingle outside the sanctuary. Keeping them balanced and separate was the only insurance against loss. An integrated Maggie meant choice, and choice was unthinkable.

Her heart had begun to beat very fast. She watched the oncoming cars with terror, certain that one of them would surely leap the barrier and smash into them head-on. What if there was an accident and Matthew was killed? The thought surfaced like the snout of some hideous swamp creature coming up for a breath of fetid air. If Matthew were dead and she survived . . . Maggie pressed the monster back into the dark waters where it belonged and thought about how much she missed David. If they could just hold out until the children were in college, Maggie thought. There'd be a divorce and the children could come home to David and her. . . . But her mind veered from the concept. Somehow David and her children seemed mutually exclusive. Fred and Susan adored their father. David had not shared the years of anxiety and pleasure that accompanied the parenting of these two particular human beings. Maggie tried to imagine Susan and Fred cavorting among David's sculptures, or sprawled on the floor watching the television that would have to be imported since David had none. No, instead the young people would sit stiffly at the round oak table staring accusingly at Maggie and David.

Her head began to ache. She inched closer to the window to let the breeze cool her face.

"You know, I really can't stand my mother," Matthew was saying.

"What?" Maggie was not sure she had heard him correctly.

"I hate her," he said, then looked at Maggie with a triumphant grin on his face. "Whoa, how terrific."

"What do you suppose inspired that?"

"I don't know. I was just remembering the way she puts on her lipstick with that kind of kissing action at the end, and I wanted to strangle her." He shook his head wonderingly. "If this is what going to a shrink does, maybe I ought to try it. I must have been saving that up for forty years."

"Well, I hate my mother too," Maggie blurted. Then they both began to laugh.

"Oh, Christ," he moaned. "I'd better pull off or we'll wind up in the ditch."

The laughter brought Maggie dangerously close to sobbing. Matthew was not permitted to indulge in sudden insights or make emotional declarations. These were David's province. She took the tissue Matthew offered, wiped her eyes, and glanced at him. But he was peering ahead already, lost in thought. If she spoke to him, she knew he would not answer her.

Maggie had surprised herself with the declaration of hatred for her mother. Whenever she had thought about the house in Stafford, there had always been a bad taste in her mouth that she interpreted as the typical vague resentment one feels for one's family. Today's particularization of the emotion caught her off guard. If anyone was going to be hated, Maggie assumed it would have to be Joanne. But examining her feelings for her sister now, Maggie found merely a kind of fond pity. Maggie's outburst over Joanne's hypothetical birthday present must have cleared the way for a more potent disaffection. Mother, Maggie thought, one of these days I will get around to you.

Their resort was carefully scattered among the trees along the top of a ridge called Frenchman's Notch. There were tennis courts, racquetball courts, indoor and outdoor pools, saunas, even a small indoor ice-skating rink. Maggie liked the place because the architects had left its wild surroundings intact. Even the parking lot had been constructed with deference to the shade trees that prevailed over the macadam here and there. Only a few spots were available when they pulled in; parents' weekend always jammed the hotel to its limit.

"I wonder if the others are here yet," Maggie said. She looked around the lot for other New York license plates. There were several.

"It's touch and go with the Brodys, isn't it?" Matthew said, hauling the suitcases from the trunk.

"Last I knew, they were coming."

But there was a message at the front desk for Maggie to telephone Robin in New York.

"Have the Wheelers arrived yet?" Matthew asked the clerk.

The young man punched some keys on his computer. "Yes, sir. Just barely."

As soon as the door shut behind the bellhop, Maggie sat down on the edge of the bed and called Robin.

"It's me. We miss you already."

"I'm sorry," Robin answered. "I kept trying to hold out until after the weekend, but I just couldn't. And then yesterday this apartment came up, and I went over there this morning and signed a lease."

Maggie was stunned to silence.

"I'm moving out this weekend."

"I didn't realize. I thought it was because of what happened. The baby . . ."

"I hated to put a damper on things, but there's no way we could have faked it. If you want to make up a story for the others until you get home . . ."

"I don't think I could do that."

"I'm sorry, Mags. Don't let it ruin everybody's fun."

"Robin, whatever made you . . ."

"Let's talk about it face to face, okay? I'm fine. Jackson's okay, too. I'll see you next week."

"All right," Maggie said. Robin, sweet Robin, who was so

intimidated by Jackson that she did not own a single pair of pants because he disliked how she looked in them.

"Are you all right?" Matthew asked. He was staring down at her as she sat motionless on the edge of the bed, her hand resting on the telephone.

"She's moving out," Maggie said.

Matthew laughed. "That's ridiculous. She would never leave him."

"She signed a lease. She's moving this weekend."

Matthew headed for the closet with an armful of clothes from the suitcase. "I'm sure she's just trying to give him a scare, that's all. But why she'd want to make Jackson miserable is beyond me. He's a terrific guy."

Maggie did not answer. When he returned for another batch of clothes, he ruffled her hair. "Don't take it so seriously, Mag. They'll be back together in no time."

"Jesus Christ!" Phyllis exclaimed. Her voice traveled in the muted elegance of the hotel dining room. "It's like Santa and Mrs. Claus getting divorced."

"Nobody said anything about divorce," Maggie protested.

"Did you have any notion this was coming?" Stephen asked. Maggie shook her head.

"She's just trying to throw a scare into him," Matthew said.

"Because he won't adopt?" Hilary wanted to know.

"I don't suppose it's as simple as that," Maggie said.

"Well," Phyllis said, "I must say I'm impressed. She really has an apartment?"

"That's what she said," Maggie replied.

"And I always thought she was your basic lapdog," Phyllis mused.

"You sound as if she deserves the Nobel Peace Prize," Stephen said.

"I think of it more in terms of the Boston Tea Party or the Slave Rebellion," Phyllis answered. "I propose a toast." She raised her glass. "To Robin Brody. The worm turns."

Matthew's jaw muscle was clamped tight shut and Stephen's face looked murderous.

"Matt, Stephen says he sent you a client," Maggie said, hoping to steer the conversation into cooler water. "Somebody getting into the movies."

"Yeah, Miles Farber. Did it work out okay?" Stephen asked.

"I meant to call and thank you," Matthew said. "Very interesting situation, one of the more challenging things I've had on my desk this year."

Stephen grinned like a small boy getting a handshake from an astronaut. Phyllis winked at Maggie.

"I hope he paid the bill," Stephen said.

"Nope, he stiffed us," Matthew said.

"Oh, my God," Stephen said. "What can I do? How much was it? Maybe I can make it up. . . ."

"Don't worry about it," Matthew interrupted. "It happens all the time. We'll sue the bastard."

Maggie began to giggle. The others looked at her. "I was fishing for a neutral topic," she said. "Screwed up. You think of something, Phyl." The giggles were expanding into choking laughter.

"Are you all right?" Matthew asked.

Maggie tried to speak but was gasping now. She gestured helplessly as tears slid down her face.

"She's upset about Robin," Hilary said.

Maggie nodded. "Upset," she sputtered. "I'm upset. Oh Lord!" And she was off again.

"Here, Mag," Phyllis said, handing her a glass of wine. "Take a few deep breaths and then drink this down in one swig."

Maggie did as she was told. Finally her breathing returned

to normal and she was able to wipe her eyes. Matthew patted her awkwardly on the back.

"Sorry, I don't know what came over me," Maggie said. "I guess I was more shook up than I thought."

"We're all shook up," Phyllis said. "We may just as well try to talk about it. I promise I won't be smug if you guys don't get defensive on behalf of mankind. Okay?"

"Fine," Matthew said.

"It's that it's so unexpected," Maggie said. "I don't know as it's the best marriage in the world, but I certainly thought of it as a permanent one."

"We're going to be hearing a lot of this," Stephen said.

"It's already started," Phyllis agreed. "Two kids in Zach's class this spring had parents split up."

"Are these supposed to be rough years?" Matthew asked. "I don't notice any particular stress. Do you, Mag?"

Maggie avoided looking at Phyllis.

"It's the times we live in," Phyllis said quickly. "We're all stuck in limbo. Our parents had this nice formula where everybody knew their slot. You just never stepped outside it. Very uncomplicated. Now everybody's telling us that women have to be more like men and men have to be more like women."

"Well, don't believe everything you hear," Matthew said.

"Can't help it," Phyllis said. "It sinks in after a while. Besides, it's true. The old way sucks."

"How would you change things, Phyllis?" Matthew asked.

"I'd be teaching physics at Columbia," she answered promptly.

Matthew looked stunned.

"She was a whiz in the sciences," Maggie said. "Top of the class."

"So why not?" Matthew asked.

"So I got married and followed my husband to New York and put him through his MBA with my nice little job at *Woman's Companion*. And then I got pregnant."

"But you could do it now," Hilary protested.

Phyllis shrugged.

"She's too busy with her tennis game and her manicure and lunch with the girls," Stephen said.

"I thought we weren't going to get nasty," Phyllis snapped.

"Truth hurts," Stephen said.

"Something happens to all that ambition," Maggie said. "It gets siphoned off by people needing you all the time."

"There are the rare exceptions," Phyllis said. "Whoever thought Robin would be one of them?"

"She's left her husband," Matthew protested. "That's not establishing a career."

"But if she's unhappy and has the courage to break away, it's a start," Maggie said.

Matthew stared at her. "They should try to work it out. It's not courageous to run out on the situation."

There was a long silence. Phyllis lit up a cigarette. There were already half a dozen cigarette butts in her ashtray.

"Kids don't help any," Stephen said finally. "Some of our worst fights are over Zach. Although I suppose that's because we're not very good parents."

"Speak for yourself, darling," Phyllis remarked.

"All right. I'm a pitiful father. I don't know, I say the wrong thing nine times out of ten. I keep meaning to thank you two for letting Zach spend so much time at your house. It's good for him, being around you and Fred."

"It'd be better for him to have a decent relationship with his own father," Phyllis said.

"Sometimes I think it'd be a good idea to get into some kind of counseling . . ."

"Ha!" Phyllis hooted. "You've been saying that for at least five years. You'll never do it, you just like to parade your good intentions. How about a public pledge? Maybe then you'd actually get off your ass."

"You're embarrassing me," Stephen muttered, his face scarlet.

"I don't mind embarrassing you if it's going to help Zach," Phyllis replied.

"You don't mind embarrassing me just for the fun of it. Besides, I don't see that eight years of therapy's done much for you."

"Listen, you two," Matthew interjected. "Why don't you slug it out in private? Any more marital discord around here and Maggie'll start giggling again."

"You're right, you're right," Stephen said. "Come on, Phyl, let's quit playing *Who's Afraid of Virginia Woolf?* and have another drink."

The remainder of the meal passed glumly but without incident. By the time the bill arrived, they had consumed three bottles of wine.

Later Matthew turned to Maggie in the dark in their king-size bed. "What a pair they are," he said.

"Stephen and Phyllis?"

"Yeah."

"I guess if I'd had to choose, I would have picked them to split up before the Brodys."

"No question about it." He placed a hand over her breast. "You think that could happen to us?"

"I suppose it can happen to anybody," she said.

Matthew was quiet for a while. Then he stared in the direction of the ceiling. "I guess I don't say it very often. I figure you know it without my saying so. But I do love you."

Maggie's throat tightened. He was waiting, she knew, for her to respond in kind. "I love you too," she whispered finally. It was true in a way, she told herself. They had lived together for a long time. You can't share that many years without loving, in a way. But as Matthew's caresses grew more insistent, she thought of David with shame. I'm doing this because I have to, she told David silently. As Matthew drew his body across her and nudged her legs apart with his knee, she thought with sickening irony of the guilt she felt in allowing her own husband to make love to her.

"Fred's gonna get best boy camper this year," Susan proclaimed from the back seat.

"I won't," Fred protested.

"You will." Susan spoke with the profound authority of her new position as counselor-in-training.

"Mom, can't you move the seat up? I'm all tangled back here." Fred seemed to have grown four inches since June. He was thinner. For the first time, Maggie thought she saw a resemblance to Matthew.

"Zachary Wheeler may make *worst* camper," Susan said. "If he doesn't get thrown out."

"Oh dear, why?" Maggie asked.

"He's got a lot of problems, Mom," Fred replied.

"I thought you liked him," Matthew said, swerving to pass a tractor carrying a load of hay.

"I do," Fred said. "But he's probably gonna get busted for smoking dope and messing around with Freda Gross."

Matthew shot Maggie an alarmed look. He had a dread of drugs anywhere near the children. "How could he get hold of anything way up here?"

"Oh, Daddy," Susan said. "Don't be so naive."

"He never does it around me," Fred said. "And anyhow, he's been warned, so maybe he'll watch it now. They already threw one kid out, and that scared Zach. They told us he had appendicitis and had to go home."

"Reuben Marshall had appendicitis," Sue said in her capacity as a spokesperson for the camp.

"That must be why he was popping all those little blue capsules," Fred said. "To kill the pain."

"My God," Matthew said.

"Don't worry about us," Fred assured him. "We're much too well-adjusted."

"Remember camp, Matthew?" Maggie asked. "Roasting marshmallows over the campfire, hikes in the fresh air, square dances?"

"Actually we got drunk in the boathouse one night," Matthew said.

"See?" Susan exclaimed. *"Plus c'est la même chose."*

Maggie twisted around in her seat to inspect her children. It always disoriented her to see them after a long absence. They had such fresh attractive faces, the kind she enjoyed looking at in airports and restaurants. By the time Maggie had reached Fred's age, she had already begun to withdraw. In every class photograph from the sixth grade onward, Maggie wore the same solemn expression. Fred and Susan had open, confident faces. They were brown from four weeks of outdoor activities, except for the mosquito bites that dotted their arms and legs. Maggie smiled.

"Remember when you both had chickenpox for Christmas?"

Susan laughed. "Yeah, and you gave us paintbrushes with calamine lotion in our stockings and had us paint each other's spots."

"Well, it worked. I just couldn't do you both every day. Together you must have had five hundred poxes. Anyhow, it kept you occupied."

Maggie noticed that Susan had pulled her hair back into a ponytail. It was streaked with gold. The soft hairs around her face were bleached white-blond. "You look very pretty, honey," Maggie said. "Being a counselor must agree with you."

"She was a pain at first," Fred declared. "Ordering everybody around, especially me so she wouldn't get accused of nepotism. But once she got over being drunk with power, she turned out to be a pretty excellent counselor."

"Gee, thanks," Susan said wryly. "He's always trying to worm privileges out of me, like not having to set tables."

"I need all the support I can get," Fred explained. "I'm entering puberty."

Matthew laughed. "God knows it's rough to set tables with puberty lurking around the corner."

They pulled onto the steep road that led up to the hotel.

"Who's the richest black man in the world, Dad?" Fred asked.

"I haven't the vaguest idea. Probably some king in Africa. Why?"

"What about the richest black *woman*?"

"Oh, Fred," Maggie said. They turned into the parking lot and the children scrambled out of the back seat and raced for the hotel entrance.

"What do you suppose that was all about?" Matthew asked as they trailed along behind.

"God knows," Maggie said. "It never changes with him. Remember 'If you dropped a penny off the World Trade Center, would it make a hole in the sidewalk?' "

"I got 'If you droped *water* off the World Trade Center, at which floor would it evaporate?' " He swung his arm around Maggie's shoulder. "I wish we could take them home with us tomorrow."

"Yes," Maggie said. As she and Matthew stood adoring their children, she struggled to think about David and what he might be doing at this particular moment. But his image flickered evasively in the powerful light of the sunny Vermont morning.

When Maggie mentioned the subject of Robin and Jackson, Matthew's hands turned white on the steering wheel.

"If she took off just because of the adoption thing, I can't work up any sympathy for her," he said. "The man already has a kid of his own. She knew that when she married him."

"Why shouldn't she have one of *her* own?"

"It wouldn't be her own. It would be adopted."

Maggie stared out the window at the blur of pine trees and telephone poles. It was like the film of a parade speeded up to an unbearable velocity. "I'm not sure it's just the issue of having children," she said. "It's his whole attitude. . . ."

"Fuck attitude," Matthew interrupted. "She's acting like a spoiled child. I don't know, you women amaze me sometimes."

"Oh, we women?"

"Jackson works his balls off trying to give her a good life and look what he gets for his pains. I suppose he's going to be paying two rents now."

Maggie was silent.

"I see it all the time in the legal profession. The poor suckers get dragged into court and never crawl out from under the alimony payments. Meanwhile, the ex-wives keep the car and the fancy co-op apartment and the clothes and the antiques . . ."

"You know damn well," Maggie broke in, "that most divorced women never collect their alimony payments *or* their child support. You're really worked up about this."

"Isn't it something to get worked up over?"

"Yes."

"Well, there's nothing we can do about it." He snapped on the radio. WPIX. Love songs, nothing but love songs. Roberta Flack was singing "The First Time Ever." The first time ever David Golden had touched Maggie, his hand had been so gentle. She looked at the angry man who was glaring out at the road with clenched jaw and thought about Robin all by herself in her very own apartment. What Maggie felt was profound envy.

17

"We're too goddamn solemn," David said to her over the telephone.

Maggie was startled enough to hear his voice at ten in the morning. His lighthearted tone baffled her further. "Oh," she said.

David laughed. "It's a beautiful day and we're going to enjoy it. Bring a warm sweater, jeans, and rubber-soled shoes, and don't ask me any questions."

"Aye, aye," Maggie said. There was sudden silence at the other end. Maggie knew that she had reached into his brain yet again and guessed correctly that they were to be on a boat.

David was already standing at Riverside Drive and Seventy-ninth Street when Maggie got off the bus.

"Where are we going?" She gave him a quick kiss and allowed him to take her arm. Lately, her vestigial fears of being seen with David had dissipated. She thought perhaps it was because her life on the West Side had become so vivid and essential it now seemed inviolable. Sometimes she wondered if there was an unconscious wish to be caught and thereafter forced into decision, but the reality of such an event seemed so horrific that she repressed such notions as soon as they surfaced.

David led her across the intersection and along a path that bisected the ribbon of Riverside Park. Suddenly they rounded a bend and blinked at the dazzling spectacle of the Seventy-ninth Street boat basin. Maggie had seen the marina from David's windows, but the aerial view left her unprepared for the sight that confronted her now. Except for the muted roar of traffic and ambulance sirens shooting past on the West Side Highway, she might have been in a quaint fishing village. Dozens of tidy sailboats and powerboats nestled against the docks and bobbed in the September sunshine. There were some square-shaped vessels as well, like boxes on platforms, a small barge with an ancient beetle-shaped Volkswagen aboard, and a jaunty red tugboat.

David followed her line of vision and gestured toward the tug. "Fellow picked that up on the Jersey shore after it spent a long career towing sand barges. It's quite a house. There's even a baby grand piano nailed down in there."

Maggie laughed. "This is like Hilary's apartment."

"Why's that?" David asked as he unlatched a gate and motioned her out onto the pier.

"Serendipity. She lives at the top of a dingy old warehouse in SoHo. If you survive the rickety elevator, you step out into this huge white space with polished floors and skylights. She's furnished it with antiques and needlepoint rugs, a real surprise, like pianos in tugboats. And this place perched on the edge of the river." Suddenly she pulled back. "David, didn't you tell me Eliza Austin has a boat here?"

"Yes. She lives on it."

"I don't think I want to do this."

"Liza's a good friend, Maggie. I want you to know each other." Reluctantly Maggie let him urge her along. "After all," he continued, "she was really the beginning of everything for us."

They made their way along the pier and off onto a spur to the left. David halted beside a thirty-foot fiberglass boat and rapped on the hull. A muffled voice called "Come!" David climbed aboard, gave Maggie a hand, then disappeared below while Maggie stood awkwardly on the teak deck wishing she could hop back on the crosstown bus. Her feet in their battered tennis shoes were pointed toes-inward like a schoolgirl awaiting punishment.

After a moment, Eliza Austin's gray cropped head appeared, then shoulders, and finally the entire six feet of her, clad in overalls and navy-blue wool turtleneck. It was difficult to accept the fact that Eliza was approaching seventy. She was slim and straight, and had the same type of face as David's, clean and spare, with nothing hidden by excess pouches of flesh. There were wrinkles, of course, but they only served to soften the severity of her high forehead and cheekbones. She might have been David's mother.

Eliza watched, amused, while Maggie made her surreptitious inspection. Then the older woman held out her hand. "Welcome aboard. The overalls are a necessity. Sometimes it gets pretty hectic alone at the helm, so I always keep a supply of emergency equipment in here." She reached into a roomy pocket and drew out two cigar-shaped pretzels and a can of grapefruit juice. "And here. And here." Another pocket held a pair of sunglasses and some Band-Aids, a third a miniature tool kit.

"It was nice of you to invite me. Us," Maggie said. But Eliza was already busy coiling lines and pushing buttons on an instrument panel.

"We'll be set in a minute. David, ready to cast off?"

David stood at the bow. "Anytime you say," he called.

Maggie sat down and watched as the two expertly maneuvered the boat away from the dock, David pushing off with his foot and Eliza reversing with one hand on the wheel. Soon they were free of the marina and heading north up the Hudson. Although it had been quite warm back at the dock, there was a stiff breeze on the water. Maggie turned her face into the wind and let it whip back her hair. A tanker, moving seaward, split the golden surface of the river, leaving a foamy wake. Far ahead, the George Washington Bridge stretched in a graceful span from New York to New Jersey. Along the shore on the Manhattan side, the trees had begun to turn, mostly yellow with an occasional burst of scarlet from a sugar maple.

Eliza slowed the engine so that it was possible to talk. "Come sit closer," she said to Maggie. "David, go get my straw hat, will you? It's on my bed."

He disappeared belowdecks while Maggie dutifully edged closer to Eliza. "Do you actually live on this?" Maggie asked.

"Yes. A lot of us do at Seventy-ninth Street. There's a big mess about who's in charge of the place at the moment, but we'll hang on no matter what. We're a tenacious lot."

"Have you always? I guess it's hard for me to imagine. Can you cook? And take a bath?"

"All the conveniences, more or less. Sometimes if there's an awful ice storm in February I'll go hole up in my studio until it blows over. These old bones are a bit intimidated by winter gales."

David returned to plunk a ragged straw hat on Eliza's head. When he sat down beside Maggie and threw an arm around her shoulders, Maggie stiffened. Eliza averted her eyes.

"So what do you think about this old tub?" David asked Maggie.

"It seems glamorous to me," Maggie answered.

"She's not even ten years old," Eliza protested. "What do you know about old age anyway, child?" She reached to ruffle David's hair and he ducked. Maggie had never seen David playful. Perhaps he had been right on the telephone this morning; their relationship was pretty serious-minded.

"People choose to live this way for a variety of reasons," Eliza was saying, "but since it's not an ordinary way to live, the people tend to be odd themselves."

"Why did you?" Maggie asked.

"I spent twenty years in a stifling marriage, another ten practically starving to death trying to meet the rent in a hideous apartment. When the building went co-op, I sold out, took the money, and bought my freedom."

"Eliza and her husband ran a very successful advertising business," David said.

"Howard ran the business. I designed packaging for our clients. On my God, how I suffered, trying to convince myself it was gratifying to draw Jell-O boxes. One time my husband came home from a trip on a sunny Saturday afternoon. He walked into the studio, looked over my shoulder, and said, 'You were supposed to have that finished yesterday.' I don't know what happened to me. I just got up, said something about how a person has to know when to walk out into the sun, and I left him. Never went back."

"Goodness," Maggie said. "Do you ever hear from him?"

"No. Why would I?"

"Well, twenty years, and building up a business together."

Eliza shook her head and waved a long tapered hand as if she were shooing away a gnat. "It was over. I never missed him for a second."

Maggie wondered how the husband felt about losing Eliza. When the image of Matthew's face bobbed into view, she tried to imitate Eliza and brush the vision away.

"But you see, I never had children," Eliza said. Maggie felt

David squeeze her shoulder. Eliza squinted at a floating carton ahead and swerved to starboard. "I don't understand the power of it myself, motherhood, especially once a child is old enough to comprehend a sentence. I can see sticking it out for little ones. They're quite helpless. But once they reach eight or ten, they should be able to manage. I know I did. I was ten when my parents separated."

The George Washington Bridge loomed high above them now. The two huge towers rose out of the water, dwarfing the boat passing far below. The structure's intricate design and immense arches seemed to echo the Gothic splendor of St. John the Divine, which dominated the riverbank just to the south. Sunlight through the cables cast mysterious shadows on the river. Maggie felt as if they were gliding across a strange floating web. "Where are we going?" she asked.

"Depends on how much time we've got," Eliza replied. "When do you have to be home?"

Maggie imagined that she detected a hint of pity, or perhaps it was contempt, in the question. "About ten."

"Good. Bear Mountain for sure, maybe farther. How about a beer?"

"Yes!" Maggie exclaimed.

"Hold the wheel, Dee," Eliza said, and slipped below.

David winked at Maggie, but kept his eyes on the river. "There's garbage floating around. I'm always afraid I'll crack into something."

"You seem to know what you're doing," Maggie said. "What did she call you?"

"Dee. Silly nickname."

Eliza emerged with three Molsons. "Hope you can make do without a glass," she said to Maggie. "I like to keep the dishwashing to a minimum since it's pretty cramped in the galley."

Maggie took a swig, enjoying the shape of the smooth glass

opening against her lips. It had been a very long time since she had drunk anything straight out of the bottle—probably not since adolescence. She took another long draw, stretched her feet out, and sighed contentedly. To the west, the Palisades made their steep ascent four hundred feet straight up. They had a raw scraped appearance as if the geological phenomena that formed them had happened in one violent night. Manhattan, far downriver now, was merely a haphazard assortment of children's blocks, like the Legos Fred used to snap together. Fred. According to Eliza's philosophy, Fred was far past the age of comprehension and Maggie was free to leave. Children were resilient. In time, they would surely adjust to a new family structure. They loved their father, but how could they not learn to care for David? She watched him now, squinting up at the sky and absorbing the shapes of the fat fluffy clouds.

Eliza, back at the helm, reached out for David's beer. He handed it to her, she took a sip and returned it. "Did David tell you about the squall we got into off Montauk this spring?" Eliza asked. "He saved this boat, not to mention our hides."

"No, he didn't," Maggie said. She was beginning to feel a rising sense of discomfort regarding David's obvious intimacy with Eliza. Here was a part of his life he had never shared with her, even verbally. She wondered why not. She chided herself for the absurd fantasy that he existed only when she was present, and somehow remained suspended each time she left, like a television set she could merely switch off as she walked out the door. Besides, was her jealousy a fraction of what David must feel about her life with Matthew and the children?

"What did you do with that bomb hoist Ben dug up for you? Was it any use?" Eliza was asking David.

"Not much. It's okay for hauling raw stone, but even then I'm afraid I'll wind up chipping it or fracturing something."

Maggie was too proud to ask for an explanation, not wanting to give Eliza further indication of how little David told her. Anyway, Eliza had now switched her attention to Maggie.

"I understand you've begun working in collage," Eliza said. "I'd like to get a look at the Hudson River piece sometime."

Maggie flashed a glance at David. He seemed free enough conversing with Eliza about her. "You have a gift for dramatic utilization of space," Eliza went on. "You'll enjoy collage and do it well."

"Your class was good for me."

"Come take another, though I don't know how much I can teach you now."

"A lot." Maggie hesitated. "Are you working?" she asked finally. She was careful about asking a fellow artist such a question. It could dip into the most agonizing area of the creative person's life. But all was well with Eliza.

"Oh yes," she replied with gusto. "David took me to see a film recently, what was it, the one about the runners?"

"*Chariots of Fire*," David answered.

"Yes, that's it. I like athletics. This was quite charming, and it got me started on some things having to do with competition."

"Eliza's an exercise fanatic," David explained.

"I must say that movie was an inspiration. I came right home and jumped into my leotard. All those slim bodies."

Maggie remembered now that on the night of her first class, she had felt curious about the nature of David's relationship with Eliza Austin. Maggie had wondered about the possibility of a sexual history between them, then dismissed the notion as foolish. But why reject such a possibility when the only obstacle to their being lovers was Eliza's age? Maggie was certain that neither David nor Eliza would find such a consideration the least bit relevant. An intimate relationship might explain David's silence on the subject of their friendship. Maggie looked from one to the other. David was staring out at a pair of gulls swooping into the wake of the Dayline excursion boat that had overtaken them on its way upriver. Eliza peered through binoculars at a swampy area on the New Jersey side. It seemed clear to Maggie that there had been something, and just as clear that it was over, leaving them both with deep affection for each other.

Eliza handed her the binoculars. "Take a look at that egret. Damn thing's always standing in the same spot. At least I like to think it's the same fellow."

"Liza used to skydive, Maggie, just like that bird," David said drowsily. His eyes were half-closed. The sun had already put a flush on his cheeks and the ridge of his nose.

"Did you really? Is it wonderful?" Maggie asked.

"Yes. I've always liked floating." Eliza laughed. "Look at where I live. But I finally broke a bone in my foot and had to give it up." She gazed into the sky. "That's a fine place to get ideas."

"I'll bet I know some of the work that came out of those dives," Maggie said excitedly. "About ten years ago, the exhibit at Higgens Gallery. God, that was wonderful stuff. Kind of ethereal patchwork, disorienting, like looking through the wrong end of these." She handed the binoculars back to Eliza.

"Yes," the older woman nodded with a grin. "How marvelous that you remember."

The river, which had gradually broadened into its widest point at Haverstraw Bay, narrowed suddenly around a long bend to the left. Mountains a thousand feet high rose up on either side of them. As they passed beneath Bear Mountain, Maggie exclaimed at the sight of a huge bronze stag's head projecting from the bare rock.

"I wouldn't mind mounting my carvings on that chunk of boulder," David muttered.

"There're lots of nice rocks in Central Park, darling," Eliza said.

A few moments later they passed Buttermilk Falls, which cascaded down the mountainside into the river. Just to the north was West Point.

"We're in luck," Eliza said. "David, give me a hand. See that mooring over there? Next to the blue yawl." As she steered the craft alongside the large Ping-Pong ball, she explained to Maggie, "There're only a couple of guest moorings here. On a weekend, it's usually hopeless."

While they tied up, Maggie stared up at the brooding monumental pile of granite that was West Point military academy. The buildings were austere but handsome. She could see a jeep slowly climbing a steep road on the edge of the cliff.

"Are you sure it's all right to be here?" Maggie asked.

Eliza laughed. "Intimidating, isn't it? Actually, they're very friendly at the office over there on the pier. Come, you must be starving. Let's eat."

Eliza had loaded up on provisions at a delicatessen. Maggie was astonished at her appetite. She wolfed down an overstuffed corned-beef sandwich. Eliza watched with a smile, then wordlessly handed Maggie a second one, turkey this time, dripping with Russian dressing. Maggie made it halfway through, and lay back against the seat groaning.

"It's the water that does it," Eliza said. "I have to watch myself or I'll turn into a tugboat." She poured coffee into plastic mugs. "Cream and sugar?" she asked, and seemed pleased when Maggie shook her head. "David," Eliza went on, "would you be a dear and see if you can do something about that shower head? It worked fine for six months the last time you tinkered with it."

"Sure," David said. "I'd just as soon get out of the sun for a while anyhow. My nose is frying."

Maggie watched him disappear below, and when she looked up, saw that Eliza had been studying her quietly.

"Tell me," Eliza said. "Do you think it's possible to be a good mother and a great artist simultaneously?"

Maggie cupped her mug and thought about it. "I don't know," she replied finally. "It's a very complex subject. A good mother and a good artist, maybe. I don't think a great one."

"Is it the logistics, like having help so you can physically get to the studio?"

"In part, but that's not all of it, at least for me." She sighed and looked up into the deep blue autumn sky. "Children are like leeches—beautiful, amazing, delicious leeches. I remember the first time I went out to dinner after Susan was born. She was three months old and I had been completely absorbed in her. I was worn out from lack of sleep and constant self-denial, and I guess I thought if I hired a baby-sitter and left the apartment, everything would be the same as before she was born. I would feel free again. It took ten minutes at a candlelit table for the truth to sink in. I wasn't free anymore and never would be, even when Susan was grown up and gone. She had become a part of my consciousness in such a profound, mysterious way that I knew I would never be able to stop thinking about her on some level, worrying about her, wondering about her. And it's been the same with Fred, the second one. It's affected my work. I can't ever be ... single-minded again. They're always in my thoughts, and it takes very little for me to be distracted away from my work if they need me. But maybe it's not the same for other women."

Four Canadian geese paddled over to the boat, one of them honking tentatively. Eliza tossed a crust overboard and it was gobbled up.

"No, I think you're probably right," Eliza said. "Look at the history of art in this country. How many women made a success of their creativity? A handful—O'Keeffe, Nevelson come to mind first, since they're so well-known. O'Keeffe never had children and Nevelson went off to Europe and left her child behind. Even Carolyn Wyeth—I'm rather fond of her work—is basically a recluse with no dependents."

"O'Keeffe used to paint from first light until the sun went down," Maggie said. "I can't imagine ever having that kind of unstructured time. Every moment I'm at work, I'm aware that there's a limit. Somebody's waiting for me to do something for them outside that door. No matter if I'm on the edge of an important discovery or if the light is just right at that particular second. The kids come home from school or I'm required at some function. I know it has a deleterious effect. But I do think about later on, when there're off on their own. Maybe then . . ."

"Do you ever imagine running away?"

"Yes," Maggie admitted. Then she added, "But never as a permanent solution, just a week or even a couple of months to myself. They're so much a part of my life, you see."

"Perhaps for you it's worth the compromise," Eliza said.

"It is."

"I always thought I'd have made a dreadful mother," Eliza said.

"Is that why you didn't have any children?"

"Yes, partly. Howard was bent on building up the business. He had no interest in babies. I saw my friends with their families, how consuming it all was. It was frightening. I believed I would have been submerged, drowned altogether if I'd added mother-hood to the stew."

"I've had that feeling," Maggie said. She glanced toward the galley. "How did you meet David?"

"At Ben Ginsburg's. He runs an art-supply store and gets artists together to drink too much and sound off about art." She poured Maggie a second cup of coffee from her thermos. "Ah, David was such a sobersides. We disliked each other enor-mously. Pompous, self-righteous type, he was. And he thought I was naive, and probably senile to boot." She laughed. "We had some real set-tos in the first few weeks he joined the circle. I remember asking Ben what on earth he saw in this idiot, and Ben just said, 'Wait.' Then one day David stopped in at an exhibit of mine on Fifty-seventh Street. It was the first I'd had after leaving my husband, and there was a work called *Flight*. A very large canvas with open sky and wings. Well, I found him staring at it pale as a ghost, and the next Saturday night he brought along this carving to Ben's, and it was uncanny how it mirrored my painting. Wings, it was, really soaring so you could practically hear the wind rush. It was soon after he'd left New Orleans and I suppose the feelings that went into both works were very similar. That was the beginning. Not that we don't have some knock-down-drag-outs even now. I think he's a dreadful teacher."

"You do? Why?"

"Well, I'm overstating it. We're philosophically opposed. He can't tolerate mediocrity of any kind, and is forever discouraging people. My feeling is that art is for everybody, and the more people who experience it, no matter how limited their ability, the better. What's wrong with some fellow making mudpies to set on his mantelpiece? He's had the joy of creating something with his hands, and he'll have a better understanding of what the rest of us are trying to do."

Maggie had sat forward. "I watched him finish off the career of a little old lady just last week. It was heartbreaking."

"What are you going to do, Maggie?" Eliza asked suddenly.

Maggie stared down into her mug. The kindness in the older woman's voice had brought her close to tears. "I don't know," she said. "I don't know."

"You're a forever thing with David," Eliza said.

"I know that."

"And how about you?"

"He's a forever thing."

"Can you go on this way indefinitely?"

"It's getting very hard. I'm not good at deception." She gave Eliza a bitter smile. "Oh, I've become an expert at lying. It's living with it that's making me miserable."

"He'd be a very good father," Eliza said. "He's always wanted children."

Maggie shook her head. "It sounds so reasonable. But it's doing it that's difficult. I must be an awful coward."

"Or else you haven't made up your mind."

"Oh but, Eliza, I see other people wait twenty-five years in a terrible marriage until the children are grown, and I think, what a waste, what a criminal waste. And then I try to imagine myself sitting down with my kids to tell them about David, and it just seems absurd. This is not how I always thought I would live my life. And there's Matthew."

"What about him?"

"I don't know what I feel. I'm very angry, I guess. Whenever I try to figure him out, I mean in relation to me and the marriage, I get this feeling as if my head has turned to cement, just a solid block of it." She looked up at Eliza. "Pathetic, isn't it?"

"Can you imagine yourself living with David?"

"Yes. I do it all the time. I have trouble with the children, though . . . they don't seem to belong in this part of my life. But that's surely a matter of adjustment. For me, for them. Oh Lord." Maggie rubbed her head. "Here comes the cement."

"Do you feel strange here?" Eliza asked. "I mean here, on the boat, with me, with David."

"It's curious, today seems like a kind of . . . nailing things down, in a way. David and I have been pretty much isolated in our own world. Today, being here with you, has made it even more real. A confirmation. And talking about it with you. I haven't talked about it with anyone except David."

"I'm very fond of Dee," Eliza said. "I would hate to see him hurt."

"Somebody's going to be, and it'll be me who's doing the hurting. It's pretty ironic, after making a lifetime career out of being nice to everybody."

David's head appeared in the galley entrance, but Eliza managed a final remark. "Forget being nice. Be honest, and you'll do the right thing." She waved at David. "All fixed?"

"Yup."

"Good," Eliza said. "You gave us a chance to pick your character apart."

"Uh-oh," he said. His face was glowing with sunburn.

Maggie pulled him down beside her. "But we decided that you have a few redeeming qualities."

"Like what?"

"Tolerance," Maggie said.

Eliza hooted. "Come over here, Maggie. As soon as we get untied you can take over."

A train whistle blew in the distance. Its ghostly echo bounced back and forth between the mountainous banks. Eliza glanced at her watch. "Amtrak, more or less on time. All right, David? We're clear?"

"All set!" he called.

Eliza started the engine and they moved away from the mooring. "We'll wait until we get out into the bay, then you'll take the helm," she told Maggie.

The craft was very responsive. "Can we go faster?" Maggie asked.

"You can do forty-five miles an hour in this thing," David said. "But let's not."

"Chicken," Maggie said. With the wind rushing past her ears and the soft purple mountains curling away behind her, she had the momentary fantasy of steering them all up out of the water like a seaplane and off into the darkening sky beyond the evening star to freedom. At the Tappan Zee Bridge, Maggie relinquished the wheel to Eliza and lay down with her head in David's lap. He stroked her hair and argued with Eliza.

"Art is explosive communication," he said. "It demands attention from the public, as if to say: Look at this and understand it the way I understand it."

"I don't care if *nobody* sees my work," Eliza retorted. "It's communion, not comunication. I only show my paintings so I can make enough money to keep doing it."

"Bullshit," David said.

Maggie's eyelids began to droop. David's voice seemed to be a buzz emerging from the firm muscle of his thigh. The sky was like a soft deep-gray canvas with streaks of gold.

"Then what you're doing is for other people," Eliza protested. "You may just as well be in the advertising business. Right, Maggie? Oh heavens, let her sleep."

I could be very happy here, Maggie thought, and surrendered to the rocking motion of the boat and the drone of the engine.

When she awoke, the sky was black. There were jagged splits in the cloud cover that allowed glimpses of stars. Eliza, whose straw hat had disappeared, smiled at her.

"How long have I been asleep?" Maggie asked.

"An hour maybe," David answered.

"Oh no. Where are we?"

"Take a look," Eliza said.

Maggie sat up stiffly. Behind them, shimmering lights blurred, then came into focus. The twin towers of the World Trade Center rose like splendid glittering columns out of the water. She turned toward the bow and caught her breath. To starboard, the Statue of Liberty stood draped in scaffolding. The intricate webbing of cables had been lit so that each strand was like a fine golden chain. Barely visible beneath the luminous veil was the shadow of the lady herself, imposing, dark, secret.

"Oh, look at her," Maggie whispered. They were all silent as Eliza moved closer, then made a long arc and headed up the East River.

Bulky shadows passed back and forth as they motored up past Governors Island, where headlights could be seen blinking through the black silhouettes of trees. "What are all those huge ships?" Maggie asked.

"Tankers. Cargo ships. This is the busiest harbor in the world, next to Rotterdam," Eliza explained.

"I had no idea," Maggie said.

"It's easy to forget that we live in a seaport," David remarked.

"Extraordinary." Maggie gazed at the Manhattan skyline. "It looks so fragile, as if it's all afloat, and could sink at any moment."

"Liza," David said. "It's almost nine. Maggie has to be back at ten."

Maggie looked at him, startled. It was impossible to imagine stepping back onto dry land and leaving this magic world of reflections and darkness. "I didn't want to hear it from you," David said softly, putting his face next to her cheek.

It took very little time, with the engine near full throttle, to deliver them back to Seventy-ninth Street. The marina glistened against West Side Manhattan like a handful of diamonds tossed carelessly against the shore. When Maggie stepped off the boat onto the dock, she felt her knees give way. The solid planks seemed cruelly unyielding beneath her feet after the gentle roll of the river. She held her hand out to Eliza. "I don't know how to thank you."

"Come again, that's how," Eliza answered. She waved and disappeared below.

David walked Maggie to the bus stop. Neither of them spoke. He kissed her once, lightly, and she stepped up into the phosphorescent glare of the crosstown bus.

18

"Forget the cards," Phyllis said. "Put them away, Robin."

Robin looked at the others.

Maggie nodded. "Phyl's right," she said. "Nobody can concentrate."

"Something tells me our bridge days are numbered," Hilary remarked.

"What's the rent for this place anyway?" Phyllis asked. Maggie noticed that she had refused a glass of wine and was drinking Perrier like Hilary.

"Five-seventy-five."

"You know you could always move in with us," Phyllis said. "We have the sofa bed in the living room."

"Thanks, you're sweet, but I need a place of my own."

The apartment was in a new high-rise that catered to young singles. Rock music pounded through the Sheetrock wall, and from the floor above, someone seemed to be dropping paper clips in a relentless rhythm. After three months, the apartment was still bare, almost ascetic compared to the friendly clutter of Robin's home with Jackson. There was the card table where they sat, which also served as a dining table and a desk. There was a couch which opened into a bed, a small portable television, and one jade plant. There was not a single hooked rug in evidence.

"I saw a bevy of stewardesses in the lobby," Phyllis said. "And somebody's having a Halloween party. The elevator had a belly dancer, a witch, and a gorilla in it. God, they're all so young." She gave Robin one of her penetrating inspections.

Robin had lost weight and given up her contact lenses. The combination of visible cheekbones and large tortoiseshell glasses lent her a sober appearance that was in marked contrast to her former little-girl softness. She had gradually removed most of her wardrobe from the old apartment and sold it to secondhand clothing stores. With the profits, she bought herself several pairs of pants and some tailored dresses. Tonight she wore plain black wool pants and a cowl-necked sweater.

Phyllis nodded approvingly. "You look fine," she said. "I've got to confess, you shocked the hell out of me."

"Leaving my husband? People do it all the time."

"Not you. Christ, I've been bitching and moaning about my marriage for fifteen years, and I'd never have the guts to do what you did."

"How's Jackson?" Maggie asked.

"He calls a lot. He wants to date."

"Will you?" Hilary asked.

"I've seen him a few times," Robin said. "But I'm not sure it's a good idea."

"It must be so strange, living by yourself after all these years," Maggie said.

"It's lonely and it's very nice. Well, Hil, you know."

Hilary smiled. "It's different if you've never been married."

"Do you know I tried practicing my shorthand today and I couldn't remember any of it?" Robin said.

"You're not going to get a *job*?" Phyllis sounded so appalled that they all laughed.

"Sure. How else am I going to pay for this place? I blew all my savings when I moved in."

"I thought Jackson was paying the rent," Hilary said.

"He wanted to, but I won't let him."

"You've lost a few bolts there, dear," Phyllis remarked.

Robin smoothed her hair but it popped right back into its springy curls. "This is *my* place. It's the first time I've ever had anything of my own, and I don't want to owe anybody, especially not Jackson."

"Let me see what I can scare up," Hilary said. "But you know, secretaries use computers now. Think you could handle that?"

"I'll learn."

"Christ," Phyllis said. "We used to wear white gloves to work every day. Imagine that."

"Yes, and getting a swat on the behind from the boss was a token of his appreciation," Hilary added.

"I don't know if there's any way I could explain how it was to my liberated daughter," Maggie said.

"She should never know," Phyllis remarked.

As the others reminisced about *Woman's Companion*, Maggie thought about David. Tonight they would be together all night long. Matthew had left on a rare three-day trip out of town, and the children were on a school outing at Sturbridge Village in Massachusetts. It was wonderful to think of falling asleep in David's arms and waking to find him beside her. She was almost sorry that it was nearly time to leave Robin's. Soon there would be no more minutes left for this delicious anticipation.

"Hil's coming home with me tonight," Phyllis was saying. "You want us to drop you?"

"No, I think I'll walk, thanks. Matt's out of town so there's no need to hurry home."

Phyllis's eyes narrowed briefly. Downstairs when Hilary stepped into the street to hail a cab, Phyllis said, "Did you put my number down as a backup for the Sturbridge trip?"

Maggie nodded.

"Good," Phyllis said. "Just in case there's an emergency, God forbid, and there's something wrong with your phone."

Maggie thought: Someday, I'll tell you how much I love you. As soon as their cab was out of sight, she flagged another one and headed for the West Side.

David was standing in the doorway in a pair of jeans and a T-shirt as Maggie ran gasping up the last flight of stairs.

"You couldn't possibly have found an apartment on the first floor," she laughed, falling into his arms.

"Just a little closer to heaven," David said.

"I'll say. No, don't kiss me yet. I'm all sweaty."

David ran his tongue lightly along her cheek. "Mm, delicious. Like sashimi."

"You don't really eat that stuff, do you? Raw fish?"

"Such a sheltered life you lead, my love." He drew her to the round table, sat down, and pulled her onto his lap.

"Not sheltered anymore. David, we have all night together."

"I know."

She wove his long dark hair through her fingers. "It's nice to be home."

"Yes." He unbuttoned the bodice of her dress and made her naked to the waist. She could feel him growing hard under her thighs.

"Take off your clothes," she said.

He lifted her in his arms, carried her to the bed, and set her down.

"How did you do that? I weigh almost as much as you do."

"You're a whole lot lighter than a quarter of a ton of Belgian marble."

"Look at you." Maggie stared at his penis, erect and slightly curved. "How did you ever get that way?"

"Practice."

Maggie laughed.

"Care to straighten me out?"

She held out her arms. "If it takes me all night."

As their lovemaking became more intense, the lighthearted mood shifted. Maggie watched David above her as their bodies did their slow dance. His face reflected the same mingled pain and joy that she felt, and as her eyes filled with tears, his did too. Afterward she cried against his shoulder while he stroked her hair.

"David, what are we going to do?"

He lifted himself away and lay down on his side so that he could look at her. "Do you really want to talk about it?"

She shook her head and held his hand hard against her cheek. Then they slept. When David woke up, Maggie was standing over him. He sat up in a panic. "What time is it?" he asked.

"It's all right. We only slept for a few minutes. Are you hungry? There's not much in the refrigerator."

"I could eat." He rubbed his eyes with the back of his fists like a child. His hair looked soft against the hard lean muscles of his shoulders. "All right, I know what," he said. "I'm taking you out."

"Out? We can't go out."

"It'll be all right."

Maggie considered. No one she knew could possibly be dining at one A.M. in this neighborhood. And then, she could not deny, there was an appealing element of danger, even of defiance.

_____

David picked up her rumpled clothes and handed them to her. She hesitated a moment, and then got dressed.

Columbus Avenue was lively, but not with the trendy elegance of the Upper East Side. Here were crowds of young people with punk hairdos and outrageous clothing, long-haired women in faded jeans walking arm in arm, and bearded men with wire-rimmed glasses talking earnestly over espresso in the windows of cafés.

"Doesn't anybody ever go to bed?" Maggie asked.

"Eventually."

The October sky was a clean navy blue. Maggie held David's arm. A black man passed in dancer's leg warmers. He let his eyes linger on Maggie and gave her a smile. She knew her body told the street that she adored this man, and that she had just made love to him.

David steered her into a tiny Japanese restaurant with half a dozen tables and a counter. The place was nearly full, but they found a table at the back.

"All right. It's time you discovered sushi."

"Oh dear," Maggie said nervously. "I was kind of thinking about a cheeseburger."

"Don't be crude. Trust me."

"I do," Maggie said. "God, I'm so in love it's sickening."

David ordered several unintelligible items and two Japanese beers.

"What are we getting?"

"Don't ask. Just eat."

Soon a lacquered tray appeared with what looked like a garden laid out on it.

"We can't disturb this," Maggie said, poking carefully at a shiny pink rectangle fastened to a ball of rice with a seaweed belt.

David lifted a piece of raw tuna in his fingers, dipped it in soy sauce, and popped it into Maggie's mouth before she could protest. She chewed bravely. The pleasant texture surprised her, and also the delicacy of the flavor. She had expected a heavy fishy taste.

"So?" David asked.

"Good. What's that?" She picked up something white and slightly translucent.

"Giant clam. It takes perseverance to get your teeth through it, but it's worth the effort."

"Life with you is an adventure," Maggie said. She worked at the tough clam while David kept his eyes on her. "Eat something," she urged with her mouth full.

"I am, in my way. . . ." His feet grasped her ankles under the table. "Tell me about your work. Did you have time this week?"

She nodded. "I couldn't fall asleep Sunday night. I guess I was all jagged up from . . ." She nearly mentioned yet another disagreeable conversation with Matthew about Robin and Jackson, but she could not bear to bring Matthew into the restaurant with them. "I was just lying there thinking about that damn black surface of the cityscape piece and how I couldn't make the shapes come alive. I wanted it thick, you know, and round in this particular spot, but not static. There just didn't seem to be a way, and then I suddenly remembered Fred's hole punch. Revelation. I bounded out of bed and sat punching holes like a madwoman until six A.M. It works, David. I paint each little circle, then pile them up one on top of the other, but not rigid. They bend and twist. It's quite wonderful."

"I want to see it."

"You will. Aren't you going to ask me why I paint all the pieces when it's only the one on top that's visible?"

"I know why."

Maggie picked up his hand, kissed it, and returned to her sushi. "Matt thought I was crazy, sitting there at Fred's desk making little piles of circles." She stopped suddenly. David's face had flinched at the mention of her husband's name.

"I'm sorry," Maggie said. "I forget sometimes. . . ."

"You live with him. He's part of your life. But it's worse when you call him 'Matt.'" He smiled ruefully and shook his head. "I'm a very possessive man."

"I know that."

"How do you know that?"

"Because you can't part with your carvings."

David drained his beer. "Your kids will be home on Friday."

"Don't be jealous of them."

"I'm not jealous. I want them in my life. They're part of you. They came from your body."

"It would be easier if they hated their father."

David shook his head. "No, it wouldn't. You can't bear to think of depriving them of anything, much less that."

"David, I want to be with you all the time, not just a few hours in the middle of the day. It shouldn't be a novelty waking up in the morning with you beside me."

"Then . . ." he began, and hesitated. "I'm afraid to pressure you. I'm afraid you'll bolt on me."

"Other people find ways when these things happen. Why am I paralyzed?"

"Because you don't want to hurt anybody." He sighed.

"He's a decent man, David."

"If you tell me that one more time, I'll have you shot."

A young woman in an elaborate kimono stood quietly beside their table. "Everything okay?" she asked.

"Everything is fine," David said. She bowed and disappeared with sandals slapping against tiny feet.

"I wish we lived in Japan," Maggie said. The ambience of the place, with its perfectly ordered decor, its carefully presented food, its beautiful polite waitress, seemed so controlled and passionless. Perhaps in Japan, love affairs were never chaotic.

David read her thoughts. "Ever take a good hard look at Japanese art?" he asked.

Maggie smiled, remembering the blood and the lust. "Yes. I guess there's no escape." They were both silent, lost in yearnings. "You know what," Maggie said finally. "I want to do a whole wall. A huge white space about eighteen by ten."

"With your hole punch?"

"Yes, and other things. It's been struggling in my head. I'm going to need too much space, though."

"Put it on my wall."

"Are you serious?" But she saw that he was. She contemplated the open white rectangle that was washed with intense river light. "It's about perfect."

"I figure it ought to take you at least thirty-five years."

"God willing." She got up. "Let's get an ice cream cone and walk back home."

She told Matthew that she was working on a project requiring space and that a fellow student from last summer's class had offered his studio for a few hours a day. Matthew asked no questions. In fact, he appeared not to have heard her.

"Did you hear what I said?" Maggie asked. Listen to me when I'm lying to you, she thought.

Matthew looked up from the *Times*. "You'll be working in someone's studio, person from class. I heard you."

Anyway, it wasn't even a lie, Maggie told herself.

Before long, David began to see her every afternoon. At first, he would stay home and wait for her. She would smile at him, hold his hand, even make love with him, but he felt all the while how she was drawn to that great white wall on the other side of the room. Soon he gave her a key and began leaving the apartment before she was due. Then when he came back to her much later, he was always rewarded with her exhausted, grateful smile.

She began by transporting the accumulation of many years' work across the park in her black leather portfolio. She kept the papers in a pile on the floor beside the wall and each evening when she had gone, David examined piece after piece, reading her past as if he were poring over a photograph album. There were early experiments with fabric designs, undisciplined but fabulously colored. There was a series in various color washes that from a distance seemed merely attractive nubbly-surfaced abstractions. Close up, however, row upon row of tiny faces, each different, peered out. There was another group portraying the surfaces of tree bark: oak, birch, pine, maple. There were several renditions of baby's hands and feet that David found particularly poignant.

Sometimes when David was sketching to prepare for a new carving, he stayed and sat at the round table, looking up every now and then to watch Maggie. At first, she did nothing but sit on the floor and cut up her work with a pair of scissors. She would make a selection from the pile, then study it carefully for what seemed a long time. When she began cutting, she often worked against the flow of the design to create movement and tension. This process went on for many days. Then one afternoon she arrived at the apartment in a state of agitation.

"What's the matter?" he asked. "Is it that I'm here? I was going to sketch today, but I can do it at the studio."

"No. I'm ready to begin on the wall today. I'm terrified."

Like the first strike into the stone, it was a commitment. Even if you changed your mind later, the initial impulse reverberated with a kind of tyranny.

"Do you want me to leave?"

"No."

He saw that it did not matter. She smiled apologetically.

"I won't let myself be jealous of your work," he said.

She kissed him, shrugged off her coat, and spilled the wild array of shapes and colors onto his floor. David fixed himself a cup of tea, and sat with the sketchpad untouched.

For nearly twenty minutes Maggie stared at the wall, sighed, sat on the windowsill and stared some more, then went to ponder the cutouts. Finally, with the acuity of an osprey after a fish, her hand dived into the multicolored patchwork and picked up a piece. It was crescent-shaped, fashioned from a fabric design of bold green and burgundy. She strode to the wall and taped the fragment to the upper-left area of the space. Then she returned to the center of the room and stared some more.

Pretty soon she swooped after another piece, this time a square of intricately woven strips from the tree series. She placed it to the lower right of the first, then retraced her steps to stare again. This process went on all afternoon. David barely sketched at all, so enthralled was he with watching her redesign the fragments of her history.

There was a kind of radiant intensity in her face that might have been frightening had he himself not experienced the emotions that produced it. As she paced back and forth, he watched the long bones of her legs swing as she walked, the flat pelvis pivot with each turn, and he appreciated their movement as he supposed only a man who loved stone could. But Maggie was living stone, warm-blooded and graceful, and her presence in his home produced a peculiar convergence of excitement and peace. Everything in his life seemed suddenly to make sense. There was coherence where there had once been restless discontent.

Maggie flung herself down at the table. "Whoa, maybe I'm too old for this. Got some tea for me?"

He poured her a cup. It was lukewarm but she gulped it thankfully. Both of them gazed at the wall for a moment.

"Why that particular spot?" David asked. "Where you began."

"I don't know, really. I always seem to work out of the upper left-hand corner. It's where my focus is."

"Ever try starting somewhere else?"

"Oh, sure, but I always wind up feeling lost. There's never any balance." She took his sketchpad and saw that he had made only a single preliminary drawing. "Oh, David. I'm not good for you."

"You are good for me. You're the best thing to fall into my life since my first hunk of alabaster. In fact, I think I could give up my work before I could live without you."

"I don't want that kind of power."

"I can't help you there."

"Besides," she continued, "I don't believe it. As long as you're still breathing, you'll be carving stone."

He considered this. "Tell you what, let's not test it, okay?"

After she left, he turned on all the lights and scrutinized what she had done. The wild collection of colors and the juxtaposition of fantastic shapes seemed to leap off the wall and dance in the air.

"I know I shouldn't call you," he said into the telephone, "but I've been looking at your wall. It's thrilling, Maggie. You're doing something extraordinary here."

"Thank you." She sounded pleased, with none of the usual strangled remoteness of other phone calls.

"I'll see you tomorrow. I love you."

His eyes kept returning to the wall. It was as if she was living there with him at last, singing, crying, and speaking in many voices from the other side of the room.

19

Maggie's fingers trembled as she picked up the telephone to dial her doctor. With one hand she gripped the receiver. The other she held unconsciously to her right breast.

"This is Margaret Hollander. I'm calling for my autopsy report. I mean, oh, sorry, my *biopsy* report."

"Just a moment, please."

While she waited with the dead air against her ear, the knot in her throat threatened to gag her. It felt a bit like the forbidden lump of laughter that used to choke her as a child at somber occasions like funerals.

"Mrs. Hollander, this is Dr. Berg. It was negative. You're fine. It's just a cyst."

"Oh God, thanks," Maggie said. "What do I do now?"

"Go on with your life. I'll see you in six months."

Maggie sat on the edge of the bed and tried to analyze her reaction to the news. *Go on with your life*, the man said, as if that was such a simple matter. Checking into a hospital seemed like a respite. Major surgery would have kept her isolated for a few weeks anyway, and after that, if it turned out that they had not managed to remove every malignant particle, perhaps she would soon achieve a permanent reprieve. No guilt. No decisions. Her heart began to thump. Death. The word flew about the room like a huge black bird, beating its wings against the walls, the windows, her face.

The phone jangled. "Hello," she said, certain it would be David.

"Hi, Mags. Did you get your results yet?" It was Matthew.

"Yes. I'm fine. It was okay." She could not remember telling him she would find out this morning. There was silence on the other end.

"That's great," he said finally. She heard the catch in his voice. "In a meeting. See you at dinner."

As soon as he hung up, Maggie began to cry. What was Matthew doing showing concern for her health? And what was *she* doing reacting with tears? She tried to imagine herself telling him about David. What was the kindest way to say it? *Matt, I'm leaving you and taking the kids.* Does one do such things over dinner? Or first thing in the morning, perhaps, when everybody is presumably stronger.

This situation is giving me lumps in my breasts, Maggie thought. I'm giving myself cancer. She got off the bed, washed her face, threw on a heavy jacket, and went out. She walked aimlessly along Seventy-ninth Street until she found herself in front of the Metropolitan Museum. It was cold and damp, but not raining yet, so she sat down on one of the benches. I will watch these other people, Maggie thought. I will observe them and I will learn.

A large yellow school bus stopped at the curb. The doors opened and released a tumbling chattering collection of Oriental children dressed in black uniforms. They chased across the plaza, settling on the empty benches like a flock of starlings on a telephone wire. Soon they were herded together by their chaperons and swept up the vast stone stairs into the museum. Two young women with strollers passed, eyed Maggie, and then sat down on a bench nearby. Out came the Smurf and Strawberry Shortcake thermoses and the plastic Baggies full of raisins and whole-wheat cookies. The toddlers, freed from their strollers, began to grab at each other's snacks.

"Jason! We want to share. Melanie always shares with you. Give her a cookie."

"That's all right," Melanie's mother responded.

As Jason continued to hoard his cookies, his mother's voice began to lose its guise of reasonableness. "Please share your cookie, Jason," she wheedled. "I'll be your best *freh*-hend." She wrenched a cookie from Jason's tiny fingers and handed it to Melanie. Jason promptly flung himself to the ground and began to wail. His mother stood over him helplessly. "Jason, this is not appropriate behavior. You know I love you, darling, but I do not love your behavior." Jason began to kick and flail. His mother looked at her friend. "He didn't have a nap yesterday. He's overtired." She picked up the howling child, ducking the swinging feet. "It's all right, Mommy loves you," she crooned. "Come, I'll take you to McDonald's and buy you a nice burger and fries."

Maggie glared at the woman and tried to transmit her thoughts through the air. I hate you, Maggie said in her head. You are so stupid, so criminally stupid. Your child will grow up sick and twisted and destructive because you are such a fool. You'll probably have three more babies and turn them all into monsters and the world will have to cope with them. I hate you.

Jason's mother turned to intercept Maggie's furious gaze. The young woman's face was full of bewildered love.

When Maggie and Matthew first moved uptown, they used to see a woman who haunted these benches and the street near the museum. It was difficult to guess her age. She was tall, slim, wore her hair in a neat pile on her head. Her face was weathered, but attractive. She was always just barely smiling, either sitting with her hands crossed in her lap or striding up Madison Avenue—in the street, never on the sidewalk. People always looked at her. But it soon became apparent that there was something off kilter. Either her otherwise impeccable attire was marred by stockings that hung in sagging wrinkles around her legs or it was mid-July and she was wearing a heavy wool scarf twisted around her neck as if it were January.

Maggie constructed endless romantic tragedies around the woman. She was an heiress driven to insanity by a lover who had betrayed her. She was a brilliant artist who had forsaken her children to paint, only to lose her great gift. Maggie searched the benches, but there was no sign of the strange elegant presence. She glanced down at her own ankles. Her stockings clung smoothly. Her jacket was buttoned tightly to her chin like everyone else's. I am an ordinary woman, Maggie told herself. What did ordinary women do in a situation like hers? There must be thousands of them, suspended between husband and lover. Perhaps there were some who could live like this interminably. If she had been raised in a cave by wolves, for instance, instead of in a suburban Connecticut colonial by Colin and Norma Herrick. Maggie imagined herself standing in a pit while two cement walls slowly, inexorably closed in upon her, creaking and scraping. It might have been a scene from an old James Bond movie. But Maggie was not a James Bond heroine, and there was no hero to rush in at the last moment and release her from her own dilemma. "What I'd better do is go home and cook dinner," Maggie said aloud. Peripherally, she saw Jason's mother turn her face away quickly, the way one does to avoid eye contact with a crazy person.

And when I cross the street, Maggie thought, careful now to keep the words unspoken within her head, perhaps I shall be run over by the Number Four bus and be crushed into oblivion.

Matthew was jaunty at the table but he did not mention Maggie's test. In fact, he barely looked at her, as if the intensity of his telephone call needed to be diluted.

"So, Frederick, your sister says you have a girlfriend," he remarked.

"She's full of it," Fred answered. His voice had begun to crack since the summer, so that the last few words emerged half an octave lower than the rest.

"I don't know why you're so defensive," Susan complained. "She's only the richest girl in school, even if she does have bow legs."

"Listen," Fred said menacingly, "I don't go mouthing off about your precious David, do I?"

Maggie's heart shut down completely for several seconds.

"Jeez, you must really have it bad," Susan said.

"The trick is to be cool," Matthew advised Fred. "You always rise to the bait, which is why your sister can't resist giving you the business."

"Don't take away all my fun, Daddy," Susan said. Her braces had been removed in late October and she had developed a dazzling smile.

"Who's David?" Matthew asked.

"If you mean David Zimmerman," Susan said to Fred, "we are strictly platonic."

"To your disgust," Fred said.

"Mother, don't you think Fred got surly over the summer?"

Maggie smiled at her son. His complexion had developed red spots, and fine dark hairs shadowed his upper lip. He was much thinner.

"It's just adolescence," Maggie said. "You ought to know all about it."

"Yeah, it sucks," Susan said.

"Watch it," Matthew warned.

"Anyway, Mom's not so normal either," Fred observed. "She's been in never-never-land since we got home. Right, Sue?"

Susan chewed her dinner roll and nodded. "We decided it was early menopause. Have you been getting hot flashes, Mom?"

"What *are* you talking about?" Maggie asked.

"You've gotten much too skinny, and you don't hear people when they talk," Sue said. "I told you three times about my play tryouts, and this morning you asked me when I was having my play tryouts. I mean, really."

"Last week Sue got my laundry in her drawers and I got all her stuff. Even a bra," Fred protested. "Size twenty-eight triple-A."

"Shut up, Fred," Susan said.

"I don't know what to say," Maggie replied.

"It was probably the breast lump," Matthew suggested. "You were probably more worried than you thought."

"What breast lump?" Susan asked.

"It's all right," Maggie said. "I got the biopsy report." She had to concentrate not to say "autopsy." "I'm fine. It was nothing."

"It's all that coffee," Susan said.

Maggie let her lecture, glad to be off the hook. At the first opportunity, she escaped into the kitchen to dole out ice cream. Five minutes later she was still standing with the scoop in her hand, staring at the three pint containers and the four empty bowls. Fred wanted chocolate chip and cherry vanilla. Susan was for pralines only. Or was it cherry? Matt liked all three kinds. No, that was wrong. The scoop fell out of her fingers and she began to cry. Suddenly Susan was beside her.

"What's wrong, Mom?" she asked.

"I can't keep it straight," Maggie choked. "I don't know. I'm so tired. I just can't keep it straight."

"I'll do it," Susan said, pretending not to see her mother's tears.

"Thanks, darling." Maggie excused herself and left Susan with the ice cream.

In the bedroom later, Matthew ruffled Maggie's hair and told her to use the bathroom first. "I think I'm going to take a shower, so you go ahead," he said. Maggie went into the bathroom with her nightgown and robe over her arm. She was washing her face when she heard the bathroom door squeak. With rising panic she realized that Matthew had come in, but she was helpless, bent over the sink with soap all over her face. She heard him chuckle as he gave her a quick pinch on the rear end. Instantly she swung around and with all her weight behind her, drove her elbow into his midriff. She heard the air exploding from his diaphragm with a cartoon "Ooof!" Eyes smarting from soap and naked body vibrating with outrage, she said, "Don't ever do that again. Now get out."

Matthew backed out of the room holding his stomach. His face was full of surprise, pain, and something very close to laughter. Maggie looked at herself in the mirror. The soap had dried in white splotches on her cheeks and her eyes were bloodshot. She looked ludicrous and formidable all at once, but she had defended herself, and it had been so easy. She wondered why on earth it had taken her nearly eighteen years to do it.

She woke up about four A.M. as usual, with the dreaded sense of disorientation that had plagued her over the past few weeks. She would snap out of her sleep as if a gun had been discharged beside her ear, and lie blinking in the dark with her heart pounding. Something was wrong, she knew. Someone had died, or there had been some other awful tragedy. Then she would remember that it was David. Not that he was dead, but that he was not beside her. Before long, she would slip out of bed and begin the prowl that had become a ritual. She checked and rechecked the children, listening to their night sounds and recalling the murmurs and sweet sighs of their babyhood. Sometimes she stared down at Matthew and tried to unlock the swollen cache of emotion now buried so deep inside her that it was no longer within reach. She was existing in two separate dimensions of time and space. During the day, it seemed almost possible to preserve the tenuous balance. But night had become a menacing expanse of hostile territory that she had somehow to cross. She woke earlier and earlier, dazed and miserable, like a prisoner in a time machine, forever repeating a futile journey between two centuries.

She sat at the kitchen table with her head in her hands. Then she got up and searched the drawers for a pencil and some paper. She found a red marking pen, but no paper, so she ripped off a paper towel, sat down again, and began making her list. It always started out the same way, with two columns, one headed D and one M. Under D she wrote Love, Peace, Fulfillment, Sex, Art. Tonight she added Self and underlined the word. Under M she wrote Years, Shared Experience. Then she crossed out Shared Experience since it fell under the same category as Years. She went on with Stability, Familiarity, Comforts, then Children underlined. One night, by way of experiment, she had tried to shift Children to the D column, but it hadn't worked. The letters seemed to march on their own back to M. With a groan, she wadded the paper into a ball, buried it in the garbage pail, and went into the living room. She stared out at the building across the street. There were only three windows lit out of many dozens of black squares. People ill, perhaps, or restless. Ordinary members of ordinary families, just like Maggie's. She felt the anguish rise up into her mouth like vomit and flung herself to her knees against the couch. She buried her face in the cushions and cried out: What am I going to do? Oh God, what am I going to do?

20

For the sixth time, Matthew slammed the squash ball into the telltale for a foul, losing the point. "Goddammit," he muttered, and swiped at his sweaty forehead with the back of his wrist. Jack Foreman gave him an odd look. In the ten years the two men had played together, Jack had never witnessed a display of temper by Matthew Hollander. Ordinarily, in fact, he rarely spoke on the court except to check the score or clarify a point.

Matthew toweled himself off by the water fountain and took a long drink. He had never enjoyed losing, but usually he could put defeat behind him with a shrug and look forward to beating the pants off Jack the next time. Tonight he felt like breaking his racket in half or smashing it over Jack's head. Jack, perhaps sensing Matthew's hostility, had already set off for the locker room.

"Goddammit," Matthew said again.

He stood in the shower for a long time and let the hot water pelt down on his face and shoulders. Perhaps the driving water would wash away the constriction in his head. He wondered how long he had been carrying it around, this not-quite headache. Many weeks, certainly. He thought he could even recall feeling it when they went to visit the children at camp. He had taken a couple of aspirin after the drive home. They hadn't helped, so he had never bothered with pills again. It was not pain exactly. There was just this constant pressure, as if his brains were expanding inside his skull. There was heat, too, which made him think of the textbook illustrations of volcanoes in his high-school geology course—seething magma trapped in an underground chamber preparing to blast through layers of rock, and up into the open sky.

Things had been out of whack in the office lately also. He had misplaced an important document. He kept calling his secretary "Marian," which was the name of his previous secretary, gone a year ago to have her baby. He lost his temper with a junior associate over the use of the semicolon and had barely restrained himself from hurling *The Elements of Style* at the poor kid as he fled the office. Matthew was not accustomed to ransacking his life in search of the discordant note. Either something was wrong or it wasn't, and there was not a single thing he could point his finger at and say: *That's it*. The children's summer had been wonderful. Fred slimmed down and gained confidence. Susan lost the belligerent attitude that had grated on him all last year. And Maggie was flourishing. She had embarked on this new, rather curious artistic adventure which he found difficult to understand but which engaged her to an extent he had not seen in years. He missed the paintings, those marvelous assemblages of color and line that so impressed him back in college, but if she was content with her output, that was what counted. She was a little run-down at the moment, but basically she was looking great—vibrant, healthy, sexy. Men had begun to notice her on the street. Maggie was totally unaware of it, of course. She was so damn oblivious of her own sensuality. But Matthew was amused by the surreptitious glances as he walked down Madison Avenue with her on a Saturday afternoon.

His head pounded mercilessly so he turned the dial to cold, hoping that would help. Still . . . still . . . perhaps something was maybe slightly amiss there, or if not quite amiss, then unfamiliar. She had slugged him not long ago. Even more shocking than the blow to the solar plexus had been the sight of her face, all twisted with what amounted to hatred. He turned off the water. They had never discussed it. Probably it was time to let up on the pinching and poking and ass-slapping. She was a grown woman, after all, no college kid. Maybe she was already beginning to experience some hormonal changes. Not that she hadn't been perfectly pleasant and cordial since that night, only it seemed almost as if part of her had disappeared, gone on sabbatical. Christ, his head hurt. Maybe he ought to try aspirin again.

"You okay, Hollander?" Jack asked him. He was blowing his hair dry at the mirror. Since his divorce a few years back, the hair-drying ritual consumed half an hour. He had explained to Matthew that erotic women relate to a well-groomed head of hair.

"Headache," Matthew said. He never bothered with the dryer, just toweled his hair fiercely and then combed it with his fingers.

Jack snapped off the machine and studied Matthew. "I don't know why I still bother to ask, but why not join me for a drink tonight? It won't kill you, and you might even enjoy yourself."

It had become a joke between them that Matthew always declined Jack's invitations. But for the first time, Matthew hesitated.

"Come on," Jack urged. "Let's cure that headache."

The children were out late. Maggie had phoned about an art

function she wanted to attend and given him instructions about heating his dinner. Matthew had half-planned on returning to the office to put in a few extra hours, but suddenly the idea of companionship appealed to him.

"Okay, what the hell."

"Attaboy!" Jack exclaimed. "We're gonna make it a veritable pub crawl straight up Columbus Ave."

Jack's enthusiasm was daunting, but Matthew admitted to a twinge of excitement. It seemed pleasantly racy to be out on the town with this self-proclaimed womanizer.

"First rule," Jack said in the cab. "No shop talk. Anybody mentions the legal profession has to buy dinner." When his marriage had disintegrated, Jack moved into a studio apartment on the West Side near Lincoln Center. He had since become the type of zealot who considered everything east of Fifth Avenue to be hopelessly dreary. "None of your tawdry Third Avenue bar scenes tonight, my friend," he said, and began to chatter about his favorite obsession, next to women. "Later you can come up to my place. I've just finished another model, Stutz Bearcat this time. Best one I've done. Real leather upholstery, brass fixtures, I'm nuts about it. I told you I finally bought my first antique car, didn't I, but it's out on the island. I can't insure it in the city."

"Yes, you mentioned it." Matthew was beginning to regret his impulsiveness. Maybe it had been a mistake to allow his circumscribed relationship with Jack to seep out beyond the thick walls of the racket club. Where would it end, this invitation to intimacy? Matthew imagined himself being dragged to antique-car conventions in Bridgehampton. His head began to pound again.

"I visit the damn thing almost every weekend," Jack said. "Good thing Virginia and I never had kids."

Matthew regarded Jack with pity. Where was the humanity in this well-coiffed fellow's life, the warm rough-and-tumble of a complex lively family? Matthew was struck with his own good fortune. If not for Maggie, he could certainly have wound up just like Jack, devoting his days to wherefores and hereinafters and nights to jigsaw puzzles or computer games. Matthew knew that there was much in his own character that reached for objects and ideas rather than people.

"I'm buying tonight," Matthew said.

"No way." Jack took out his wallet to pay for the cab.

"How're things going on that co-op conversion on Eighty-fourth Street?" Matthew asked.

"Okay, I get the point," Jack said. "But the drinks are on me."

"Deal."

The cab let them off on Columbus Avenue in front of a place called Thimbles. It was dark inside, with a long oak bar and tables in the rear. Jack was right. The people here bore little resemblance to the natty Upper East Side crowd that gathered at Uzie's or McMullen's. In fact, Matthew and Jack were the only patrons wearing suits. A young woman with a clipboard stopped beside Matthew. "Dinner?"

"Christ, look at this," Jack complained. "Rose, why is it I can never find you when I come in here alone, and now I've got this guy with me you're on us like flies on a cowpie?"

"You're so poetic, Jack," Rose observed.

"A drink first, then dinner," Matthew said.

"I'll put you on the list." She smiled up at Matthew. "Name?"

"Foreman," Jack answered.

"You make yourself at home and I'll slip you in whenever you're ready," Rose said to Matthew.

As she squeezed through the crush toward the tables at the rear, Jack muttered, "Bet she would, too. Hollander, you just may be a liability to a horny single man. I've been trying to score with that piece of ass for two years now."

They made their way to the bar and ordered a couple of beers.

"She's a class act, that one, a violinist when she's not at this place. I keep telling her it's not just for a quick stab in the dark. She's marriage material."

"You want to get married again?" Matthew asked.

"Sure I do. Who wants to be stuck in an empty apartment with a pile of plastic model pieces and a tube of airplane glue? I was the one who screwed up the first time. I drove Virginia crazy."

Matthew lifted his glass in salute. "This was a good idea. Thanks for pushing it." It was agreeable standing here with Jack surrounded by lively intelligent-looking people. While Jack began a comical litany of his faults as a marriage partner, Matthew studied the mob. An earnest-looking group of middle-aged people in jeans moved off to be seated. It was then that Matthew got his first clear glimpse of the dining area. It used to be difficult to make out the faces through the haze in a place like this, Matthew thought. Maybe people were finally beginning to heed the voices of reason and cut down on cigarettes. Off in the far corner, his eye caught the outline of a familiar profile. There was the usual rather pleasant jolt to the consciousness that he often experienced on the street or in a crowded department store. The eyes, minding their own business, pass over the milling faces, come to a halt, retrack, and hold on a particular arrangement of nose, mouth, line of jaw. *We know that person*, the eyes tell the brain, *just in case you're interested*. Sometimes he was, most often he was not, and would lose himself in the throng so as to escape a meaningless exchange with someone he cared nothing about. A moment too banal to qualify as even a minor event in a busy man's busy day.

So why in this darkened place with the warm air full of animated voices had this ordinary moment of split-second recognition suddenly sucked the breath from his lungs and set the wooden-plank floor tilting and shifting under his feet? *If I look away*, he thought, in words slow and deliberate inside his head, *the sideways movement of my face will obliterate the scene before me like an eraser swept across a chalkboard.* But he could not avert his eyes. He stood immobilized like a jammed, malfunctioning lighthouse that could focus on only one particular wedge of treacherous sea.

The woman was distressed, perhaps in tears. She talked, mouth twisted in anguish, then listened with eyes that fastened on her companion's face as if she were drowning and he possessed the world's sole life raft. The man's face was angled away, but Matthew could see the shoulder-length hair. No mistaking him for a woman, at least not for long. There was too much sinewy muscular power in his body. As he spoke, he gestured with his hands. Once he caught the woman's fingers between his own and held them to his mouth. Her face crumpled, she dropped her eyes, and hid them with her other hand.

Jack had stopped talking. His eyes followed Matthew's to the corner table. "See someone you know?"

Matthew exerted enormous effort and forced his gaze to meet Jack's. "I thought maybe, but I was mistaken."

Breathing was Matthew's immediate problem. His chest was paralyzed. So he ordered his brain to tell his lungs to expand. They did, and he gasped. But his upper body refused to take the next step without further instructions. Exhale, he told his brain to tell his lungs. They did, and his body relaxed with a sigh. He kept his eyes focused on Jack's face, but what he saw was the replay of an incident he had witnessed several years ago in a subway station. Matthew had stood in the rush-hour crowd waiting at Eighty-sixth Street for the downtown express. There was a distant rumble, and finally the appearance of a bright headlamp at the far end of the tunnel. Then a scream as a young man in a red windbreaker was shoved off the platform onto the tracks. Women's shrieks mingled with the sound of brakes, but before the train could stop, the man had lost his leg. The whole thing took five seconds, maybe less. What Matthew found so horrible was the guillotine speed of the tragedy. There was no prep-aration. If the fellow had suffered frostbite, for instance, there would be the hospitalization, the medical consultations, with warnings that gangrene might ensue. Then, if weeks later the leg were amputated, at least there would have been some groundwork.

Five seconds, and a life was altered forever. Everything would now be sorted into two categories: before and after. So while Jack Foreman related his exploits concerning an apartment full of "stews," Matthew watched the news feature of the day unreel in the flat air an inch in front of Jack's face: *Intense Conversation in West Side Bar*, starring Margaret Hollander, longtime wife and best friend of attorney Matthew Hollander. Costar unidentified.

He had to get out. Now.

"Go," he interrupted Jack.

"What?" Jack said.

"Gotta go. Don't feel so red-hot. Do it again sometime. Next week. Sorry."

He fled. It had begun to sleet, but the ice felt good against his face. He tried not to think, just walk and taste the cold air and breathe until the process became automatic again. He walked south past the damp glitter of Lincoln Center with its limousines and fountains, then across Central Park South, ignoring the sodden horses and their half-frozen buggy drivers still hawking for rides. Next he headed downtown on Fifth. The apartment waited for him like a beast huddled in the dark up on Seventy-ninth Street. He wanted to avoid it as long as possible. Perhaps he never had to go back there.

By the time he reached Fifty-first Street, he had begun to think that, of course, Maggie was in love. What a fool he had been not to see it. Or perhaps he had merely chosen not to see it. A businessman with well-trimmed hair and sensible horn-rimmed glasses passed by. Why not him? Matthew thought. Betray me if you must, but let it be one of my own kind, not that bohemian with the sensitive hands and the turtleneck sweater. He was probably an artist, no doubt the "fellow student" who had loaned her his studio. So many lies there must have been. So much deception.

Matthew began to shiver. The shock and the cold had penetrated his topcoat. He ducked into a restaurant on a side street near Radio City Music Hall. It was a glossy place that catered to the theater crowd who had long since left. Only half a dozen people sat at the bar. The bartender poured goldfish crackers into wooden bowls in preparation for the mob that would arrive in an hour's time. Matthew ordered a double Scotch, swallowed it in a hurry, and ordered another.

"You okay?" the bartender asked before complying.

"I have hate in my heart," Matthew said. "Other than that, I'm fine."

The bartender studied Matthew dubiously. The sleet was melting off Matthew's hair and dripping onto the polished surface of the bar.

"Look, I forgot my hat. I'm an attorney. Lost a big case today due to deceit and corruption. I don't usually drink much so it won't be long before I'm totally blasted. I'm a very quiet drunk."

"Got a car?"

"Nope. I'm on foot and I live right up the street."

"Okay."

He poured and Matthew drank. The liquor felt good going down, but seemed to have little effect on Matthew's thoughts. To no avail, he huddled over his glass as if the whiskey's warm comfort could reach into his soul. After he had finished his second double, a young woman sat down next to him and shrugged out of her wet trench coat. She wore an expensive navy silk suit with a Liberty-print tie and a bow at her collar. She smiled at Matthew.

"Bad day?" she asked.

"Bad of prodigious proportions."

"You're an attorney, right?"

"I'm dismayed that it shows," Matthew answered.

"Can't help but recognize a fellow traveler."

"Oh shit," Matthew said.

"You don't like women lawyers?"

"Don't like any lawyers. Minds like steel traps, hearts like basalt."

"I play the harp in my spare time. Professionally."

"That's different," Matthew said. "My wife's fucking around."

The woman looked at him.

"You hardly know what to say."

"That's right," she said.

"Neither do I. What're you drinking?" Matthew asked.

"Vodka on the rocks."

He ordered her drink and another double for himself. "It's what's on my mind this evening. My wife's fucking."

"There're a whole lot of questions I'd like to ask," the woman said.

"You're an educated woman. Know how I can tell?"

"No."

"Most people would say *'there's'* a whole lot of questions, not *'there're.'* "

"Ah." She waited. "About those questions."

"Fire away."

"When did you find out?"

"Tonight. I saw them. He's a fucking hippie."

"How long have you been married?"

"Eighteen years."

"What are you going to do about it?"

"Drink."

"You're extremely attractive. I suppose you know that."

Matthew was silent.

"I mean, if you need bolstering in the confidence department, I'd be very happy to oblige. I've had a long day myself."

Matthew took a closer look at her. She had a soft face, not bony like Maggie's. She was blue-eyed, rosy-skinned, and rather fragile-looking. Her mouth was pink and full. It had been a very long time since Matthew had kissed anyone other than Maggie. He could take her to bed, no doubt about it. A soft round body might be a welcome change from Maggie's angularities. A sweet form of vengeance. The woman moved her chair closer to his. His face was no more than six inches away.

"Try it," she said.

"Okay." Matthew leaned forward and kissed her gently. His lips were numb from the liquor. It felt as if someone else owned his mouth.

"Nothing, huh?" she asked.

"Sorry. Should have tried it before the last round."

"I have a feeling it wouldn't have made a difference."

"The trouble is . . ." he began.

"Go ahead," the woman sighed.

"I keep wanting to tell Maggie about it."

"Who's Maggie?"

"My wife."

"I see your problem."

Her face expressed patient sympathy, but practiced, as if she had heard it all before.

"The humiliation of it. Everybody always thought we were the perfect couple. Well, almost everybody, as it turns out."

"What went wrong?"

"Nothing."

"There must have been some . . ."

"Why?" Matthew interrupted. "Maybe she just has the hots for him. A temporary hormonal derailment." He caught a glimpse of the coat rack by the door. There were only two coats hanging, a woman's fur, and over that, a man's Burberry trench coat, the arms of which draped the fur in a protective embrace. The tenderness of it was too much for Matthew to bear. Once again, he was overwhelmed with the urgent need for flight. Pain kept tracking him down. If he could only find some respite, however temporary. He paid the bill and stood up.

"Good luck," the woman said.

"I hope some nice violinist sits down in a minute. Stay away from lawyers." He leaned over and kissed her again.

He stopped beside the railing at Rockefeller Center and looked down at the skaters. They were teenagers mostly. They fell a lot, but seemed immune to pain. At the west end of the plaza, a team of men pounded at the scaffolding surrounding the giant bare Christmas tree. Matthew imagined Maggie and her lover crucified, hanging there from the wooden braces like macabre holiday decorations. Christ, how maudlin it all was. He wanted to kill Maggie, and yet all the time there was this need to go straight home and tell her all about the miserable night he was having.

He could picture her at the kitchen table, leaning forward on her elbows, her expressive eyes watching him carefully as he spoke, so as not to miss a word. She was the perfect person to unload on because she never trivialized the complaint. If he was having a difficult time with a new secretary, Maggie never said, "Oh, but it will soon get better, you'll see," which, of course, he knew. Instead the response would be something like "It must be difficult adjusting to someone you're so dependent on." If his shoulder stiffened so that he could not play squash, she never said, "Aren't you lucky it's not serious?" Instead it was "You really count on that game. You'll miss it this week, won't you?" She had such a gift for making him feel understood. How he longed for her tonight.

He wondered suddenly about Maggie. Where did she go with her pain? The question struck him full force. He supposed she confided in her friends. He remembered her stunned silence when he called to check on her biopsy report the other day. Clearly, she had been shocked at his interest. The fact was, he only remembered because his secretary had used her lunch hour to have a mole removed and was terrified it was malignant.

Matthew crossed Fifth Avenue and stood looking up at the spires of St. Patrick's Cathedral, resplendent with its recently cleaned facade. He had liked it better grimy and gray, but then perhaps he was just uncomfortable with change. Christ, how long since he had wondered how Maggie was doing, or looked at her with careful eyes? He thought of her companion in the bar tonight. He was watching her, listening to her.

"Oh, God," he heard himself moan, and a passerby gave him a suspicious glance. He sat down on the stone steps in front of the cathedral, not far from a bag lady who picked idly through her tattered belongings and sorted them into piles beside her feet. But all Matthew could see was Maggie's tormented eyes as they clung to the face of her lover.

"All right," he said aloud, but the bag lady did not seem to hear. It was time to sort this thing out. He had a legal mind. Then be a lawyer now.

Maggie had met this man, been strongly attracted, resisted, but finally succumbed, with what terrible guilt he could only imagine, knowing her deep family commitment. It made Matthew's stomach turn to think that another man had discovered the joys of this woman's sensuality. But no, he would not think of that. He needed to understand, not torture himself. He stared down at his hands. They were capable, straight fingers, but not long and sensitive like that other man's. How casually Matthew had abused her body, he thought, pinching, wrestling as if she were some kind of toy.

Perhaps Maggie was attempting to give him up, this lover. There was conflict between them. Perhaps she was trying to remain in the marriage, even if only for the children's sake. Assuming this was so, did Matthew still want her?

He thought of her face, the way she looked at the children with a kind of shy adoration, the way she stood all rumpled and sleepy at the kitchen counter each morning, her gentle voice. Whatever beauty there was in his life, she brought it. She was good and loving, and, yes, he wanted her. More than ever in his life, he wanted her, and Matthew put his head in his hands and cried on the steps of the cathedral.

It was two A.M. when Matthew was finally sober enough to leave the all-night coffee shop on Seventy-fifth Street. It had begun to snow. At the corner newsstand, there were tubs of flowers now lightly sprinkled with white. Matthew stared at them for a moment, then swooped them up, daisies, carnations, irises, lilies. His arms were so full of dripping blossoms that he could barely get his money out, but soon he started off up Lexington Avenue toward Seventy-ninth Street.

Matthew bid the doorman a pleasant good morning as the flowers created a puddle beside the elevator. He studied himself in the elevator mirror on the way upstairs. He barely looked drunk.

Maggie was waiting by the door. She was ashen, with dark circles under her eyes. "Oh my God, Matthew, where have you been?" She did not notice the flowers. "I've been calling the office and the squash court and Jack didn't answer his phone. Oh God, Matthew." She began to cry, standing in her bathrobe with her arms stiff at her sides. Matthew handed her the flowers, which she took, opening her hands blindly. Matthew held her face between his hands and kissed her carefully. She wept with the flowers crushed between them.

"I thought you were dead. Oh, Matt, don't ever do that to me again. I was so scared, so scared. . . ."

"Shh, shh," he soothed her, touching her hair. "Here, let's put these in water."

She saw the flowers for the first time, stared down at her

arms and their contents as if she had no notion how they got there. "What's this?"

"Flowers."

"Flowers," she echoed. "What are they for?"

"For you."

"Flowers for me," Maggie repeated.

"Yes, at two-thirty in the morning, flowers for you." He put his arm around her shoulder and led her to the kitchen. "Come on, let's get us all a drink, water for them, whiskey for us."

They sat at the kitchen table while Matthew tried to tell her what happened without telling her what happened.

"I think I had a mid-life crisis or something tonight," he began. "Oh, it sounds ridiculous, like some born-again nut. I hardly know how to describe it."

Her eyes were beginning to lose some of their terror. She held her tumbler of Scotch with both hands. "Where have you been all this time?"

"Walking mostly. I even sort of went to church."

She waited.

"I don't know, Mag, I just suddenly realized that I've lost touch somewhere along the line. Or maybe I never was in touch." He reached across the table and took her hand in his. She dropped her eyes as they both thought of the darkened table in the restaurant on Columbus Avenue. "I don't want to go to my grave a successful lawyer and half a human being."

"What happened tonight, Matthew?"

"Oh, Christ, I don't know. Some silly bastard of a client was in today. Lost his whole family in an ugly divorce and he's falling apart. It's his own damn fault. He's not what you would call a thoughtful human being. He's about as tractable as a totem pole. I looked across my desk at him and suddenly I saw myself. . . ." Matthew took a long pull on his drink. He had made it through the worst part. The lie was behind him now, and he saw that Maggie was eager to believe him. "I need you, Maggie. I want you to help me be more of a person. It's a heavy load, I know, and I've got some hell of a nerve. Can you help me?"

"I don't know," she answered softly.

"I can't lose you."

"I'm glad you're safe, Matt."

"We've been together a long time. That counts for something."

Maggie drew her hand across her eyes. "I'm so tired."

"Come. Let me put you into bed." He walked her down the hall, helped her into bed, and sat down on the edge beside her. He bent over to kiss her, then snapped off the light. Her eyes stared up at him in the darkness. "Please, Maggie," he whispered. "Don't let it be too late."

Then he got up and left her, closing the door softly behind him.

But Maggie did not go to sleep. She lay on the bed with her heart beating so hard that she could almost feel the tug of her nightgown with each pulse. The fear had left a taste in her mouth, acrid and bitter like the chalky film from an aspirin that would not go down. For so long, she had been trying to resurrect her feelings for Matthew so that she could examine them. Had she truly spent eighteen years married to a man she merely respected? It seemed unlikely, and yet nothing surfaced to deny it. Until tonight, in the long hours when he did not turn his key in the lock and she became certain he was injured or killed—that there might never be Matthew on this earth again. The thought—in fantasy the solution to her dilemma—was in fact unbearable. The implications of her terror had been too complex for Maggie to deal with. I'll worry about all that later, she had thought. Just please, please, let him come home.

With the growing conviction of tragedy had come the flood of memories, long buried beneath the heavy cloak of anger. She remembered the first time she had found a lump, years ago, in the other breast then. Dr. Berg drained off some fluid and had it analyzed. The first report was inconclusive, and they had had to wait two dreadful weeks for the verdict. Matthew was a man who could not bear sleeping with anyone touching him. Nevertheless, every morning for fourteen days, Maggie had awakened with his arms tight around her. He never spoke of it, and when the good news came, he reverted to bounding out of bed first thing.

She remembered a game he used to play with the children. He would place an object, a shoe perhaps, on the cocktail table. The children, delighted, would pounce on it and take it back to its closet. There in the empty pouch of the shoe rack they would find something else, perhaps a jar of spaghetti sauce. Off they would go to the kitchen to discover a pair of Susan's socks where the spaghetti sauce belonged. The game continued until they reached the treasure—a box of chocolates or some silly wind-up toy. Maggie once asked Matthew where he had learned such a game. He shrugged and said he made it up.

"Don't ever tell me you have no imagination," she had told him then.

She remembered when she was first pregnant with Susan, going to spend a week by herself with her parents. The second day she began to experience stomach cramps. The local doctor prescribed bed rest, assuring them there was no reason for alarm, yet when Maggie telephoned Matthew that evening, he rented a car and showed up in the driveway at five A.M.

Recollections kept appearing one after the other, like marching bands in a raucous Fifth Avenue parade. Still Matthew did not come to bed. It was nearly light outside before Maggie remembered that last night she had spent two hours in a bar with David trying to figure out how to tell Matthew she was leaving him.

21

Matthew and Jackson Brody walked downtown on Fifth Avenue. It was hard going, what with the slush underfoot and the crowds of holiday shoppers.

"Sorry to just drop in on you," Matthew said. "Christ, is it always like this around here?" He was nearly shoved into the street by a bulging shopping bag.

"Always at Christmas," Jackson said. "We'll be out of it in a minute though." He guided Matthew along Thirty-seventh Street and through the doors of a restaurant called Mary Elizabeth. "Ah, we're early enough. Ten more minutes and we'd have been out of luck."

While they stood in line to be seated, Matthew looked about. There were long rows of tables in a large wainscoted room. Most of the patrons appeared to be elderly ladies wearing hats. He spotted one man, but he was accompanied by a woman and a child who was asleep in its stroller. "What is this place?" Matthew asked.

"A little off the beaten track, isn't it?" Jackson replied.

There were two large glass cabinets on the wall above their table. One displayed a pair of green porcelain chickens and the other faded paintings of houses over which a poem was superimposed. Matthew strained his eyes but could make out only the first line: *To think I once saw grocery shops with but a casual eye* . . . None of the waitresses was younger than forty-five. Theirs flew past in frilled white apron, dispensing menus in her wake. But she reappeared in seconds.

They ordered. After the waitress whisked away, there was a long silence. The men smiled at each other and then quickly averted their eyes. Matthew took a deep breath.

"Silly to feel bashful after all these years," he said.

"I guess we're used to having the girls with us," Jackson said.

"Jesus, keep your voice down, man. You're taking your life into your hands, using that term in here."

Jackson looked at the sea of bobbing felt hats and smiled.

"What are you doing for the holidays?" Matthew asked.

"Just hanging out," Jackson answered. "With Robin away . . ." He let the sentence go unfinished.

"Come spend Christmas with us," Matthew said.

"Oh, thanks, I appreciate it, but I think I'm better off just . . . hanging out."

There was another silence. Matthew was finding this more difficult than he had expected. He had figured that once he finally picked up the telephone and asked Jackson if he was free, the rest would follow easily enough. And Jackson had seemed genuinely glad to hear from Matthew.

"I'm not accustomed to . . ." Matthew began. He hesitated,

and tried again. "I don't have friends. Men friends. I'm used to just Maggie. There's a lot I'd like to ask you about, but God damned if I can get started."

Two bowls of vegetable soup swooped under their chins and settled on the table. "I know," Jackson said. "After this . . . thing . . . with Robin, I really got myself tied up in knots. The only person I could talk to about Robin was Robin."

"Exactly!" Matthew exclaimed. "So what did you do?"

"Spent a lot of money drinking so I could complain to the bartender."

"Well, look, I'm sure it's cheaper than psychotherapy."

"There's a guy in a place on Madison and Eightieth who's not half bad," Jackson said.

Matthew surveyed the roomful of women chattering eagerly together. A lady at the next table kept dabbing at her eyes with a white lace handkerchief. "They don't have any difficulty," Matthew observed.

"They're analyzing their real-estate portfolios," Jackson explained.

Matthew tried submerging himself by gradual steps. "So what about you and Robin? Are you . . . is she . . . if you don't mind talking about it."

On the contrary, Jackson seemed eager. His voice was deep and rich. Matthew liked listening to it.

"She's got this job, you know," Jackson said. "With a film company. She's wild about it. They do a lot of public-service shorts for television, things on the environment, health care, that sort of thing."

"Doesn't sound like Robin to me."

"Have you seen her lately?" Jackson asked. "She wears glasses and these godawful turtleneck sweaters. Hasn't put on a dress in two months as far as I can tell. I figured if she wanted to work I'd set her up in a little business of her own, maybe with crafts. Needlepoint, macrame, knitting. Not a chance. She wanted to do it completely on her own."

"But didn't Hilary Vonderhyde get her the job?"

Jackson shrugged and smiled.

"It sounds as if you're still in touch," Matthew said.

"Oh yes. We date." Jackson smiled again, but he was forcing it. He had ten years on Matthew, but sometimes he seemed even older. "It's not wonderful."

Matthew decided that by now he was in up to his ankles. Time to go for the knees. "Aren't you pissed off?"

"Yes," Jackson answered. "But not as much as I was at first."

"But you were always so good to her, gave her every damn thing she wanted. You always treated her like a princess, unless you beat her when nobody was looking."

"She says I gave her what I wanted her to have, not what she wanted."

"So what does she want then?" Matthew's voice had risen. In his agitation, he nearly knocked his water glass over.

"She doesn't know. She's working on it."

"Oh my God."

"I know," Jackson said. "I've gotten to the point where I read the *Hers* column in the *Times* every Thursday."

Matthew laughed. "Me too. What the hell, I figure I may learn something."

The empty soup bowls turned into plates of toast smothered in melted cheese. "I keep telling myself it's not easy for her, either," Jackson said. "Robin can't inflict pain without suffering herself. She's got plenty of things to sort out right now." He reached into his pocket, took out a roll of Tums, and popped two into his mouth.

"Maybe we should talk about the stock market?" Matthew said.

Jackson laughed. "I would guess they spend a lot of time on us. Maybe if we dedicated a few lunch hours to discussing our wives we might even figure them out someday."

The melted cheese and toast points had transported Matthew back to the dining hall at Andover. Life had seemed manageable then. It was easy just making grades and shooting balls through hoops. "Do you think . . . this is none of my business . . . did she, was there someone else?"

"I don't think so. I'd know if there was."

"One would think."

Jackson studied Matthew as the younger man tapped restlessly on the place mat with his fork handle.

"Of course, you and Maggie are an institution," Jackson said. "It must be tough for you to understand what I'm talking about."

"Every marriage has its rough spots, ours included." Matthew set his fork down too hard and it fell to the floor with a clatter.

"How about a commune? Men only," Jackson suggested.

"Sign me up," Matthew said.

"One of those rough spots?"

"Nothing we can't handle, but it's a pain in the ass." Matthew looked down at his hands. It should be so easy to let the words spill out of his mouth, but they would not come. Still, he was sitting across the table from Jackson, wasn't he, after all those years of promising? It was a start.

They finished off their Welsh rarebit without speaking, but it was a comfortable, thoughtful silence now. For the first time in days, Matthew thought he felt a stirring of hope. It was elusive, like the tiny shimmering reflection of his watch crystal that danced on the wall beside him, but it felt good nonetheless. He looked up from his plate to see Jackson staring at him intently.

"Since we're into it," Jackson said slowly, "Robin's pregnant."

"Oh, for Christ's sake."

Jackson smiled sadly. "What a mess. She doesn't even know if she wants it."

"You have most certainly been in touch."

"Once. We got a little boozed and forgot we're not supposed to be lovers."

"Do you want it?"

"I wouldn't mind having a baby around," Jackson replied.

The waitress handed them the dessert menu and moved on.

"Any projections about what'll happen over the next few months?"

"Damned if I know," Jackson answered. "I'm taking it a day at a time. The only thing I know for certain is that I'm going to have the gingerbread. Try it. It'll remind you of the days when Grandma spent her afternoons baking goodies in the kitchen instead of producing documentary films or running for Congress."

"With lemon sauce, no less," Matthew read from the menu. "My grandmother was a golf pro."

"Mine drove a cab."

Matthew laughed and raised his glass. "Well, here's to grandmas anyway. The myth and the reality. May they rule the world someday and give us a break."

Jackson touched his glass to Matthew's and drank. "If they don't already."

"You feeling okay, Mom?" Fred asked as they stepped out of the taxi in front of the Higgens Gallery.

"A little queasy," Maggie said. "Must have been the Christmas pudding I had for dessert." She ushered Susan and Fred up the steps ahead of her and wondered if David was already there. Under his steady pressure, she had finally agreed to bring the children to Eliza's retrospective exhibit. He had convinced Maggie that the gallery was an ideal place for a preliminary meeting.

"It's friendly and public," he had said. "You can ignore me if you like, or introduce us if you think you can. Just relax, look at Eliza's pictures, and let me stare at the kids."

All night, Maggie had been practicing a possible introduction. "Fred, Susan, this is David Golden, a friend of mine from art class." It seemed so simple. She had tried it aloud in the bathroom this morning, but her voice trembled so violently that she never got past the word "friend."

"Hey, Mom," Susan was saying. "Your stuff is just as good as this. How come you don't get a show?"

"Patience, patience," Maggie said. So far, no David. But there were two rooms. He could be lurking just around the corner.

Fred drew her over to an abstract of white-yellow color slicing through a black background. "Pretty excellent," he commented.

Maggie thought of the Montauk lighthouse Eliza had spoken about on the boat. "What do you suppose she was getting at?" she asked Fred.

"Does it always have to mean something? Maybe she was just having fun with the colors."

"I bet it has something to do with inspiration," Susan suggested. "Kind of like the cartoon with a lightbulb going on over somebody's head."

"Crude," Fred said.

Then she saw him. He was leaning against the far wall. Maggie watched his eyes move from one child to the other. There was the merest flicker when his gaze intercepted hers. Maggie felt her face flush red-hot. She was certainly not ready for an introduction today, she decided. Let this be the first step. He could see them with her, and perhaps the next time it would be easier for Maggie to initiate an actual confrontation. She steered Fred and Susan in the opposite direction. The next time Maggie checked, David had disappeared.

"Maggie Hollander," he said.

Maggie jumped. "Oh," she said.

"I'm David Golden," David said to the children. "I know your mother from art class."

"Yes," Maggie said. "Fred, Susan, this is David Golden."

"He said," Fred remarked, giving his mother a sideways glance.

Susan held out her hand and stared up into David's face. Maggie had begun to feel far removed.

"What do you think of the exhibit?" David asked.

"Extremely excellent," Fred said.

"She has a fine sense of color, hasn't she?" Susan said.

David nodded seriously. "It's one of her greatest assets."

"If you know Mom from class, you must paint too," Fred said, as if he were not quite sure he was getting the full story.

"Sculpture," David said.

"A sculptor! How exciting!" Susan exclaimed.

Maggie said in a strangled voice, "It was nice running into you. We haven't seen the other room yet."

David's expression closed up; he waved to the children and turned away.

"He's *cute*, Mom," Susan whispered. "He looks just like a sculptor's supposed to look."

"And how's that?" Maggie asked.

"Incredibly romantic, with that long hair and those wild eyes."

"Probably hasn't had a bath in weeks," Fred commented.

At the dinner table, Fred passed the rolls to his father, glanced surreptitiously at Maggie, and said, "We met a friend of Mom's at a gallery today."

"Oh?" Matthew said. Something in Fred's tone made him look up from his dinner.

"Yeah, the neatest-looking sculptor," Susan said.

"He was far from neat," Fred muttered

Matthew stopped buttering his roll. He stared at Maggie, who was poking carefully at the mounds of food on her plate.

She tried to swallow a mouthful of zucchini, but it stuck just above her Adam's apple.

"You should've seen the way he looked at Mom," Fred began.

"Oh, Fred, don't be absurd," Susan said. "It was a terrific exhibit, didn't you think so, Mom?"

Fred excused himself before dessert. Maggie tried to keep her eyes off Matthew's face until she felt her expression return to normal.

Matthew caught Maggie's hand as she started for the bathroom with her nightgown draped over her arm.

"Why, Mag?"

She looked startled.

"This." He touched the soft folds of her nightgown.

"I'm just going to change."

"I know that. Why do you hide in the bathroom?"

"It's more . . . I'm just in the habit, I guess."

He drew her over to the edge of the bed and sat down beside her.

"Do you have something to tell me?" he asked.

Her eyes filled with tears. She shook her head.

"Are you sure?" he pressed.

"No."

Matthew cupped her chin with his hand and forced her to look into his face. "You're not sure, or you don't have anything to tell me?"

"I'm not sure."

He released her chin, but took her hand in his. "Maggie, you and the children . . ." He was silent for a moment. "Are we going to be all right?" The words caught in his throat.

Maggie squeezed her eyes shut and tried to steel herself against the anguish she heard in his voice. David, she thought, what am I supposed to do now? Matthew pulled her into his arms and rocked her on the edge of the bed. She could tell by the sound of his breathing that he was crying.

Later, as they were finally succumbing to exhaustion in the dark, she heard Matthew say something. "What?" she asked groggily.

"I had lunch with Jackson Brody the other day," he said.

"You did?"

"Yeah."

"Well," Maggie said. "Well."

Christmas morning, Matthew handed Maggie a large envelope. Inside were two airline tickets and a brochure for the Spindrift Hotel on Key Biscayne. Maggie stared at the papers in her hand as though the writing was in a foreign language.

Fred and Susan laughed. "You know what our present is?" Susan asked. "We're not going with you."

"But where will you stay?"

"Here. Grandma's coming."

"Grandma," Maggie repeated.

"Grandma Rhoda," Fred said.

Maggie looked incredulous.

"Don't worry, Mom," Fred said. "We'll take good care of her."

"I thought she was in Santa Fe."

"She was," Matthew said. "I told her it was an emergency."

"Well, when? Oh, I guess it's on the tickets. January third. My goodness, so soon." Matthew was beginning to look disappointed. "Thank you, Matt," Maggie said hurriedly. "It's a lovely present. I'm just stunned." She was already wondering how she would break the news to David.

*

"He knows," David said over the telephone.

"How could he?" Maggie asked.

"I can't imagine. Christ!" David's outburst sounded un-characteristically violent. "I wish I could throw down a gauntlet or something. I'd like to take him on face to face and get it over with."

"I'm the one who has to sort it out, David."

"The man's not used to losing."

Maggie was silent.

"Don't let him . . . Oh dammit. I wish I'd stayed away from that gallery."

"I wasn't ready," Maggie said.

"You wouldn't ever be ready," David said. "It's not that, it's Fred. I'm sure he guessed there was something. Can I see you before you leave?"

"No. I've got Rhoda here. I'm supposed to show her the ropes. It's so silly, the children are far more mature than she is. David, I don't want to go. It'll be ghastly."

"I have to say I hope so."

"I'll be back in a week. We've been apart longer than that."

"That was before he knew."

"Happy New Year, David, my darling."

"Happy New Year," he said gloomily.

On the plane to Miami, Matthew said, "This week is for fun only. No decisions. Real life is hereby suspended. Okay?"

"Okay," Maggie said.

Before dinner, they walked on the beach, picked up shells, and talked.

"What do you think about psychotherapy?" Matthew asked. "Think it could help ease the mid-life miseries?"

"I would think so," Maggie answered. "But does this topic fall under the category of fun?"

"We're just not allowed to get grim," he said. "God, that sand feels good on my toes. Maybe this is better than going to a shrink."

"I always thought you were pretty much set against it in principle," Maggie said. She pulled her sweater more tightly around her. The sun was nearly down, sending red streaks blazing across the sky. The breeze was thick with the smell of the ocean.

"I was." He flung a flat stone into the surf and watched it skip four times. "Not bad for an old duffer. What if I quit law?"

"Quit law!"

He laughed.

"That's like telling me you'll quit eating, sleeping, and breathing," she said.

"I met a fellow the other day, used to be with a big uptown firm. He's chucked it all and started a maple-syrup farm in Litchfield County."

"Oh, Matt, I can't see you in maple syrup."

"You know what, Maggie?" He was suddenly serious. "I'm trying to climb out of a whole bunch of ruts. Don't keep stepping on my fingers when you see them coming over the edge."

"I'm sorry," she said.

Over dinner, he asked her if she thought there was hope for modern marriage. "Theoretically," he added.

"Some people seem to manage it," she replied.

"Name three," he said.

Maggie thought hard. She might once have counted the Brodys. "How about Ethel and John Miller? And the Epsteins. The Wilkersons?" She paused a moment. "Well, maybe not the Wilkersons."

"You can only name them because you don't know them very well." He ordered two espressos. "Remember when we used to sit up half the night drinking wine and planning our lives? Back in that minuscule apartment when we first moved to New York?"

Maggie nodded. "I was going to be a great artist and you a criminal court judge and we'd raise children together, taking turns walking them to school and waking up with them in the night."

"Well, Christ, look what happened."

She was silent.

"What can a man do?" Matthew asked. "What do you women really want from a marriage?"

"Theoretically?" she asked, with a touch of bitterness. The candle on the table hissed and flickered.

"I don't manhandle you anymore," he said. "Give me credit for that."

"Am I supposed to be grateful?" Maggie asked. "After pleading for seventeen years and being ignored? You only quit it because I slugged you as hard as I could. Is that what I have to do to get your attention?"

"Not anymore. I'm asking you to talk to me."

Maggie glared at him.

"Come on, talk," he challenged her.

"What I have to say isn't fit for elegant surroundings like these."

Matthew stood abruptly, dug in his wallet, slapped two fifty-dollar bills on the table, and held out his hand. "All right. Let's go someplace that is."

Out on the beach, the wind had quickened. Waves at high tide beat up against the sand and retreated. A full moon dodged the clouds to provoke weird shadows on the shore. Matthew spun Maggie around to face him. She could distinguish every whisker and every wrinkle on his face in the strange light.

"Let's have it!" he shouted over the wind. "What do you say?"

"You're an insensitive bastard," Maggie began. "No, you're not a bastard, that's what makes it even more terrible. You're a nice guy, but you don't *see* people. We're all factors, items, that get arranged to suit your convenience. If somebody says something you don't like, you don't bother listening. Being married to you is like flailing at the wind. Jesus Christ, Matthew, how could you not remember that Susan got her goddamn period!" It was all exploding out of her. She felt her face contort with the screaming and knew that nothing could stop her. "You don't know your own daughter, or Fred, or me, you don't even know yourself! Maybe you *should* see a psychiatrist! Maybe that'd be a start!" She began to run. She felt wild, exhilarated, but it was hard going with the sand sliding away beneath her feet. She could hear Matthew just behind her.

"You can't lay it all on me," he was shouting. "You're a silent brooder. It's deadly. It eats you up and destroys everything around you. Yes, I heard you when you jabbed me in the gut. You should have done it years ago."

"People shouldn't have to scream to be heard," Maggie yelled back.

"Sometimes they do." He grabbed her arm and she struck out at him.

"I hate you!" Maggie howled. She pummeled his chest with her fists. He pinned her arms against him and they both fell to the sand. She struggled, but he held her fast.

"I hate you, I hate you," she sobbed again and again until finally all the energy went out of her and she lay still.

"Anything else?" he asked her after a while.

"Yes," she sniffed, and sat up, brushing sand out of her hair. "You were my friend and you let me down."

Back in New York, Maggie realized that during the entire week, Matthew had not once tried to make love to her.

22

The evening was unexpectedly mild for January. Maggie wore her down coat open, while Matthew was content with a wool sports jacket over his sweater. As they walked down Lexington Avenue toward the Ice Studio, Maggie took a deep breath. She always drew hope from the false spring contrived by a January thaw. It assured her that winter would truly end one day.

Matthew took her hand. His was smooth compared to David's bony roughness. Guiltily she glanced down the sidewalk, as if David might materialize to find her walking hand in hand with her husband.

"What are you thinking, Mags?"

"Oh, I don't know. About springtime, I guess."

"Pretty sober face for such a pleasant topic."

"Do you know, Matt, I bet you've asked me what I'm thinking half a dozen times since we got back."

"Have I? I'm curious, that's all. You get this Mona Lisa expression and I don't know where you are."

"I'm not complaining," Maggie said. "I'm just not used to it."

"Are we on time?" Matthew asked, checking his watch.

"Early, actually. Zach's skating lesson is over at seven-thirty and we don't have to have him up at school for the show until eight-fifteen."

"How come Stephen isn't taking him straight from the rink?" Matthew asked.

"He's got a dinner meeting and Phyllis is at the hospital with her mother. I didn't think it would kill us to go four blocks out of our way."

"Okay, okay," Matthew said. "Just asking."

They walked half a block in silence. The scratchy brown carcasses of discarded Christmas trees lay in a heap at the curb.

"Do you think I could ever be more like you, Mags?"

"I don't understand."

"You're in it up to your neck. You've had babies. I mean felt the pain and bled. You've mopped up their vomit and worried all night with them."

"You have too," Maggie said.

"I worry until I get out the door in the morning, and then I leave it all to you."

"But you care about your clients."

"My clients. That's not family, that's pieces of paper. They come and go. There's no impact on my life, just ripples on the surface. You make things, beautiful permanent things, with your hands. You're involved with . . . your friends. Get all messed up in their lives. You're not afraid of that, of the mess. You feel things, I know, so deeply, and you suffer. . . ."

Maggie dropped her eyes. Matthew's grip on her hand

tightened. "I'm like one of those bugs that skates on the water, we used to call them skimmers," he said. "I've never really gotten wet. You think it's too late for me to submerge? Once a skimmer, always a skimmer?"

"Come, it's up here," Maggie said, opening a heavy wooden door with a narrow staircase behind it.

At the top, another door opened into a frosty room with benches, and beyond that, a picture window overlooked a small square rink. Three girls sat on benches unlacing their skates and giggling. A gum-chewing attendant leafed through *Variety* at the desk. "Help?" he asked Maggie and Matthew without enthusiasm. The sound emerged from his mouth in a mist of condensation that smelled of Juicy Fruit.

"We're just picking someone up," Matthew said, approaching the window. "It's colder in here than it is outside. Hey, that's Stephen."

"Yes, he always skates with Zach. He doesn't trust anybody else to teach him," Maggie said.

"What's he going to do, wear his skates to his meeting? Christ, he's pretty good," Matthew said.

Stephen executed a neat jump. The piped music was barely audible outside the glass cage. "It's like a silent movie," Maggie said.

Zachary watched his father carefully and tried to imitate him, but his ankles kept collapsing inward. He could barely stand, let alone attempt the tricks Stephen was urging on him. Suddenly the boy fell. His ludicrous version of Stephen's leap had caused him to catch a pick in the slushy surface, and he went down hard. He grasped his knee and tried to bite back the tears. Stephen stood above him, talking and gesticulating while Zachary huddled in his wet jeans, one hand on his knee and the other extended to his father.

"Help him up," Matthew muttered.

But Stephen ignored the hand. Tears were forming raw

streaks on the boy's face. He tried to struggle onto his feet, but the weakened knee would not support him and he went down again. His cry penetrated the heavy plate glass.

"Goddammit," Matthew said, as Stephen angrily thrust Zachary's hand away. Matthew rapped hard on the window. Stephen turned in annoyance, but Matthew beckoned insistently. Once Stephen recognized Matthew, his face rearranged itself into a friendly smile. He came to the door and opened it while Zachary began a painful crawl to the side of the rink.

"Hi. We're learning the first rule of skating. How to get up after you fall on your ass."

"Yeah," Matthew said. "Hey, Zach, you ready?"

"But we've got another fifteen minutes," Stephen protested.

"Sorry, but we've got an errand to run on our way to the show." Matthew held his hand out to Zachary, who gratefully clutched it and made his way to the nearest bench.

Stephen's face was at war between irritation and hero worship. "Well, thanks for picking up my little klutz here," he said. "Sorry I can't make the show, Zach." He glanced at the wall clock. "I've got a little time before I have to be downtown. Think I'll just stick around in there for a couple of minutes." He escaped back onto the rink.

Outside, Matthew ushered Maggie and Zachary into the coffee shop across the street. "Here, sit in a booth and order something gooey," he told Zachary.

"Is this our errand?" Maggie asked.

"Mm," Matthew said.

Over a butterscotch sundae, Zachary bemoaned his lack of athletic prowess. "My father can never figure out how I can be so bad when he's so coordinated."

"I'm sure you're good at other things," Matthew said.

"I suppose I have my strengths."

Maggie watched Matthew study the boy. "Can I ask you a personal question?" Matthew asked.

"Yeah, sure." Zachary rolled his cherry in the butterscotch sauce and popped it into his mouth.

"How'd you get your name?"

Zachary looked up, his face darkening. "Old family handle from Mom's side."

"You don't like it?" Maggie asked.

"My father says it's a faggot name."

Maggie noticed that Phyllis was always referred to as "Mom" while Stephen was invariably "my father."

"What about our esteemed president Zachary Taylor, Old Rough-and-Ready?" Matthew asked. "He was pretty tough."

Zachary stared at Matthew with his mother's piercing intensity. "Do you think a name can make you . . . can make a person into what . . . well, say your name is . . . uh, Mike or Jack or something, like, strong. You think that has an effect on you so you end up being like your name? Say I had a name like Chad Stallion or maybe like that guy John Wayne. His name could've made him real solid, I bet."

Matthew thought for a moment. "First of all," he said, "I don't imagine John Wayne's real name was John Wayne. It was probably Percy Higgenbottom."

Zachary laughed. The sound was light and clear.

"I suppose it would have an effect if you let it," Matthew went on. "But after all, a name is only an arbitrary label. You can change it anytime you like."

"Nah, Mom loves it. It was the name of about the only relative she didn't hate."

"Well, then, maybe you could compromise. Keep Zachary for your middle name, for instance."

They watched him think this over.

"What name would you choose if you changed?" Maggie asked.

"John," Zachary said promptly.

"John Wheeler," Matthew said. "John Zachary Wheeler. It's nice."

Zachary topped off his sundae with a Coke. Then Matthew paid the bill and said, "Okay, John, let's go get some culture."

When they got to the auditorium, Zachary saw Susan and Fred waiting near the stage and took off for them.

Maggie pulled on Matthew's elbow. "Matt?"

"Yuh," he said, searching for two empty seats.

"I don't think you'll always be a skimmer."

He put his arm around her shoulder and squeezed it.

She woke herself up screaming. Matthew snapped on the light.

"What is it?" he asked.

"Nightmare." Maggie's face was soaked in sweat. Damp tendrils of hair clung to her cheeks like claws.

"What about?"

Maggie sat up and tried to unpeel the nightgown from her back. "I was me, now, but sort of a child, too. I was in this kind of tent, I think at my parents', and I was all alone. This person came and he . . . no, it was a woman . . . she had a long knife, and she cut a circle in my stomach and pulled out my insides. I was eviscerated. Emptied out. There was just this dark hole left. I looked down into it. The odd thing was, I didn't fight her at all. I was completely passive. There was this sense of inevitability. It just had to be, that's all."

"Can I get you something? A glass of milk, maybe?"

"No, thanks, I'll be fine." But when Matthew turned out the light again, she lay next to him and thought about David and how he had made her feel rich and full. She pressed her hands flat against her stomach and hoped that he was lost in the sweet oblivion of sleep on the other side of the park.

23

"I have to see you," Maggie said into the telephone.

"What's wrong?" David asked.

"I can't talk. Matthew's still here."

"I was just about to leave for the studio. Meet me there."

"All right." She hung up and moments later Matthew came into the kitchen to pour himself a cup of coffee.

"Who were you talking to on the phone?"

Maggie buried her face in the newspaper. "Phyllis."

"Isn't it a bit early in the day to call Phyllis? I didn't think she ever crawled out until noon."

"Just confirming our lunch date." Maggie's cheeks were flaming. It had been so easy when Matthew was indifferent. She knew that if his eyes could penetrate the op-ed page, he would

---

surely guess the truth. But Matthew did not press her. It seemed that whenever he came close to the truth, he backed off or circled around it. Sometimes she wondered if David was right, that Matthew knew.

"How about dinner tonight?" Matthew asked. He glanced at his watch and bolted the last of his coffee.

"With the kids?"

"No. Just us."

"Where?"

"I'll surprise you. Call at six and I'll tell you where to meet me." He bent to give her the usual brief morning kiss, then lingered to kiss her again, slowly and thoroughly. Finally he went off down the hall bellowing, "Will you still need me, will you still feed me, when I'm sixty-four?" A minute later she heard the front door slam.

Her body felt like stone, but leaden, not full of movement and grace like David's carvings. She dragged herself to the bedroom, pulled on a pair of pants and a sweater that did not really match, slung her bag over her shoulder, and left. She was deaf to the doorman's good morning, and his bewildered concern went unnoticed.

As soon as she stepped out of the freight elevator, Maggie heard David's air hammer pounding. It was a comforting sound. The only thing she ever truly dreaded for David was that he could not work. Creative silence was the great unendurable terror, and she believed that he would prefer annihilation to the death of his art.

She had to beat on the door to be heard over the din. David was covered with marble dust. It clung to his hair in streaks and frosted his eyelashes and eyebrows.

"Where's your mask?" Maggie asked.

"I forgot," he said. When he closed the door, a choking

cloud swirled around them. Maggie began to cough. "I'm sorry," he said. "Let me get you some water."

She sat on the folding chair and drank. It was painful to look at David's face. Sweat and dirt traced deep lines beside his mouth. His eyes seemed to have sunk into dark caves beneath his forehead. Maggie tried to calm the sick trembling of her stomach by concentrating on the uncut stones that lay in jagged heaps on the floor. She knew that if David were to rinse away the thick film of dust, their rough beauty would be revealed. The texture and translucence would emerge, veined in lovely patterns of blue, rust, gray, white. David had performed that magic trick with her, too, she thought, when she had been as drab and inert as that raw marble.

"Do you want to see what I've been doing?" David asked.

"Of course."

In the two months since she had last been here, ten new pieces protected by canvas drapes had filled the long shelf. One by one, David removed the covers and wet the sculptures with a spray bottle. Each was carved from dense black marble. Some were sharp spears, like shards split by lightning. The others were perfectly round highly polished masses whose interiors had been roughly gouged out. The gaping holes were all the more disfiguring in contrast to their serene surfaces.

Maggie took David's arm and buried her face against the chalky denim of his workshirt. "I'm so sorry," she murmured. "How long have you been . . ." She gestured at the dark shapes.

"Since we met in the bar that night." He touched one of his carvings. "I call these pieces *Omens*. They are omens, aren't they?"

Maggie took his hand in both of hers and held it to her breast.

"Do you love me, Maggie?"

"Yes."

"Why can't you leave him?"

"Because he's trying so hard. Because he's the father of my children. Because I can't imagine my life without him."

"He's a habit, not a lover. Not even a friend. It's the children."

He extracted his hand, and it hung like a dead thing against his side. Maggie felt the strain of sharing the same space without being physically connected.

"It's not just Fred and Susan," she said. "It's Matthew, too. He's so much what I am." She saw David flinch. "Oh God, I have to tell you, don't I?" He nodded, and she went on. "If I had met you years ago—David, don't you know it would have all been different? But we didn't meet, and I married Matt and had a family, and they're as much a part of me as my hands and eyes and bones. I can't start all over again, pulling all the pieces apart and redefining myself."

He took a step backward as if seeking shelter from the black stones.

"There's another one I haven't shown you," David said. He lifted the drape that covered a medium-sized carving in a corner by the window.

Maggie gasped. It was a bust of two young faces, one elevated slightly above the other. The top of the boy's head was level with the girl's temple, and each pair of eyes gazed out at Maggie with the penetrating confidence of youth. David had even captured the asymmetrical shape of Fred's eyebrows.

"Oh my God," Maggie said, and began to cry.

David reached for a manila folder and handed it to her. Her fingers trembled, and the folder slipped to the floor. The preliminary sketches of Susan and Fred lay at Maggie's feet.

"You can keep those," David said, kneeling to gather them together. "But not the carving." He stood and put his hand on the statue, his fingers gently cupping Fred's chin. "It's all I'll ever have of them."

"What you don't really believe," Maggie said through her

tears, "is how much I love you and how much I wish there was a way. My heart is breaking . . . it sounds so pitiful and lame, but it's true. I wasn't even half a person when I met you. David, are you going to be all right?"

"No," he said. One of the hooks on his overalls had come undone. She longed to fix it for him. She would never touch him again, never see him grow older.

"I'll never see you get old," he said.

"Oh, David." The cry was wrenched from some primitive place inside her in a voice she did not recognize. She took one last look at him, and fled.

Maggie dutifully called Matthew at six o'clock. She was to meet him in the bar at Windows on the World at the top of the World Trade Center. She went through the motions, bathing, dressing, checking the pantyhose for runs.

Her cabbie was friendly. When he asked how she was this fine evening, she wanted to reply, "In mourning." Instead she answered, "I'm well. And you?" As she had hoped, the question set off a monologue that lasted the entire trip downtown.

The cavernous elevator at the base of One World Trade Center catapulted her up a quarter-mile of concrete and steel. Matthew was waiting at a table in the bar. He rose to kiss her.

"I wanted to see what kind of a night it was going to be before I decided on this place. Spectacular?"

Maggie gazed out over the pinpoint lights of the harbor. There was still enough twilight left to reflect off the water, turning it into a shiny slate-gray mirror. Helicopters winked far below like fireflies knee-high on the immense Goliath pillars of the twin towers. Maggie felt the comfort of being suspended far above the earth. She closed her eyes and listened to the music from the three-piece jazz band—"Fly Me to the Moon." They seemed halfway there already.

"Come on," Matthew said. He stood up and held out his arms.

"We haven't danced in a hundred years," Maggie protested.

"Time we got back into shape."

They had enjoyed dancing in the early days in New York, but once the children arrived, they got out of the habit. Maggie was usually so exhausted from sleepless nights that an evening out seemed most appealing if it required nothing more than sitting down for two hours and being served something edible on dishes she did not have to wash herself.

After so many years, she was surprised at how easy it was to let Matthew guide her around the tiny dance floor, expertly, graceful as he always was. They had once choreographed a dance of their own, an elegant lindy-like combination of steps. When the music swung into a Cole Porter medly, Matthew began the first moves and she found herself remembering, gliding along with him. It was gratifying, this effortless collaboration of movement. Maggie remembered David's accusation, that Matthew was really no more than a habit.

"Can we sit down now?" she asked Matthew. "I could use a drink."

She sipped her wine and looked out the window. Jewels scattered on black velvet as far as the eye could see. So many lights, so many people, so many tragedies. She was tinier than that speck landing way off at La Guardia Airport. What did her pitiful love affair signify in the face of all that vast glittering display? But she felt herself slipping down, down, as if she were back in the drafty elevator, plunging down the shaft, through the bottom of the building and into the black dense suffocating swamp of lower Manhattan. She glanced up suddenly, feeling Matthew's eyes on her. She smiled at him feebly.

"You okay?" he asked.

"Yes," she answered.

"Nope," Matthew declared.

He took her hand, laid it flat open on the table, and traced the lines. "About your lunch date today," he began slowly. Maggie's heart started to thump. "Did you manage to set up a bridge game finally?"

"No."

His voice was casual, but he still did not look into her face. "Do you think there'll be any more?"

Maggie could feel the thundering reach her temples now. "They're over," she said.

"That's sad." Matthew picked up her hand and kissed it.

"Yes, but life changes. Things happen to people. They grow and change."

"If I can help, Maggie. If you get lonely those times you would have been ... at the bridge table. Will you call me? I promise I won't put you on hold."

"You are a good man."

"I love you, and that's a fact."

"I know."

"Do you really know?"

"Yes. Now tell me about your day."

"What do you want to know?"

"What you did, whom you talked to, which clients."

He leaned back in his chair. "Well, let's see, first I worked on a merger agreement between two little film companies. Do you really want to hear this?"

"Yes," Maggie said, "but I have a confession. At least half the things you tell me about your work go right over my head. I used to try to look as if I knew what you were talking about, but really I didn't." Over the years, Maggie had learned little catch phrases to give the impression that she understood him. She was like her deaf grandmother, nodding brightly as if she had heard every syllable when in fact there was merely a bewildering hum. "You'll think I'm incredibly stupid when you see how much I don't know, but I'd like you to explain it all to me as you go along. If you've got the patience."

"Why?"

"I want to understand what it is you do for that huge chunk of time I'm not with you every day."

Matthew smiled at her but did not talk.

"Well?" Maggie said.

"In a minute," he replied, and kept on smiling.

That night in bed, he held her without making love to her, just allowing her to snuggle against him for comfort like a child with a nightmare. She could not help but think about David and wonder where he was now, with no warm reassuring body to curl up to. She imagined him standing alone among the cold stones in his darkened apartment, looking out over the icy water of the Hudson. She shivered, and felt Matthew's arms tighten around her in his sleep.

24

Maggie walked north on Fifth Avenue past the wrought-iron gates of the Frick Museum with its soft green lawns and flowers blooming thick along the verges of the formal gardens. There was still a bite in the air, but the exercise of walking from the Fifty-seventh Street galleries had warmed her. She switched her heavy portfolio to the other hand and drank in a deep breath of early June that was only slightly polluted by traffic. Surely Robin would be outside on such an afternoon. Maggie turned into the park at Seventy-sixth Street and strolled down toward the boat pond.

A painter had set up his easel halfway down the hill. Maggie glanced curiously at the pleasant if unoriginal oil rendering of the silvery water. Though she had been required to work in public several times, she had never enjoyed painting under the eyes of inquisitive onlookers and sidewalk critics. Still, there was no point attaching herself to a gallery if the idea of public display intimidated her. She smiled at the artist and moved on.

There was no Robin on the benches circling the pond, only nannies and here and there a drunk stretched out to bask in the sun. Maggie turned right and was nearly knocked over by a roller-skater with a bare chest and earphones. But the *Alice in Wonderland* statue reposed unperturbed in bronze splendor on its vast platform. As always, children clambered up Alice's slippery surface, clinging to sides worn shiny by the many wriggling bodies that preceded them.

Maggie climbed the steps, and there beside the statue sat Robin. Maggie watched her for a moment, smiling at the scene. With one hand, Robin held a copy of *People* magazine unopened in her lap. With the other she rocked the baby carriage. Her face had the vacant exhausted look typical of new mothers. She seemed stunned, as if she had been confronted with some monumental fact that she could not absorb.

Maggie sat down on the bench. "Hi," she said.

Robin blinked. "Hi. Well, hi!"

"I figured I'd find you at your usual spot on such a pretty day."

Robin squinted up into the sky. "Yes, it is nice, isn't it?"

Maggie laughed. "Did you sleep last night?"

"Oh, we're doing much better. She made it from eleven until three, her first four-hour stretch."

"You've been up since three?"

Robin nodded. "Mostly, and look at her now, the little beast, peaceful as can be."

The minute figure in the carriage was barely visible under her quilt. Tiny spiky eyelashes lay against a pink cheek.

"I wish she'd get up so I could hold her," Maggie said.

"Drop over anytime between three and six A.M."

"When are you going to get some help, Robin? You'll wear yourself out."

"We're doing all right. Jackson's a big help." Robin stood and leaned over the carriage to fuss with the baby's quilt. "Come on, Phoebe, let's walk Maggie home." They started up the path away from the boat pond. "I always knew a baby would make me happy, and she has. I wish you would be happy too, Mag."

"I'm not unhappy. What makes you say that?"

"There's something. But I've been so preoccupied . . ."

Maggie laughed. "I'll say. Listen, one of these days we'll have a very long conversation, but in the meantime, don't you worry about me. I'm fine."

Truly, the searing pain of those first months without David had eased. When she was miserable, she turned to Matthew and he was always there to comfort her, requiring no explanation other than her feeling low. And she found relief, and sometimes even joy, in her work. She felt like an amphibian who was slowly, inexorably evolving into a land animal. She would drag herself out of the surf only to stagger as the heavy spray broke over her head. She splashed about for a while, then touched the sand beneath her feet and began the struggle all over again. It was sad, abandoning that watery world, and sometimes she longed to flip back into the waves and let them wash her down, down. But dry land rose ahead, and she liked the firm feel of it, liked directing her own steps rather than drifting with the current.

She and Robin strolled slowly north along the plaza in front of the Metropolitan Museum. Sunshine was glistening on the fountains when Maggie's heart suddenly caught in her chest. It happened often, and each time the jolt left her shaken and tearful. There was always some familiar feature, a lanky walk, an angular face, a gesture from long fingers. She strained to track him as up ahead he glided through the throng like some slim and elegant sea creature swimming among the reeds and tall grass, only to disappear forever in the shimmering light of the water. As always, she lost him, but there was a rainbow dancing in the spray from the fountain as they passed.